MRS SOMMERSBY'S SECOND CHANCE

Laurie Benson

MILLS & BOON

First Published in Great Britain 2019
by Mills & Boon, an imprint of HarperCollins*Publishers*
1 London Bridge Street, London, SE1 9GF

© 2019 Laurie Benson

ISBN: 978-0-263-26925-3

MIX
Paper from
responsible sources
FSC® C007454

This book is produced from independently certified FSC™ paper
to ensure responsible forest management.
For more information visit www.harpercollins.co.uk/green.

Printed and bound in Spain
by CPI, Barcelona

Laurie Benson is an award-winning Regency romance author, whose book *An Unexpected Countess* was voted Mills & Boon's 2017 'Hero of the Year' by readers. She began her writing career as an advertising copywriter. When she isn't at her laptop, avoiding laundry, Laurie can be found browsing antiques shops and going on long hikes with her husband and two sons. Learn more about Laurie by visiting her website at lauriebenson.net. You can also find her on Twitter and Facebook.

Also by Laurie Benson

Secret Lives of the Ton miniseries

An Unsuitable Duchess
An Uncommon Duke
An Unexpected Countess

The Sommersby Brides miniseries

One Week to Wed
Convenient Christmas Brides
His Three-Day Duchess
Mrs Sommersby's Second Chance

Discover more at millsandboon.co.uk.

For my editor, Linda Fildew,
for trusting me with this idea and for
frequently making me smile with your notes.

Thank you to Harper St George for being there, and
to Anabelle Bryant for listening to me work through
this plot on that long road trip. Shout out to my
agent, Courtney Miller-Callihan, and to my team at
Harlequin Historical. To my friends, who understood
when I disappeared to write this. Thanks for your
patience. And to my family. I'm grateful for you every
day. Finally, thanks to my awesome readers! For those
of you who said Clara deserved to find love again,
regardless of her age, this one's for you.

Chapter One

❦

Bath, England—1820

It wasn't as if a small sip of water was capable of changing one's life. In all the years Clara Sommersby had stood in the Pump Room to have her daily drink, she had never witnessed anyone perform such an intense inspection of a glass of the spa's mineral water.

She had seen the tall blond-haired gentleman accept the empty glass from the attendant and approach the fountain out of the corner of her eye. Many people entered Bath each day to stay for an extended amount of time to take advantage of the waters in hopes of alleviating their ailments. There were also those who came to the fashionable town to experience the noted assemblies and various entertainments. She would firmly place this gentleman in the latter category.

While Clara normally took note of newly arrived visitors, this morning she awoke with a soreness in her lower back and had only been thinking of a long soak in the thermal baths to hopefully relieve her discomfort—until she saw this man swirl the water in his glass and sniff it as one would do while studying a glass of wine.

As he held the glass up and brought it to his eye, he caught her staring at him through the clear liquid. Too amused to look away, Clara tried to flatten out her smile. The gentleman across from her cleared his throat and went back to studying the contents of his glass.

'The water is an exceptional ancient vintage,' she offered, not even bothering to hide the amusement in her voice. 'It might be a bit odd on the palate at first, but people have been praising its quality for ages.'

He lowered the glass and the faint spark in his blue eyes told her that he understood her jest. 'I was simply trying to determine the mineral content.'

'Are you a connoisseur of water, then, or perhaps a scientist of some sort?'

'Neither. I was just comparing it to the waters from the Chalybeate Spring in Tunbridge Wells. The water there is also reputed to have healing properties.'

'Reputed?' She raised her hand to her chest and

gave him a false look of indignation. 'Sir, I would refrain from making such a statement here unless you're prepared to endure long lectures by numerous patrons on how restorative this water truly is. You'll be advised on how it has eliminated painful symptoms of the gout, how drinking it has reduced a bilious gut and how it has miraculously helped with a variety of other diseases, half of which you might not have ever heard of and quite possibly might not even exist. Scepticism is met with radical belief here in Bath.'

As he tipped his head at her, his serious expression softened just a bit. 'I'll make note of it.'

Bath was losing too many visitors to Brighton since the royal court, and George in particular, had made that town fashionable. Clara owned one of the finest hotels here, although she kept that fact a secret from Society. For all she knew, he might be staying at The Fountain Head Hotel. It was in her best interest to create a favourable impression of the town.

'I'm sure whatever it is that ails you, you will find relief here.'

He seemed surprised she assumed he was here because he needed help. 'I have no ailments that I'm aware of.'

Two finely dressed young ladies approached Clara's side and dipped their glasses into the streams of water, while trying to catch the gentleman's eye. Instead of offering them some form of encouragement, he reverted his attention back to studying his glass until they walked away, giggling and whispering as they went.

When they were alone once again, he eyed Clara across the fountain. 'And you, madam, certainly you are much too young to suffer from any of those ills you spoke of. What brings you to the spa?'

'I am not as young as you might think.'

'Come now, you're not any older than I am.'

Ah, so he was one of those gentlemen who liked to flatter women. She had run across many of them in her life. By her estimation he appeared to be in his midthirties, which was ten years younger than she was.

'Perhaps this fountain also holds the key to a youthful appearance,' she teased. 'I have been drinking from it for many years now.'

A small smile tugged at the corner of his lips and softened the hard angles of his features. 'Then the waters here are far better than those in Tunbridge Wells. I don't believe they'd dare to make that claim.' Suddenly, his features hardened once more as he appeared to study her. 'Perhaps you are one of those charlatans, like the men and women selling miracle elixirs outside in the streets, only you are employed by the Pump Room to convince people they should drink this odd-smelling liquid.'

'I assure you, sir. I am not. I am simply an honest patron here for my daily dose.' And to recommend a certain hotel to those who happened to be in need of one whenever she was here, but that was neither here nor there. 'And how do you think our water compares to those of Tunbridge Wells?'

He peered out of the window behind him, down at the steaming spa waters below which, if it weren't for the rain, at this hour would have been full of bathers who had come at this early hour of the morning for the restorative benefits. Once again, his attention was back on his glass. 'The smell is similar. However, the water is cold there, not hot like this, and that water comes from a small spring. People do not bathe in it.'

'You will not find hair in your water, if that is your concern. This water is not piped in from the baths.'

His face scrunched up as if that disgusting thought hadn't occurred to him. 'I am much relieved.'

Quite deliberately, Clara raised her glass and took a long sip of the hot water. It was not exactly a pleasant taste, but over the years she had grown accustomed to it. She wondered what he would think of it.

His gaze rested on her lips as she lowered her

glass. Then he fixed his attention on her face and it appeared he was trying to determine what she thought of the taste. She would not give him any reason to think the water people were consuming in Tunbridge Wells was better than the water that flowed here. Bath needed people to believe in the waters, if the town was to continue being a popular destination. And, as the owner of The Fountain Head Hotel, she needed those people—those gentlemen—to keep returning to her establishment. The Hotel meant everything to her. It was her security for financial independence and its success was something she took great pride in.

'I'm trying to determine if you're a good actress or if indeed the water is not as bad as I've been imagining.'

Had anyone ever been this hesitant to try the water? His procrastination was rather amusing. 'There is only one way to find out.' She cocked her head to the side and gave him an encouraging nod.

It wasn't as if a small sip of water was going to change his life. It might keep him close to a chamber pot for a good part of the day, but that would pass. At least that's what Mr William Lane silently hoped was the case as he had accepted a glass from the attendant and walked over to the King's Spring fountain in the Pump Room in

Bath. Water cascaded down from spigots at the top of a pale stone urn into the open mouths of painted fish below. It was a clever feat of design engineering to get the water to fall just so and Lane took note of it, along with the other observations he was making of the interior design of this public space.

He dipped his glass into one of the streams of water, breaking the flow and filling his glass with the warm liquid. He had yet to try the thermal water his workmen had uncovered underneath the building he had just purchased, but thought it wise to try the popular water in the King's Spring first so he would have something to compare it to. If he offered it to customers to drink and reap the reputed benefits, he knew people would expect it to taste the same.

Lane raised the glass slowly to his lips and gave it a sniff as if he was sampling a fine bottle of wine. The bouquet in his glass was nowhere near as appealing. Instead of fruity notes or the scent of the oak barrels that wine was stored in, this water possessed a metallic scent. He had tried the water at the spring in Tunbridge Wells, when a friend procured a glass for him after an evening of too much ale at a local tavern. He didn't know if it was the water that had caused him to be violently sick shortly afterwards. That was not a sensation he had enjoyed and he would rather not do anything to bring it on again. Certainly not all of these people would be coming to the Pump Room and drinking this water if they knew they would be sick afterwards.

Just as he was about to ask the woman in front of him, an expensively dressed, slight, elderly woman and two older gentlemen joined them at the fountain, forcing him to step closer to the striking, petite brown-haired woman he had been conversing with. The faintest scent of roses replaced the metallic scent of the water, giving him a brief reprieve. It brought back a vague memory of laughing while running through a garden surrounded by roses, as a small child. Lane couldn't recall much of that memory. It was one of the earliest ones he possessed and remembering it always seemed to somehow create a sense of longing for a time that was best forgotten.

Pushing back against the sensation, he took note that the three new guests nodded a greeting to the woman beside him before they filled their glasses with water and immediately began to drink it as if they were returning from a long trip in the desert. At five pence for a glass and with the crowds of people standing about in the classical, sparsely decorated room, offering a similar arrangement in the spa he might build appeared to be an excellent idea. Perhaps if he charged four pence per glass for the first few months it would be a way to entice patrons of this spa to the one he might build. He just needed to find a way to convince his partner that this was a lucrative investment.

'Drink up, my boy,' the balding man wearing spectacles called to him from the other side of the fountain. 'You will experience none of the benefits of the water if you simply hold it in your glass. The water needs to be hot to be at its most effective.'

Lane must have been eyeing the room longer than he realised for it to be remarked upon. Out of the corner of his eye, he could see the woman beside him take another sip from her glass.

'You find the water beneficial? I admit I've been hesitant in trying it.'

There was a faint tsking sound from the woman next to him and he could see her shake her head ever so slightly, right before the white-haired, portly gentleman answered him.

'Nonsense,' he replied, his runny pale blue eyes narrowing on Lane under his thick, bushy, white eyebrows. 'There is no reason to hesitate. This water will not kill you. It cures rheums, palsies, lethargies, apoplexy, cramps, forgetfulness, trembling of any manner, aches and swelling of the joints, and even deafness.'

'What was that?' the other man asked him.

'I said the water has been known to cure those who are deaf.'

The balding man shook his head. 'Well, it helps with ailments, does nothing for theft.'

'Deaf. I said it cures deafness,' the other man said louder.

'Oh, rightly so. I've been coming here every day for a year and drink three pints a day. Works wonders.'

The calculations of revenue started to happen in Lane's head. 'You've been coming here for a year?'

'Near to what?'

'He was verifying that you've been taking the waters here for an entire *year*,' the elderly woman chimed in, rolling her eyes. The diamonds in her earrings sparkled as she shook her head.

The old man waved her off with his hand. 'I heard him. I heard him.'

How many patrons in this room had been coming to the spa that long? Repeat customers were a boon to any business—and this particular one was drinking more than a glass a day. What exactly was it that kept a gentleman such as this coming back? Was it something more than his belief in the water?

The elderly lady broke into his thoughts as she addressed the woman beside him.

'Good morning, my dear. Lovely to see you, as always.'

'Good morning, Your Grace.' The woman gave a slight curtsy and the sleeve of her scarlet-silk spencer brushed against his arm. 'It's a pleasure. I wasn't aware you had returned to town.'

'Just arrived yesterday and haven't sent my cards around yet. My grandson was interested in showing his wife the sights in Bath. She's never been. I saw it as a wonderful opportunity to enjoy the restorative effects of the waters and spend time with my family. Pity it's raining today.'

'Yes, it is. I was looking forward to a long hot soak when I awoke this morning.'

So, she had intended to bathe here today. He couldn't understand why. She couldn't be any older than his thirty-seven years. She appeared fit and her movements, while graceful, were spry. Perhaps she just enjoyed the feel of the hot water.

An image of the woman with her dark hair piled high on her head, soaking in the large stone bath as her skin glistening with the steam of the water, filled his mind. Did they bathe naked here in the spa? He imagined the smooth swell of her breasts submerged partially in the hot water and he swallowed hard, thinking about swimming up to her and licking the water from her soft skin. The pool of water he spied below was large, which would leave them with plenty of room to explore one another below the surface of the water or on one of the stone steps leading down into the bath. In his mind, he pictured them in there, after the spa had been closed up for the night. Those musings quickly ended with the words of the white-haired gentleman across from him.

'Blockage of the bowels.'

Lane blinked a few times, bringing the room back into focus as he felt his eyebrows rise. 'Pardon?'

There was a soft sputter of laughter from the woman he had been daydreaming about, before she covered her mouth with her gloved hand and pretended to cough.

'I said blockage of the bowels,' the man repeated a bit louder. 'It also cures blockage of the bowels. Is that why you're here? Or is it for the women? Many fine women here in this town.' The man eyed the Duchess on his right.

She raised her chin and arched a very regal-looking brow at the man who appeared older than her advanced age. Her expression had the effect she intended since he moved a few steps away from her and shifted his attention back to Lane. None of them had been introduced to him and yet they all seemed perfectly content to speak with him about the advantages of taking the water here. Was all of Bath like this or was it something unique that happened while you were all partaking in a glass of water that might, or might not, have you attached to a chamber pot for an undisclosed amount of time?

'Leave him alone,' said the elderly Duchess. 'Let the man enjoy his water in peace.'

Enjoying it was probably a gross exaggeration. 'I don't mind,' Lane said, feeling a need to speak with these people to better understand what motivated them to frequent such an establishment. 'I've come to Bath at the suggestion of a friend. He thought I was sure to find something I'd like here.'

'Plenty of things to like in Bath,' the man who was hard of hearing replied back. This time he eyed the brunette to Lane's right.

'I am not a thing, Mr Falk,' she said, surprising Lane with her way of directly addressing the man's comment.

More surprising was the way the tone of her voice and her confident demeanour made the man redden with embarrassment at her chastisement. Although that did little to stop him from continuing.

'You will never find another husband with that outspoken nature of yours.'

'I am glad to hear of it. That is more reason to speak my mind.'

'A man doesn't like a woman who speaks her mind. A man likes a woman who is docile and deferential.'

'What nonsense,' the Duchess interjected. 'A man would be bored with such a woman in less than a week.' She shifted her attention to Lane. 'What say you, sir? Do you agree with his proclamation?'

The two elderly gentlemen leaned closer and watched, as if they were warning him not to side with the two women in this odd little party.

Lane glanced at the woman beside him before addressing the Duchess. 'I've never given it any thought.'

'But surely you have preferences in the women you spend your time with.'

He was being watched too closely by the four people in this group. Why couldn't they still be discussing the benefits of the water? He downed the contents of the glass in his hand, forgetting it was the spa water. If only he could wipe his tongue on his sleeve to alleviate the coppery taste in his mouth. He had learned not to care what other people thought of him a long time ago, but he found he didn't want the woman beside him to think him lily-livered. It was not the impression he wanted to leave her with.

'An interesting way to avoid answering a question,' she commented. Her brown eyes held that now-familiar hint of amusement under her arched brow.

Lane had come here to gather information. That was all. How had he become a source of entertainment for her?

'Well?' she asked.

'I've never given much thought to the type of women I prefer.'

'I meant the water.'

'Oh.' There were no mineral deposits at the bottom of his glass. And, thankfully, no strands of hair. 'It was not what I expected.'

'You'll grow accustomed to it. You may find you prefer it when it's hot. Since you held it for so long, I'm certain it would have cooled off in your glass.'

He hadn't planned to come back to this spa to find out. One visit should be enough to see what features he might want to recreate in his. With enough information, he was certain he could convince his partner that this was a lucrative investment. And the more time he spent here, the more he was certain that it made sense to expand their operation to include bathing. In order to do that they would need to buy The Fountain Head Hotel which was next door. A spa needed to be large. His one solitary building would never do and there was a church to the left. There was no possible way he would be expanding his enterprise in that direction. They would need to purchase the hotel that sat on the adjacent property on the right if they were to have any chance of making this a highly profitable venture. He was already staying there to assess it.

Just as he was about to begin asking the people around him what features kept them coming back to this particular spa, the attractive woman in scarlet took a step back from the fountain.

'Well, do have a pleasant day, everyone.'

She was leaving? Suddenly conversing with the other three standing around the fountain didn't seem as appealing as it had moments before. He didn't even know her name or where she was from—or how he could find her again.

It shouldn't matter. He was in Bath for a short time and he never let anything or anyone distract him from business. He had no time to spend in the company of such an enticing woman—even though his thoughts once more drifted to the image of her in the hot, steaming water. Tendrils of her wavy dark hair were grazing the glistening skin of her shoulders.

She was a distraction he couldn't afford right now. Hopefully soon he would be devoting all of his attention to convincing the owner of The Fountain Head Hotel to sell him their successful enterprise as inexpensively as possible.

Chapter Two

The sun had finally come out from behind the clouds and was shining high above the garden that was behind Clara's house in the Royal Crescent. This lovely garden, with a large variety of colourful roses, was one of her favourite places to spend her time in the warmer weather. On this spring day, she was enjoying the company of Eleanor, the Dowager Duchess of Lyonsdale, who she had run into at the Pump Room the day before. They were seated across from one another at the small round table that was set out on the gravel circle at the very centre of the garden.

The women had become friendly five years ago when they had worked together on a committee raising funds for the Foundling Hospital in London. Days were never dull when Eleanor was around and, for that, Clara was grateful.

'You always do have the most exceptional tea,' the Dowager commented, lowering her fine porcelain cup into its saucer and placing it on the table.

'Thank you. I've blended a few special types of oolong for this pot.'

The weight of the head of Clara's Cavalier King Charles spaniel rested on her foot while Humphrey stretched his small, exhausted, black furry body down beside her after having spent the last fifteen minutes chasing a butterfly along the garden pathways. While he rested on Clara's foot, his big brown eyes looked up at the Dowager.

'My, you are a handsome fellow,' she said, breaking off a piece of her biscuit and placing it down near the ground.

Humphrey looked at the offering and back up at the Dowager.

'Come now,' she said to him. 'If you want it, you have to come to me to get it.'

Clara had never owned a dog before and she was learning how to manage Humphrey through trial and error, but she knew she didn't want him begging for food at the table. She had been around enough houses with dogs to know that the experience as a dinner guest could be annoying. But before she was able to request that the Dowager not give him any food, Humphrey jumped up and padded over to her to gently take the piece of biscuit she offered.

The Dowager rubbed his little head and brown ears. 'That's a good boy. How long have you had him?'

The little imp yawned and went back to Clara's foot where he stretched out again and closed his eyes. Apparently chasing butterflies and eating a biscuit was an exhausting endeavour for one so small.

'Only a few weeks now. Juliet gave him to me for my birthday. I think she assumed that I was lonely now that she is no longer living with me and somehow she believes Humphrey will help.'

'How many years has it been since you took Juliet in?'

'Four years. She lived with Elizabeth and Skeffington for two years after their parents passed, but we found it was better for her to stay with me in Bath than with them.'

'I suppose living with one's older sister can be trying at times and Skeffington certainly did not have the nicest disposition.' The Dowager broke off another piece of her biscuit. 'At the time that the two of you left London, I thought it might've had something to do with the Duke of Winterbourne's youngest brother, Lord Montague. But Juliet and Monty are married now, so perhaps that assumption was incorrect.' Her gaze held Clara's for a few breaths longer than necessary before she placed the piece of biscuit in her mouth.

'I don't know what you mean.'

How was it that this woman always seemed to know things that should have been a secret? Clara's niece Juliet had suffered terrible heart-break at the hands of Lord Montague Pearce when her guardian refused to allow them to marry. At the time, Clara had taken Juliet out of London to spare her the pain of having to see Monty. The experience had created a close bond between the two women and while Clara had been so delighted that Juliet had finally found her happiness with Monty years later, Juliet's absence had left a hole in her heart.

The Dowager waved away her statement with a carefree movement of her hand. 'Very well. Keep your family secrets. They married in the end and I have seen them at various balls in London. It is apparent that it's a love match so perhaps her time here in Bath *was* for the best.'

Clara was not about to divulge her niece's secret. The secrets the Sommersby women shared with each other stayed within the family. She had never betrayed Juliet in the past and she wouldn't do so now. 'I think Juliet enjoyed her time here. There is talk of them finding a home in Bath in the future.'

'How lovely for you,' the Dowager responded

with sincerity. 'However, having them in town will not be the same as having companionship in this house, and I am not referring to that little fellow at your feet who has been charming us today,' she said, gesturing to a sleeping Humphrey.

'Have you run out of people to pair up in London so now you think to turn your attention to me after all these years of knowing one another? My friends and the visits from my nieces are enough for me. I do not want a husband.'

'Perhaps you just haven't found the right gentleman.'

'Perhaps neither have you.'

The elderly woman with the mischievous smile let out a small laugh. 'Perhaps I already have.'

Clara wasn't certain if the Dowager was having a bit of fun with her last comment or if indeed the woman had found a gentleman caller at her advanced age. Regardless, Clara was not interested in wading through the waters of another relationship. 'I will not lose my independence. I have managed my affairs very well over these last ten years. And I have done so going against some of the wishes my husband had while he was alive. I've discovered I possess a keen ability to make sound business decisions, placing me in firm control over a comfortable future. I will not give that up for any man.'

She would never turn over control of The

Fountain Head Hotel to a husband. That hotel was her security and as long as she owned it, she would never have to worry about being thrown in debtors' prison—the way she had when her husband Robert was alive.

A murmur of voices drifted over the garden wall and Clara knew the Collingswood sisters had come out into the garden of the house their parents had recently begun leasing next door. She wondered if Mrs Collingswood had stood by her window and peered through her sheer muslin curtains and spied them in the garden. The girls were of marrying age and she noticed that Mrs Collingswood was fond of throwing them in Clara's path whenever she had the opportunity. In fact, she had spotted them yesterday heading towards her in the Pump Room and had walked away from the fountain before Mrs Collingswood approached her, presumably hoping for an introduction to the blond-haired gentleman she had been speaking with—a man whose name she did not know.

Even though the sisters' voices weren't loud, Humphrey's sleepy head popped up and he trotted slowly towards the garden wall between the two properties.

'You left the Pump Room rather abruptly yesterday. I do hope nothing was amiss,' the Dowager said, picking up her teacup.

'No, I just saw people that I preferred to avoid and thought it best to leave before I was obligated to speak with them.'

'Nothing troubling, I hope.'

Clara leaned closer so her voice would not carry on the breeze over the garden wall. 'No, just my new neighbours,' she replied in a low whisper.

The Dowager's expression filled with interest and she, too, leaned forward. 'Neighbours can be so trying at times. Tell me about these.'

'It is the new family who are leasing the house next door.' She motioned with her head to the low garden wall where Clara suspected the Collingswood sisters were instructed to spend part of the afternoon. 'The family is nice enough, really. Except the mother seems determined to introduce her daughters to every eligible young man in Bath.' The fact that Clara had noticed the focus was always on the prettier younger daughter made her amend the statement. 'Well, she attempts to promote the younger one, at any rate. The older is practically ignored in those situations.'

'What a pity for the girl. It is not easy living in the shadow of someone else.'

'No, it isn't. I recall feeling that way when I would attend a ball or other social engagements with my older sister, Mary. Conversing with others came very easy to her. It was not so with me when I was younger. Because of that, I often disappeared into the background like wallpaper.'

'You? I find that hard to believe. Did you behave in such a way even with Mr Sommersby? I remember him when he was younger. He was a bit of a charmer.'

'I was like that with everyone *except* him,' Clara replied with a smile. 'He was very easy to speak with. I do think being married to him helped me become more assertive and outgoing.' She had been forced to become that way when she would regularly have to find ways to convince the shopkeepers that they would eventually get paid for their wares.

'Maybe you can help Miss Collingswood?' the Dowager suggested.

'And they say *I* have a fondness for matchmaking...'

'Oh, you know I do. Everyone knows that I do. I've never really made it a secret. You, however, are subtler. I have witnessed it. Perhaps you could introduce her to that gentleman you were speaking with yesterday.'

'You mean in the Pump Room? Why would you mention him?'

'My dear, he is a handsome man. I may be old, but I am not dead. What can you tell me about him?'

'The truth of the matter is that I know nothing about him. We had not been introduced before we began speaking.' Clara took a sip of tea to give her guest time to process that statement. 'You don't look shocked.'

'I'm not. I suspected as much when no introductions were made.' She tilted her head and looked Clara in the eye. The Dowager was of an advanced age, but she never seemed to miss anything that was going on around her, no matter how insignificant. 'You did speak with him, surely you must know something about him?'

'All I know is that he has spent some time in Tunbridge Wells.'

'That's all?'

Clara nodded while considering once more who he was and what had brought him to Bath.

'Did you check the registry book? Surely he must have signed the book in the Pump Room. Everyone who comes to town knows to do that.'

'There were a number of gentlemen who signed the book yesterday. There is no way to know which one he is.'

'Then you do not know how long he will be staying in Bath or if he was merely passing through.'

'I do not.'

'What a pity.' The Dowager's keen eyes settled on her again. 'I saw the way his gaze would drift to you while we stood about talking and I noticed the way you studied him when you thought none of us was looking.'

There had been a few moments when Clara was speaking with him that she had felt he was giving her his undivided attention—the way you did when you were attracted to someone. It was a lovely feeling to think it might have been possible that she had caught the eye of a handsome young gentleman at her age. Not that she was particularly old or that he was exceptionally young, but she was certainly older than he was. She knew any attraction that might have been there was short-lived and he must have forgotten all about her the moment she had walked away from the fountain.

But if she was honest with herself, she would have to admit that there was something about their encounter that had stayed with her and she even found herself looking for him in the Pump Room this morning as she stood by the fountain and was disappointed when she didn't see him. Perhaps he had left town already.

'I thought you wanted me to arrange for him to meet my neighbour's daughter?'

'Well, you've said you do not want to marry again. There is no sense in me matching the two of you together. Unless you are open to having an affair with him.' That mischievous look was back on her lined face, making her appear almost childlike. 'I can help you with that endeavour if you like. You did bother to look for his name in the book. That has to mean something.'

'That signifies nothing and I am certainly not looking to have an affair,' Clara replied, not even trying to hide her indignation. 'And he is much too young for me, regardless.'

Humphrey padded down between the rose bushes from where he had been by the garden wall. The small dog stopped near one of the pots on the edge of the border that held lavender. He raised himself up on his hind legs and proceeded to thrust himself against the clay pot a number of times, eliciting a laugh from the Dowager.

'Humphrey, no!' Clara called out to him, while a hot flush crept up her neck. She had to repeat his name a number of times before he stopped and looked over at her with those big brown eyes. She walked over to him and picked him up. When she returned to her chair, she placed his small body on her lap. 'Please forgive him,' she said to the Dowager. 'He has developed a habit of doing that. I suppose I should be grateful he does that only to things and not people, but I don't know how to get him to stop.' The dog in question curled into a ball on her lap and lowered his head.

'I'm afraid I cannot help you with his problem. I've never owned a dog. Would it help if you walked him some more? Perhaps if you tire him out?'

'I already take him for a long walk every morning and then I walk him at four o'clock along the Crescent and into the park every day. It has done no good.'

The Dowager smiled up at Clara. 'I am certain you will work out the best course of action to take. In the meantime,' she continued, lowering her voice, 'I need something to keep me occupied while I am here in Bath and playing matchmaker for your neighbour's daughter sounds like the perfect challenge. Why don't you join me in helping her find someone special?'

'Harriet is a lovely girl. I doubt it will be a challenge. We just need to separate her from her sister.'

'And hopefully your mystery gentleman from yesterday will still be in town and we can find out if he is a suitable prospect for her.'

The idea that he could still be in Bath shouldn't have mattered. He was a stranger she had spoken to for less than thirty minutes—and yet the notion made her smile.

Chapter Three

Lane stood in the cellar of the coffee house that he had purchased with his friend and business partner the Earl of Hartwick and looked over at the man in question, who was holding a glass of hot mineral water up to the sunlight that was streaming in through the window.

'When I told you to go to Bath because you might find something that would interest you, I didn't mean the water,' Hart said, narrowing his sharp blue eyes and taking a cautionary sniff of his glass.

'I know what you meant.'

'Women, not water. I meant go to Bath to find a woman…or two. I'm not one to judge. But this water…are you certain it is safe to drink?'

'I had a glass of it myself only yesterday and I am here today.'

Hart peered at Lane over the glass. 'Yes, but

you appear agitated. I have no wish to become agitated.'

'I am agitated because you have yet to tell me if you agree that turning this coffee house into a spa is a wise business decision,' he replied in a clipped tone.

'People truly do drink this hot water that smells like a pocketful of pennies?'

'The room was full of people paying five pence per glass to drink it.'

'And they go there every day?'

'Some do and drink multiple glasses. And some bathe in the hot thermal water as well.' Lane dug his hands into the pockets of his green-linen coat. 'How is it that you were the one to tell me to go to Bath and yet you know nothing about the hot springs or the Grand Pump Room?'

Hart arched his brow. 'In the seven years that you have known me, do I truly look like a person who would bathe with strange old men in ancient pools or drink water that appears to have been boiled with currency?'

'Well, no, not really.' Lane shifted in his stance.

'Then what makes you believe I know anything about the water here?'

Lane had been introduced to Hart by Lord Boundbrooke, who was on the board of the Foundling Hospital and had helped secure Lane's apprenticeship at a bank when he left the Hospital. In the years following, he had kept his eye on Lane and had told him that he thought both Lane and Hart would benefit from a friendship with each other. He was right. In Hart, he had found a rare aristocrat who didn't care that Lane did not come from a family of consequence or that he didn't even know what family he came from at all. But even though he was very fond of the man, there were times Hart could try his patience.

'You must know of the reputation of the town, Hart, and you've seen the numerous visitors that come here by the thousands because of water such as that.'

Hart brushed a lock of his black hair out of his eyes. 'Do I really have to drink this?'

'Not if you don't want to.'

'What I'd prefer is a nice glass of brandy somewhere where we can discuss this further.'

Lane motioned to the white-skirted table with two chairs that was tucked against the stone wall and Hart followed. He broke out into a broad grin when Lane reached under the table and produced a bottle of brandy and two glasses.

'You knew I wouldn't drink the water.'

'I suspected as much and, even if you had, you would need this to wash the taste out of your mouth.'

'If that water is so vile, why are all these people drinking it?'

'Because they firmly believe that that water is going to cure all their ailments.'

'And, do you believe that?'

'I am keeping myself open to the possibility.'

Hart poured himself some brandy. 'Then why not just operate a place for people to come to drink the water? Why do we need to purchase the hotel as well?'

'If we don't offer bathing as well, it might not be enough of an incentive to draw people here. They could very well continue to go to the spas where they can have a drink and bathe. And, more importantly, there is more money to be made from people bathing in the water. Look here.' He took out a paper with his financial calculations from his pocket and laid it on the table. 'I stood outside the King's and Queen's Baths and counted how many people went in over a two-hour period this morning. I used that number to estimate how many people go in each day.' He pointed to the number of people and then the column beside it. 'This is how much they charge for a person to take to the waters there and this is how much money they might have made today. It is not an accurate number, mind you, but it is a logical estimate.'

Hart's blue eyes widened as his gaze travelled across the numbers. 'Surely that can't be right?'

'It is. I tell you, we need to expand. It is the

logical thing to do. We need to buy The Fountain Head Hotel and then construct a bathhouse on the property. It is as if divine providence has given us a gift with that water for a reason.' He leaned in and rested his forearms on the table. 'Hart, we could make enough money to start that race-course you and I have dreamed about. The one that will rival Ascot.'

He knew that the mention of horses would be enough of an enticement to grab his friend's interest in the project. They had been business partners for seven years. The investments he had orchestrated for them allowed his friend to live on a very nice income and not have to rely solely on his winnings at the gaming tables to support himself and now his wife as well. He knew Hart trusted his business sense, but he could still be unpredictable at times.

Lane rubbed his hand across his chin and waited.

'While we might be able to afford to purchase the hotel,' Hart said, 'we certainly can't afford the hotel *and* the construction of the bathhouse. Not after buying this place only weeks ago.'

'Do you have any ideas?'

Hart took a sip of his brandy and then stared down into his glass as if he would find his answer there. 'Sarah and I are staying with Lyonsdale and his family for a few days. I will mention it to him tonight and, should he be interested, I will arrange a meeting with the three of us. You can lay this plan of yours before him then.'

Lane rubbed his hand on his thigh as if he were rubbing out a spot on the soft buckskin of his breeches. He didn't want to have to wait to settle this matter. He wanted to approach the owner of the hotel now and begin searching for an engineer competent in the systems they would need to manage the flow of water. He would need a survey of the property next door to present to the engineers. But he couldn't do any of that until he knew how much money they had at their disposal.

While Hart with his charm and pedigree was perfect at enticing investors to fund their projects, Lane was infinitely better at executing them—and this plan was exceptional. It was easy money. Once the new spa was complete, it would practically run itself. He would hire a competent manager and return to London in search of his next financial investment.

The Duke of Lyonsdale had helped them fund a few of their larger business ventures in the past. He would certainly see the potential in this one. If only Lane did not have to wait so long for his answer.

'How much money do you think Lyonsdale will be willing to give us?'

Hart gave a slight lift of his shoulder. 'How

much money do you think we will need? I'm sure you have a number in mind.'

Lane pointed to another number further down the page.

Hart's brows rose. 'Yes, we will definitely need help with that. Let me see what I can do and I will let you know what he says.'

As he stood to leave, Lane checked his watch.

'What time is it?' Hart asked.

'Half past three.'

'I should be off. I'll send word to you in the morning on the outcome of our discussion. In the meantime, don't look at any more properties. We can't afford for you to get another one of your brilliant ideas.'

'I won't. This idea has my full attention. I think I'll go for a walk. After spending a good part of my afternoon in this dusty space, I could use the fresh air.'

'Lyonsdale is up near the Royal Crescent. You might want to explore that area. I don't believe there are any businesses to distract you.'

'I'll consider it.'

'You might even consider finding a woman or two. That should keep you out of trouble until you hear from me.'

'I have better things to do.' But even as he said it, an image of the woman from the Pump Room popped into his head. He consciously pushed thoughts of her aside. 'I'm determined to find a way to improve the productivity here at the coffee house. There is no sense in missing an opportunity to increase our income with this property until we change it to a spa.'

'*If* we change it over to a spa.'

'*When* we change it. I have faith that you will find a way to get us the money that we need.'

'We shall see.' Hart downed the rest of his brandy. 'Even if we get the money, what makes you believe the owner of The Fountain Head Hotel will be interested in selling it to us? I've heard it's the finest hotel in Bath and a haven for single gentlemen. With all the unmarried men visiting this town, it must turn a pretty profit.'

'They'll sell it. I'm good at brokering deals such as this and I want that property.'

Chapter Four

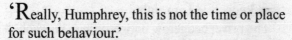

'Really, Humphrey, this is not the time or place for such behaviour.'

The feminine voice came through the thick shrubbery in the wooded area with views of the Royal Crescent that Lane found himself walking in almost an hour later. After living in London all his life, he felt more at home on cobblestones or on horseback than he did walking along a wooded path. But the wide promenade in front of the Crescent was so congested with finely dressed people of all ages that Lane grew weary of the slow pace of those walking in front of him as they strolled along under their parasols and in their beaver hats. Something told him that he was better off heading out into Barton Fields, the huge expanse of lawn opposite the long curved row of honey-coloured terraced stone residences that formed the Royal Crescent.

The air was fresher and cleaner here in Bath

and being outside exerting oneself through a brisk walk felt invigorating. Because of that, when he reached the end of the field, Lane uncharacteristically decided to continue on to the wooded area beyond. And it was there that the voice of the unknown woman caught his attention. The tone she used to address her companion had him slowing down. What behaviour had this gentleman committed that warranted such exasperation?

'Don't look at me like that,' she continued. 'You know that I am right.'

The privet hedgerow between them was about ten inches higher than his six-foot frame and too lush to peer through the leaves to the other side.

'Honestly, I would have stayed at home if I knew this was your intention.'

The gentleman in question remained silent. Or, if he spoke, it was too low for Lane to hear. He stepped closer to the hedgerow and listened intently for any response. He heard a bit of rustling, like the sound of the fabric of a lady's skirt being moved. Although he devoted his attention to business, Lane wasn't a monk. He had lifted a skirt or two…or three or four, in his time. That was a sound that a man didn't forget.

'Oh, now you have me in a tangle. I do wish you would stop.' The woman's tone had shifted from that of exasperation to pleading.

It was in really bad form to listen to what was

happening a few feet away from him. He should walk away. He should not be picturing the escapade those two were having in the woods—in the very public woods.

His thoughts flashed to an image of the woman from the Pump Room and how he had been picturing the two of them together yesterday—in the very public bath. At least his fantasy involved an empty building, after it had been closed for the day.

'Humphrey, no! Don't you do it. Humphrey!'

There was an urgency in her voice that gave him pause. Perhaps the silent Humphrey was manhandling her. Suppose she did not want him to lift her skirts here in a public garden. Lane's right hand drew up into a tight fist.

'Is everything all right?' he called through the hedge. 'Are you in need of assistance?'

The rustling stopped and there was a marked silence. The only sound now was the faint chirping of birds in a far-off tree.

'Now do you see what you've done?' Her voice dropped and, if he hadn't been standing with his ear practically in the bush, he wouldn't have heard it.

'What am I to do about you?' Her faint voice continued. 'You are incorrigible. I should give a swat to that backside of yours.'

Lane's brows rose. They were more of a daring couple than he had originally thought. Perhaps she wasn't coming to any harm after all. Perhaps he should just go on his way and forget he had ever said anything. This would teach him to venture out into wooded areas. No one would be having these types of assignations in the middle of the day on public pavements. He turned to walk further down the path when the woman called out to him.

'Sir, are you still there? I could use your assistance.'

What had the silent Humphrey done now? And did Lane really want to see? This was what he got for having no tolerance for brutes who thought they could exert their power over others.

Shoving his hands into his pockets, Lane made his way around the hedgerow and stopped.

'It's you.' It came out of his mouth before he had a chance to stop himself.

There, before him, was the woman from the Pump Room wearing a jonquil and white dress with a deep blue shawl draped over her right arm, her brown eyes widened with apparent surprise when she saw him. 'What are *you* doing here?'

'You said you needed assistance.' He scanned the surroundings for the persistent Humphrey, but the man must have had the sense to leave before Lane made it around the hedge or he was hiding somewhere while he set his wardrobe to rights.

Apparently, this woman would probably think nothing of having a scandalous encounter in the public baths. And that thought only served to have him picturing her smooth skin glistening with the steaming bath water once more.

It was bad enough Clara was in the predicament she was in. Did she really need to be stuck like this in front of the handsome gentleman from the Pump Room?

Humphrey's leash had got tangled in the privet hedge and, if that wasn't annoying enough, when she went to try to untangle it the back of her dress had got caught on a branch as well. She had tried to release it, but that particular section of lace was at a point of her back that she couldn't reach.

When the gentleman called out to her through the hedgerow, she hesitated at first to answer. A scoundrel could take advantage of her very precarious predicament. She could be robbed, or worse. Hoping that if he tried anything, her small puppy would bite his ankles and scare him off, she accepted his invitation of assistance. Only now her puppy had disappeared into the hedge and the possible scoundrel turned out to be the man the Dowager wanted her to introduce to her neighbour.

'How can I help?' he asked, tilting his head a bit as he looked at her with a furrowed brow.

'I'm stuck.'

'Pardon?'

'On the hedge.' She motioned to her back with her gloved hand. 'The lace on my dress is caught on a branch and I can't move. Would you be so kind as to release me?'

He glanced around the small wooded area she was in and even appeared to peer over a few of the lower hedges as he made his way closer to her. When he stood a few feet away, the faintest scent of his cologne drifted across her nose as it travelled on the soft breeze.

Clara was petite in stature and had to look up at him as he stood less than two feet from her. Facing him, without the busyness of the Pump Room, she was able to get a better look at him. His firm and sensual lips rose a fraction in the right corner, softening the angles of his square jaw. Although he was clean shaven, there was a hint of stubble on that jaw and on his cheeks. She appreciated impeccably groomed men so it was surprising that she had the urge to brush her fingers against his skin to see what that stubble felt like.

He leaned over her and her breath caught as his lips drew closer to her eyelids. His finely made arms, defined through the linen of his blue coat, came around hers. He could have easily stood to the side of her to free the bit of fabric, but being surrounded by all his quiet masculine presence, she was glad he had decided not to.

'You truly have got yourself caught.'

He looked down at her and flecks of gold were visible in his blue eyes. 'I know I haven't spent much time in your presence, however, this is the quietest I think I have seen you,' he said with a slight smile.

'I don't want to distract you.'

'You already have.'

She lifted her chin and now their mouths were a few inches apart. The warm air of his breath brushed across her lips. The last time she had kissed a man was ten years ago. And even then, she couldn't ever recall her pulse beating like this at the thought of kissing her husband.

Just a few more inches and their lips would be touching. Just a few more inches and she would wrap her arms around his neck and let herself sink into his embrace.

His arms tightened around hers and she felt the tugging of the back of her dress. 'I think I have it,' he said, his breath caressing her lips.

So close, their lips were so close.

A loud yapping broke the moment and the gentleman she was thinking of kissing reeled back and it was then that she realised she was free. Free of the shrub and the spell that had been cast over her. Free of desires that left her forgetting where she was or the fact that she didn't know who she was with.

She was a respectable widow and respectable women did not go around kissing gentlemen behind some shrubbery in a public park.

Humphrey's small black and brown body was hidden within the bottom branches of the thick hedge beside her, but his little black head and brown ears were visible. He continued to bark at the gentleman who had come to her aid.

'Where did you come from?' He looked between the small dog and Clara. 'You might want to step away. It doesn't appear very friendly.'

'It's fine. He's fine. He belongs to me.' She looked down at Humphrey. 'Now hush. The nice gentleman was helping me,' she said to the creature who was responsible for this awkward encounter.

'I don't think he likes me.'

'He just wants to get out from under the bush.'

The gentleman lowered himself to the heels of his top boots. The muscles of his thighs flexed in his cream-coloured breeches when his coat parted with his movement. He held his gloved hand out to Humphrey, but didn't say a word, giving the dog the opportunity to sniff him.

'He won't go to you. He's stuck in the bushes.'

'He's stuck, too?'

Clara held up the loop of Humphrey's leash

that was wrapped around her wrist, giving a slight tug to the bit of the red cord that was free of the tangled mess for him to see. Humphrey let out a series of barks as if he was trying to explain to the gentleman how it happened.

'First your dress and now your dog's leash? You two are quite a pair.'

'If we are being precise, it was his leash first and then my dress.'

Lane stood up and strode towards her. 'Can you untangle it?'

'I had been trying to when my dress got caught. I wasn't having much luck.'

'Let me see if I can help.' He squatted just out of Humphrey's reach and then held out his hand to the puppy. 'What have you done to yourself, little one?'

Instead of sniffing the gentleman's hand, Humphrey appeared to try to explain how it had happened before lowering his head to his paws.

'I see. Well, let's free you from this mess so you and your mistress do not have to spend the night here.' Humphrey looked up at him as he traced the red cord from the dog's collar into the hedge and moved some of the branches around to study the tangled mess. 'How did he do this?' he asked, his attention still focused on untangling the cord.

'I'm not sure. He was chasing a butterfly and

the next thing I knew I was pulled practically into the bush.'

'Your leash is too long. You need a shorter one.' He motioned for her to hand him her end and then he worked it through the branches.

Not wanting to inadvertently get caught in the bushes again, Clara adjusted her blue shawl around her shoulders. 'Do you think you will be able to free him or should we just untie the leash from his collar?'

'I think I've got it. Just a few more twists… There, he is free.'

He handed her the end of the leash just as Humphrey let out a few barks before charging the gentleman's leg and resting his paws on his knee. He was rewarded with some scratching behind his ears and Humphrey whipped his head around and licked the man's hand.

'No more chasing butterflies for you, young man.'

Humphrey gave an excited bark as if to say he agreed the adventure had not been worth it.

Clara took a step closer to them and prayed Humphrey would not embarrass her with more of his inappropriate displays. 'Thank you very much for your assistance. I'm not sure what we would have done if you had not come along.'

'Well, I'm just glad I did.' He moved his hands

to scratch Humphrey's neck and the little dog wagged his tail.

'Humphrey loves having his neck scratched. If you keep doing that, he won't allow you to get up.'

He looked up at her. 'Humphrey? This is Humphrey?'

'That's his name,' she said, nodding.

'Well, it's nice to meet you, Humphrey.' He held out his hand to the dog, with his palm up. 'Can you shake?'

Humphrey barked and licked his hand.

'Come now, gentlemen shake when they meet. Give me your paw.'

Humphrey barked again.

'He doesn't understand what you're asking.'

'Then we will teach him.' He tapped Humphrey's right paw. 'Paw.' He held his hand out to Humphrey. 'Give me your paw.'

Once more Humphrey barked and a few more times the gentlemen tapped his paw and repeated the word.

Each time, Humphrey barked. But the last time when the gentleman held out his hand and requested his paw, Humphrey placed it in his hand. He closed his fingers around the little paw and gave it a small shake, while he scratched Humphrey's neck with his other hand. The dog let out a series of happy sounds as if he was letting him know how proud he was that he learned a new trick. Then he looked at Clara with his big brown eyes and let out another bark.

'Yes, I see. You've learned something new.' She took a step closer as the gentleman gave one last pat to Humphrey's head before standing up.

'You seem quite at ease with him. Do you have a dog of your own?'

'Not any longer. I did for a while a long time ago. I travel too much now.'

'Travelling a lot sounds like an adventurous life.'

'I suppose some people may see it as such. Most times the travelling is rather tedious.'

'I'm surprised to see you here. This small stretch is not typically frequented by visitors. They normally enjoy promenading up by the Crescent.'

'Crawling might be a better word. They were moving much too slowly for my liking.' He took a step closer.

'Moving at a sedate pace can be enjoyable when you find your companions entertaining.'

His eyes held hers for a few heartbeats before he looked around for Humphrey. 'But when you are alone and have some place to be, walking behind people being entertained is irritating.'

The candid statement was made with such a gruff delivery it almost made her laugh. 'I imagine it would be. So where did you need to be?'

'Today?'

She nodded and waited for him to respond.

'Nowhere…exactly. But that doesn't mean it was any less bothersome.'

A small laugh crept out before she could hold it back. 'So, you came here to avoid the people out there enjoying themselves.'

His brows drew together and he crossed his arms. Standing tall with his legs apart, he appeared to be preparing for battle. 'You seem to enjoy having fun at my expense.'

'I am not having fun at your expense. But you must admit you take the most benign things quite seriously.'

'I do not.'

'You do. I have lived most of my life in this town and not once have I witnessed anyone inspect the water as carefully as you did yesterday. And today you couldn't even enjoy a walk along the Crescent.'

'That does not mean I have a serious disposition.'

She crossed her arms in return. 'How would your friends describe you?'

'That is neither here nor there.'

'That tells me that you know they would not be describing you as jovial.'

'I should have left you in the bushes.'

The off-the-cuff comment didn't insult her, but

made her laugh instead. 'So perhaps you aren't so serious all the time. What have you found enjoyable while you've been here in Bath?'

'I have yet to have the opportunity to see much of the town.'

'How long have you been here?'

'Eight days.'

'Eight days and you haven't seen much of Bath? What have you been doing all this time?'

'I'm here on business and haven't really got out much.'

'Apparently. I think we need to remedy that. It might help with that disposition of yours.'

'And what do you think I'd find enjoyable here?'

My company is enjoyable, she wanted to say. 'I suppose it depends on what you like. Perhaps it would be better to ask what kinds of activities you find enjoyable.'

He gave a slight shrug of his shoulders.

It seemed he was not going to make suggesting what he should do an easy endeavour. 'Well, one can assume you do not enjoy long strolls.'

'No. That is not true. I do enjoy a brisk walk. It helps me clear my thoughts.'

'Then we will put brisk walking on the list. Perhaps you would enjoy visiting the Lower Assembly Rooms. They are near the bowling green and close to some lovely walks that are laid out by the river. If you time it just right, you might be able to walk the pathways before the crowds descend. And the public breakfast that is served there every Wednesday is quite good.'

'That's a much too leisurely way to spend my days.'

'Well, you could always attend the dress and fancy balls in the evenings in the Upper Assembly Rooms. I prefer the dress balls, myself. And there are cards rooms at those if you do not dance.'

'What makes you think I do not know how to dance?'

'Forgive me. I meant if you were not inclined to dance.'

'I find balls rather tedious. Too much talking about the weather and the state of the roads.'

'Of course. Who would want to speak to all those people enjoying each other's company?'

His lips pressed together which made her laugh again.

'Then perhaps you would prefer a concert or the theatre. Bath has a vast array of ways to entertain yourself while you are here. Your wife might enjoy those activities.' She waited to see if he would confirm that he was married. It hadn't occurred to her that he might be until now.

'Was that your way of finding out if I am married?'

She was not one to hide her inquisitive nature so she smiled up at him. 'Are you?'

Instead of appearing affronted by her question, the hint of a small smile played on his lips. 'No. I am not.'

'Neither am I.' Clara held back a groan. Why, oh, why had she offered that bit of information? It wasn't as if he had bothered to ask her.

'I know. I assumed from the Pump Room that you are widowed. I'm sorry for your loss.'

'Thank you, but my husband passed a long time ago.'

The small creases at the corners of his eyes deepened as they looked at one another.

Humphrey's head nudged her ankle, drawing her attention down to her dog. When she saw him eyeing the gentleman's boot with that expression she had come to know, a sense of dread filled her chest. She held tight to his leash and tugged him back, closer to her.

Humphrey let out a series of barks in protest.

'I really should be taking him home. He is probably hungry.'

'Would you like me to escort you back from where you came?'

'No, thank you. That won't be necessary. I don't have far to go.' Humphrey pulled on the leash in the direction of the gentleman, making their departure all the more urgent. 'I do hope you'll take my suggestions. It would be a pity if you spent your time here without enjoying some of what this town has to offer.'

His eyes seemed to darken momentarily. 'I'll consider your suggestions.'

'I'm glad to hear it.'

There was something about being around this gentleman that made it hard not to smile. She was just glad this time she did so only after she had turned to walk away.

'Wait. I do not even know your name,' he called after her.

Clara pulled back on Humphrey's leash and turned around. 'Mrs Clara Sommersby. And you are…?'

He tipped his head and held the brim of his hat. 'Mr William Lane.' A smile softened the hard planes of his features.

There was no reason to hide her smile now as she bobbed a curtsy. 'Good day, Mr Lane. Perhaps we shall meet again.'

It had taken all of Lane's restraint not to follow Mrs Sommersby out from behind the hedgerow in their secluded spot in the park. As it were, he watched her slowly walk away from him with her small dog trotting along beside her until she reached the end of the hedge where the dirt path they were on merged with the gravel pathway that would take her out of the park.

There was something about being around her that had him wanting to talk with her some more and not rush back to the coffee house as he had originally intended. But now, running back to the coffee house was the furthest thing from his mind as he wondered if she walked her dog here often. When he reached the edge of the wooded park, he looked left and right, trying to catch sight of her, but to no avail. She was nowhere to be found. Digging his hands into his pockets, he resumed his walk. This time he didn't mind the slow pace, since, instead of focusing on reaching his destination, his mind was filled with thoughts of Mrs Sommersby. And the fact that for those few moments she was stuck to the bush, more than anything, he had wanted to kiss her.

Chapter Five

Two days later Lane sat across from Hart and the Duke of Lyonsdale in the office in the back room of the coffee house and tried his best to decipher the man's expression. Lyonsdale had listened intently to what Hart and Lane had to say about the planned spa—but he hadn't asked any questions. The Duke had invested his money with them in past ventures and in prior instances he always had some questions. However, today he sat with his arms crossed and a neutral expression on his face. It couldn't be possible that Lyonsdale was going to turn them down. This spa had the potential to become one of their most profitable ventures yet.

Tapping his finger on the proposed budget that laid between them on the table, Lane leaned closer. 'You have yet to tell us your thoughts. You see the potential, do you not?'

Lyonsdale nodded and sat back in his chair.

'Those numbers are impressive—however, I'm afraid I cannot invest in this.'

Lane could feel his composure start to slip and he almost had to bite the inside of his cheek to stop himself from calling this well-respected member of the House of Lords an ass. 'Might I ask why?'

'Because I have been coming to Bath for years and I see the changes that are taking place here. How many times have you been to Bath, Lane?'

'I just started visiting recently.'

'I see. Well, let me tell you what I've observed. This town was once overflowing with members of the *ton*. Parading along the Crescent resembled making your way through the crowds at Almack's on a Wednesday night. But do you know what I see now?'

Lane shook his head, wishing that he could tell Lyonsdale that he didn't want to know. Those numbers on that page spoke louder to him.

'Now I see a town fading somewhat in its glory as the most fashionable place to be outside of London. There are not nearly as many members of the *ton* here as there once were. Brighton is where the Regent is. Brighton is where the growth is. Do not mistake what I am saying. Bath is still a desirable destination, but for how much longer? It may be profitable now, but can you truly tell me it will continue to be profitable ten years from now…or twenty?'

While Lyonsdale, unlike many members of English Society, always treated Lane with respect, Lane had never felt the divide in class as acutely with the man as he did at this very moment.

'There are no guarantees in business,' Lane replied, looking Lyonsdale directly in the eye. 'I cannot say with one hundred per cent certainty that this venture will be profitable ten years from now or twenty. But what I can guarantee is that right now…now, those numbers are sound. And while people of your class and position may not be flocking here the way they once were, people of my class are. The merchant class and those who are discovering ways to make money through industry, we are all here. And there are many more of us than there are of you.'

He liked the man. He truly did. But how could he not see what was right in front of him?

'I didn't mean to appear so singular in my vision.'

'But you did.'

Hart shifted in his chair beside Lyonsdale. He was the one who possessed all the finesse and charm. He was always the one who would petition the members of the *ton* to invest with them. And this was part of the reason why. The look in Hart's eye told Lane that he might have overstepped himself with the Duke. It told him he should stop talking, lest they lose the man's help in the future.

Lyonsdale came from one of the most prestigious families in Britain. He was a well-respected member of the House of Lords. He was a duke and not the type of man who was accustomed to being talked to in this way. Yet Lane's pride was too great. He might have been raised in a Foundling Hospital, but that didn't mean that he and those like him were not important. They had a place in towns like Bath and Brighton and anywhere else they saw fit to inhabit.

Yes, the look in Hart's eyes said to just shut up—but in this matter, Lane was not about to brush aside the Duke's ignorance.

'With that singular vision of yours you have discounted everyone who is not like you. We have our pleasures, too. We have our place in this world and in time you may find that we are the ones who possess the majority of wealth in this country. Your title and pedigree will not put food on your table for ever.'

There was a loud groan from Hart as he lowered his head and a lock of his black hair slid across his forehead as he pinched the bridge of his nose. By keeping his head lowered and not looking at Lane, it was apparent he was contemplating where he would hit Lane first, once Lyonsdale left.

Silence descended over them, cloaking the room with an air of foreboding.

Finally, the Duke let out a loud breath. 'You can pick your head up, Hart. I'm not about to storm out. This is just becoming entertaining.'

While Hart's head jerked up, Lane had the urge to reach across the table and plant a facer on Lyonsdale. He was not entertaining. None of this was entertaining. Why were people all of a sudden considering him entertaining? First Mrs Sommersby and now Lyonsdale.

'And stand down, Lane. I did not mean to imply that the world outside my circle isn't important. But certainly you know that the *ton* sets the fashion for the rest of England. If those of English Society move out of Bath completely, it will only be a matter of time before others follow suit. That was what I meant. My comments were not intended to disparage anyone with a position in Society under me.'

The tension in Lane's shoulders began to ease a bit even though Lyonsdale was right. Lane was not an unreasonable man. To succeed in business, you had to have an open mind and view a situation from another point of view. 'It is a valid point—however, I have been to the spas. They are filled with the infirm and aged. And they keep coming. This is not just a town that attracts people for the fashionable entertainments. This is a town that people believe will cure their ills. I cannot say if they are right or wrong. I have not witnessed it myself, but what I have seen is the look in the eyes of those who I have spoken to that shine with hope. A hope to be free of the aches and diseases that have plagued them. They believe the water works. And if it doesn't cure them completely, soaking in it offers some relief. Even if for just a little while.'

Lyonsdale looked over at Hart and eyed him up and down. 'Why are you the one who always tries to convince me to invest in these endeavours of yours? Lane is much more logical than you are.'

Hart appeared completely affronted. 'Not true. I appeal to your need to make money. What is more logical than that?'

'Lane has appealed to my sense of justice.' He looked at Lane and arched his brow. 'He has almost made me feel that by investing in this I will be performing some sort of civic duty.'

'Well, we all know how much you pride yourself on your civic duty, so let's go with that, shall we?' Hart replied. 'We can look to see how many widows and orphans take to the waters.' After he said it he glanced at Lane and looked down, as if he realised immediately that he had spoken out of turn considering Lane was an orphan.

'You really should let Lane speak to me about your future investments,' Lyonsdale said, shaking his head.

'Then what will I do? Stand around and exude silent encouragement?'

'You should try that. I'd be interested to see how long you could stay in a room with the two of us and not say a word. Silence is such a foreign concept for you.'

'Not true.'

'True,' both Lyonsdale and Lane said in unison.

Hart glanced between the two of them and pressed his lips together. 'You are both wrong. And to prove it, I will sit here in silence while the two of you discuss how much money Lyonsdale will give us to build the spa.' He raised a challenging brow at him and smirked.

Before his interest waned or Hart provoked him too far, Lane needed to secure Lyonsdale to this project. 'Do you now see the potential we have here?' he asked, taking the Duke's attention away from Hart.

Lyonsdale drew the sheet of paper with the budget closer to him and his gaze slowly moved from side to side as he scanned the page. When he sat back, it was Lane whom he focused on. 'I will fund some of this, but I am not willing to give you all the money you need. And it will be on loan to you for five years.'

When he told them the amount of what he was willing to give and the interest he would charge them, Lane's heart sank. It was not an unusual arrangement that Lyonsdale had offered. Most of the time Lyonsdale preferred to be conservative in his investments. It was just that this time—with this opportunity—Lane had hoped Lyonsdale would see the full potential and take the risk.

'Come now,' Hart said, breaking his self-imposed silence. 'If you give us the full amount we think we will need, then you can become a full partner and reap all the rewards when this spa becomes the sensation of all of Bath and word of it hits London and this town becomes fashionable again.'

'I thought you were going to sit there and offer your silent support?' Lyonsdale said, shifting his weight on his chair away from Hart.

'You knew that was never going to happen, so there is no need to pretend you expected it to. It is early in the morning. You haven't had your breakfast yet. Why don't you go home, have something to eat and think about it some more?'

'No amount of food is going to make me change my mind. While I do believe, for now, it is a sound investment, I still have reservations about the long-term success of this venture. I'm sorry, but this is all I am willing to offer.'

It wasn't enough. They needed more money if they were to purchase The Fountain Head Hotel and convert it into a spa. The hot spring was running under their property for a reason. Lane had discovered it for a reason. And that reason was to make money.

After Lyonsdale left, Hart seemed to have taken the news much better than Lane. 'Do not look as if the world is crashing down on you, Lane. You always take these things too much to heart.'

Lane's reputation and the success of his business ventures were what kept him acceptable in the eyes of certain members of Society. Hart would never understand the prejudices he faced as an orphan with no family connections at all. His business success was a way of proving to them that he was just as good as they were. He believed that and, on some level, he knew some of them did as well.

'Come with me, Lane. It's Wednesday and my wife has told me that they serve a good breakfast at the Lower Assembly Rooms today. I think I need to get you out of this place for a few hours to improve that foul look on your face.'

Chapter Six

~~~~~~~~~~~~~

The Lower Assembly Rooms were located close to the banks of the River Avon, not far from the King's and Queen's Baths and Bath Abbey. The large room Lane found himself in with the tall windows held balls on Tuesday and Thursday evenings, according to Hart. It wasn't until they stepped inside that he recalled Mrs Sommersby mentioning it to him when they spoke in the park.

While they were being escorted past the small round tables of two-to-four people to get to their seats, he found himself scanning the occupants to see if she were here and found it oddly disconcerting when his spirits dropped even more than they already had when he didn't see her.

'Have something to eat. It might help to improve that mood you're in,' Hart said after they settled in with their steaming mugs of coffee and buttery-smelling breads.

'I'm fine.'

'You don't appear to be fine. You look as if you will rip apart our waiter should he offer you more coffee. Which is rather inconvenient since I believe I will be having more than one cup.'

'Lyonsdale is wrong about this. You know that, don't you?'

'Lyonsdale will never change.' Hart brushed a lock of his black hair out of his eyes. 'You know he is not one to part with his money easily.'

'But how could he not see the immediate value in this?'

Hart picked up his knife and began to spread marmalade on his bread. 'Instead of obsessing over the fact that Lyonsdale would not give us all the money we require, let's talk about who we should approach next. You always get so offended whenever someone doesn't see your vision or care to invest.'

'I do not.'

'Yes, you do.'

'No, I don't.'

'Yes. Yes, you do. You should see how that vein in your temple is pulsing right now.'

Lane rubbed his temple before he caught the mischievous glint in Hart's eye. 'You're an ass. And if it is pulsing, as you say, it's because I'm with you.'

His response only served to make Hart laugh.

'You, my friend, view life far too seriously. Stop trying to prove something. There is no need. You already are successful.'

'I'm not trying to prove anything. I am trying to make money for you and me and I would think you would appreciate that.'

'I do. However, we both know that there is more to this than that and that's why you've taken Lyonsdale's decision so hard.'

'And when did you suddenly become qualified to say what my motives are? You, of all people. You are a complicated wreck and you know it.'

'Correction. I was a complicated wreck. Now, I'm just complicated.'

'How does Sarah live with you?'

'She finds my complications endearing.'

'At least someone does.' To avoid having to look at Hart's cocky grin, he turned his attention away from his friend.

And spotted Mrs Sommersby, sitting not far from them.

She was wearing a pink and green dress as she sat with a red-haired young woman. Both women appeared to be enjoying each other's company as they placed their orders with their waiter.

'...are much less conservative in their investing than Lyonsdale,' he heard Hart say, breaking into his study of Mrs Sommersby. 'I believe there is a good chance that I can get them to commit to this.'

'Who?'

'Weren't you listening to me?' Hart scanned the area of the room where Mrs Sommersby sat as if he were trying to determine what had captured Lane's attention. With so many people sitting near them, it would be impossible for him to work it out. Hart must have come to that conclusion as well, since he looked back at Lane. 'I'll be heading back to London in two days to handle some additional affairs that need my attention and will speak with a number of potential investors then. Hopefully, soon, we will have the funds we need to create this spa of yours.'

At the mention of the spa, Lane found it hard to swallow the bread in his mouth. 'Hopefully they will be more willing to invest in it than Lyonsdale was.'

Not wishing to dwell any further on his aggravating day, Lane's attention was drawn back to Mrs Sommersby, who was now speaking in an animated fashion to her companion. Narrowing his focus on to her lips, he tried to determine what she might be saying. Some people were proficient in reading lips. Lane discovered he was not.

'I propositioned the older one once. Years ago, before I met Sarah.'

The fact that Hart had leaned closer to him when he said it made it hard to ignore the comment.

'Who?'

'The dark-haired woman sitting with the red-haired chit you've been staring at.' With his head, he nodded in the direction of Mrs Sommersby's table. 'She's a widow by the name of Sommersby. The beauty beside her with the flaming hair and full lips I've never seen before, so I cannot help you there.'

The idea of Hart and Mrs Sommersby together made Lane's stomach drop. It shouldn't matter to him who this woman chose to spend time with. He didn't even know her. 'What makes you believe I was staring at any woman in this room? Perhaps I was simply staring off, not wanting to continue to look at your face.'

The studied expression Hart was giving him made him shift a bit in his seat.

'My mistake.'

'Do you have any particular investors in mind that you'll be contacting?'

'I do. There are two gentlemen in particular that—'

'What did you say when you propositioned her?' Lane felt his forehead wrinkle as he continued to try to push away the image of Mrs Sommersby with his friend.

'Pardon?'

'Mrs Sommersby? What did you say to her... exactly?' Having the need to do something with his mouth so he would just stop talking, Lane took a sip of coffee and waited.

His friend chose that very moment to take a bite of bread, prolonging the time it took him to answer. 'I don't remember my exact words.'

'Well...what is it that you think you might have said to her?'

'Well... I *think* I might have asked if she'd care to take a turn with me in the darkened gardens during a ball we attended together. It was probably a cold night and I may have offered to keep her warm as we looked at the stars.'

'Have you had much success with that suggestion?'

'You'd be surprised.' Hart took another bite of bread.

An inexplicable lump formed in Lane's throat. 'So you are intimately acquainted with the woman?'

'Mrs Sommersby?' Hart shook his head. 'No, I thought you were just referring to the suggestion in itself. I'd had a bit of success with it in the past.'

'But not with her?'

Once again, Hart shook his head, but this time the movement was slower. 'No, no. If I recall correctly, she was flattered, but I am certain she definitely declined.' Picking up his cup, he looked over to where Mrs Sommersby was sitting. 'Before Sarah, I had a marked preference for older women.'

'She's not that old,' Lane replied, sounding almost indignant, which was strange since he had no reason to feel insulted on her behalf.

'Well, she is certainly older than the girls the mothers try to throw into your path when you are an earl attending a ball, I can tell you that. I found older women more at ease with themselves and they know their desires much better than a girl out of the schoolroom usually does. And if you find the right one, you don't have to fear being trapped into marriage.'

'Is that why you spent your time with married women?'

'I had no desire to deflower a virgin and then leave her reputation in tatters. And I never saw the appeal of paying for sex. Married women whose husbands had mistresses were my haven.'

'But you said you propositioned Mrs Sommersby and she's a widow.'

'Yes, but she's a widow who had made it known that she was not interested in marriage. With her looks and lively character, and that bit of information, I was taken with her for an entire Season.'

'An entire Season?'

'It was a number of years after her husband died and as I said, years ago. And just because

I was taken with her doesn't mean that I was celibate for all those months.' The smile on his face reached his eyes. 'Perhaps that was why she turned me down. She's a shrewd one, that one.'

'Perhaps she simply didn't find you attractive.'

'We both know that cannot be the reason.'

'Have you always been this confident in your charms?'

Hart appeared to give the question consideration. 'Yes. I suppose I have been. But that doesn't signify now. Now I am a contented married man who can look back with pleasant nostalgia on the life I led. What about you? You are not one to place your relationships out for the world to see. Are you as confident with women as you are with business? I've not witnessed that side of you in all the years we've known each other.'

The waiter came to their table to clear away their plates, saving Lane from having to answer.

'Lane?'

Damn. He hated the thought that went into answering questions like this. Years ago, Lane learned no good came from analysing his feelings. It was best to move through life without thinking too much about what anything made him feel. He had become quite skilled at it.

'I do well for myself.'

The vague comment made Hart laugh. 'With

the money you've made I'm sure you do and I've been told you are not hard on the eyes.'

Lane sat up a bit taller. 'By whom?'

'Miss Violet Westfield, one of Sarah's friends. She saw us together some time ago. I can introduce you when you are back in London, if you like?'

Was his wife's friend as attractive as Mrs Sommersby? Not that Mrs Sommersby was an outstanding beauty, but she was pretty and there was just something about her. He turned back to take a look to try to determine what it was.

'If we can get the funding we need, it might be some time before I'm back in London,' he replied, keeping his eyes on Mrs Sommersby.

'And your decision is based solely on your need to remain here on business?'

When Lane looked back at Hart, he wanted to hit that all-too-perceptible smirk off his face.

'Yes.'

'Hmm. Well, I'm sure you have things that you need to address back at the coffee house and I promised Sarah that I would be home by noon to go with her for a drive around the countryside, so why don't I ask for the bill and we can leave?'

'I'll take care of it. Why don't you go on ahead? I'm going to sit here and finish my coffee.'

'Your coffee?' That smile was back on Hart's

face. 'I see. Well you wouldn't want to leave any coffee in that cup of yours, now would you?'

'No, I would not. And stop looking at me like that. I told you, I'm just finishing my coffee.'

'If that's what you want to call it, that is fine with me. I can't imagine where you might find another cup of coffee in this town.'

'You really should go. It would be a pity if you returned late to your wife and caused her to bar you from your bedchamber tonight.'

'That is not likely to happen—however, I'll let you enjoy your coffee in peace.' He stood up and adjusted his cuffs. 'I will stop by to see you before I leave for London.'

'When do you expect to have an answer for me?'

'Sarah and I had planned to leave on Friday. You'll have your answer in about a week or so.'

A week of not knowing if they would be able to proceed was going to feel like an eternity. His grip tightened around the handle of his cup. One of the worst things about needing other people to help finance his business ventures was that it put him at someone else's mercy. More than anything he hated having to depend on other people. After living the first sixteen years of his life in the Foundling Hospital, he had learned very early on to live his life without being dependent on anyone for anything. It took a great deal of effort to relinquish some of his control.

'Do try not to be such a curmudgeon while I am gone. You wouldn't want Mrs Sommersby to find out what a grump you can be.'

It was very tempting to trip Hart on his way past him and as his friend walked towards Mrs Sommersby's table he almost wished he had done it. In true Hart fashion, he looked back at Lane with a smile before he altered his course slightly, missing the table where she sat.

Every nerve in his body was strung tight. Relying on others was not something he was comfortable with, but unfortunately it was part of doing business. And now he would have to wait a week before he knew if they could move forward with their plans.

As his vision began to clear, Mrs Sommersby came into focus. How long he had been staring sightlessly at her, he had no idea. She was listening intently to what her companion was saying. What did women talk about when they weren't in the company of men? The question had never occurred to him until now. Once more, Lane tried to read lips and once more he failed miserably.

She had this way of gracefully moving her fingers as she continually spun her cup in her saucer. It was distinctly possible that she wasn't even aware she was doing it, but oddly enough watching her movement was easing his agitation. Suddenly she looked his way and, as their eyes met, a slow smile spread across her face. Something inside him shifted and it felt as if the sun had come out for the first time during this very gloomy day.

Chapter Seven

Spotting Mr Lane sitting approximately four tables away from her in the bustling Lower Assembly Room had made a fine morning even better. It had been quite some time since Clara had captured the attention of an attractive man in his thirties—at least one that was unaware of her lofty family connections or her very comfortable financial position. And even though she knew his attention had more to do with the fact she was probably one of the only people he recognised in the room, it still was a wonderful feeling.

When she dipped her head as a silent greeting, he returned the gesture with the smallest of smiles.

'I would so love to see *The Rivals*,' Miss Harriet Collingswood said, drawing Clara's attention away from Mr Lane and back to the conversation she had been having with her new friend. Harriet was the older daughter of her neighbour; the one the Dowager had suggested might be in need of their help finding a husband. 'My mother doesn't like Mr Sheridan's work and has refused to take us to see the play,' she continued. 'She had seen two of his plays in the past and found little humour in them. However, I heard they are quite amusing and I do so love to laugh.'

Giving Harriet a sympathetic smile, Clara resisted the urge to see if Mr Lane was still watching her. With a concerted effort, she focused all of her attention on the woman sitting across the small round table from her.

The more time Clara spent with the young woman, the more she discovered she liked her. Taking her to the spa this morning to drink the waters with her and then bringing her here to the Lower Assembly Room for breakfast had proved to be a wise decision. It had become apparent that spending time with her while Clara searched for potential husbands for the woman would be rather enjoyable.

Although, currently, it was proving to be impossible to keep her attention on her for very long. The urge to glance over at Mr Lane was too great and her gaze slid over to him once more.

His eyes were still on her.

She needed to appear composed and unaffected by his attention. She was a middle-aged woman. His attention shouldn't make her want to smile, yet it was taking great effort on her part to keep her expression neutral as she quickly looked back at Harriet. 'And your sister? Does Ann have a desire to see the play?'

'No. Ann prefers operas. She tends to favour whatever is considered the height of fashion at the moment and has heard that many women of the *ton* favour it. Have you seen any of Mr Sheridan's plays?'

'I have seen all of his work and every production.' This might be just the opportunity Clara was looking for to remove Harriet from her family long enough to introduce her to potential suitors. 'Do you think your mother will be willing to spare you for one evening? If she would, I'd be happy to take you to see it at the Theatre Royal. I have a box there.'

The invitation appeared to embarrass Harriet, who lowered her eyes to the table. 'That is very generous of you, but I don't want to impose on your time that way. Please do not think it was my intention to try to garner an invitation from you.'

'The thought never occurred to me and it would be no imposition at all. I'd enjoy your company.' She fiddled with her cup in its saucer, trying to decide how to best ask the question that sprang out of her curiosity about the sisters. While she was thinking how to tactfully phrase her question, Harriet took matters into her own hands.

'Might I ask you a question, Mrs Sommersby?'

'Of course, my dear.'

'I am very grateful that you invited me out this morning, but I am curious as to why you singled me out with this favour? Most people, you see, tend to pay more attention to my sister Ann.'

And with that brief declaration, Clara was saved from finding a way to delicately bring up Harriet's sister. 'I noticed as much the times I have been in your family's company. I, too, had a sister who garnered all the attention while I was of a quieter nature. Although, I confess, I thought you were far quieter than you truly are.'

Her observation appeared to have embarrassed Harriet again. When she placed her hand gently over the young woman's as a comforting gesture, Harriet seemed surprised. Clara had always been a person who drew comfort from a touch. She had to remind herself once more that not everyone felt that way.

'I did not say that to censure your behaviour. It was simply an observation. I believe people can shine brightest when they step out of the shadows of others. I just wanted to give you a place to take that step.' She removed her hand with a pat and took a sip of her tea.

Harriet was an attractive girl with warm brown eyes and hair the colour of the setting sun. Clara knew men well enough to know that they would find her rather full lips a seductive feature, even though the young woman herself was probably unaware of the allure. Could Mr Lane have been staring at her in hopes of garnering an introduction? She already knew he wasn't married. Peering over her teacup, she moved her gaze in his direction and became disappointed when she found that he was no longer there.

However, her disappointment was short-lived when he suddenly approached her side from behind.

'Good morning, Mrs Sommersby,' he said over the sounds of the conversations going on around them.

'Mr Lane, I see you have taken my advice and come here to have breakfast.' She gave him a bright smile to show she appreciated that he had followed her recommendation.

He took a quick glance around. 'I actually accompanied a friend here. He had suggested this establishment. I stayed after he left to finish my coffee.'

There was nothing quite like humiliating yourself in front of a new friend. The man had probably forgotten all about her recommendation of this place the moment she'd left him in the park.

'Forgive me for imposing on your time,' he said with a slight hesitation, 'but you dropped this.'

When he held out her white napkin, Clara was

reminded yet again that she had been a fool for thinking even for a minute that he had fancied her. As she took the napkin from him, she was careful not to brush her fingers against his so he would not assume that she might be attempting to flirt with him in any way. It was bad enough that she found his appearance and mannerisms striking. She didn't need him to sense that she did.

'Thank you.' Out of the corner of her eye she could see Harriet looking down at the table. Now was the perfect opportunity to start introducing her to eligible gentlemen. 'Miss Collingswood, may I introduce you to Mr Lane. Mr Lane, this is Miss Collingswood. She is a visitor to Bath, like yourself.'

He executed a bow in the limited space that was available. 'A pleasure.'

'It's nice to make your acquaintance. I hope I'm not overstepping when I say that you look rather familiar, Mr Lane. Do you mind if I ask where you are from?'

'London.' For a man who moments before appeared to be leisurely sipping his coffee, a sudden sense of unease settled over his demeanour.

Perhaps he was unsure where to direct the conversation. The woman herself was not offering him any further words of encouragement after his one-word response. This wouldn't be the first time Clara had found herself helping a couple along. It was what she normally enjoyed doing.

'I realise that you were just leaving, but would you care to join us for a bit?'

'No.'

The response was abrupt and his tone caused her to start.

'Forgive me, ladies. I really must be going.'

She had thought he had enjoyed speaking with her in the past. Now, it was apparent, he had no desire to hold a conversation and was counting the seconds before he could leave.

Wanting to save them all from the awkwardness of the situation, she turned away from him and signalled her waiter with the tilt of her head. 'Do enjoy the rest of your day, Mr Lane, and the remainder of your time in Bath.'

'Mrs Sommersby. Miss Collingswood.'

She felt, rather than saw, when he walked away from their table. How was she to bolster the confidence of Harriet with men like Mr Lane around? His demeanour just now was best described as gruff. For a man who had been staring at her minutes earlier to behave in such a manner when they had an opportunity to converse was puzzling.

It wasn't long before she had the chance to confront him on his behaviour when she stepped outside the Assembly Room and spotted him not far from the entrance with his hands in the pockets of his long green coat, presumably waiting for his carriage or a sedan chair.

Early on in her marriage to Robert, Clara's husband had tried to shield her when the state of their finances became grim. The dire truth during those times would often surface unexpectedly when she was in one of the shops in town. The mortification she would feel at those moments led her to understand the value of open and honest communication. And now the truth she wished she could uncover was why Mr Lane had been watching her so intently during breakfast, only to practically run from her once they spoke.

She looked over at him and adjusted the brim of her bonnet to shield her eyes from the sun that was shining high in the bright blue sky. The movement must have caught his attention, since their eyes met immediately after she lowered her gloved hands. He gave her an almost apologetic smile, as if he knew his behaviour had been rude. At least the man was conscious of his actions. She gave him a playful chastising shake of her head and was about to turn back to Harriet when he took a single step towards her.

Chapter Eight

Lane knew he had behaved horribly with Mrs Sommersby, but the minute Miss Collingswood asked where he was from that defensive instinct inside him kicked in and he wanted to do whatever he could to avoid talking about himself. Miss Collingswood was much too young to have remembered him from the Foundling Hospital. It wasn't possible she was recalling the time he spent growing up there. However, whenever someone said he looked familiar, a prickling sensation would run along his skin and his instinct was to run.

He had faced many disgusted looks and received the cut from people in respectable levels of Society once they were made aware of his origins. Most of the children abandoned and left in the care of the Foundling Hospital were there because they were by-blows whose fathers would not or could not marry their mothers. This was common knowledge and it changed how many people treated you when they found out you were raised there. From the time that he was a young child, Lane had formed a hard shell around his emotions. But today, that shell had a crack in it and deep down he knew for some reason he didn't want Mrs Sommersby to treat him that way.

When their eyes met just now, he wanted to apologise to her for his behaviour. But after taking a step closer, he realised he had no idea how to explain his actions. There wasn't anything he could say that would make sense.

And now thanks to his decision to find a hack or one of those sedan chairs to get back to the coffee house, he wasn't going to escape having to explain himself because she was walking his way.

She strolled towards him with a teasing smile, leaving her friend behind. It wasn't until she stopped in front of him and looked up into his eyes that he was once again aware of how petite she was.

'Would you care to explain your abrupt nature just now, or would you prefer I draw my own conclusions on the matter?'

Bracing himself for this discussion, he crossed his arms. 'And what conclusions might you draw?'

'Indigestion.' Her voice was low, as if she was sharing her darkest secret with him.

'No,' he replied with a trace of laughter.

'Back to one-word replies, I see. Then it must be that you find my company dull. However, it was unkind of you to be so sharp with Miss Collingswood. You had not been in her presence long enough to form a poor opinion of her.' She would make a very good governess since she had the ability to chastise him while appearing to simply offer him some helpful advice.

'I assure you that I do not find you dull nor do I have a poor opinion of Miss Collingswood. And I do apologise for my behaviour.'

Wisps of brown hair framed her face under her bonnet and with the sun shining on them he could see streaks of mahogany mixed in. As she tilted her head, some of that hair slid across her cheek. 'I accept your apology and I am sorry I placed you in an awkward position. I assumed you were in a better disposition and even thought you might have actually smiled at me while you were drinking your coffee.'

Had he smiled at her? It had brightened his day when he had spotted her…but shortly afterwards he remembered his discussion with Lyonsdale and knew his time was better spent attending to business. 'I had received some disappointing news this morning. My friend thought having breakfast here would improve my disposition. I believe you would say that it has not.'

'I hope it was not bad news from home. Your family is well?' Concern was etched on her face and shone in her amber-coloured eyes.

'It was nothing like that. It was a business matter.' That was one more reminder today that, unlike most people, he had no family.

'I see. Well I am sorry none the less.'

A shiny black-lacquered carriage pulled up and she held up her finger to the driver, indicating she would be a moment longer. She bit her lip and appeared to be deciding if she should say something else to him. He arched his brow in encouragement and waited.

'Would you consider allowing me to try to improve your current grumpy state?'

'I don't believe we agreed I was exactly grumpy, but tell me what you had in mind.'

'Tomorrow night I will be attending a performance of *The Rivals* at the Theatre Royal, not far from here. It's a wonderful play by Mr Sheridan and one that I believe might lift your spirits. If you are still in town, would you like to join me at the theatre to see it?'

Lane couldn't remember the last time he was in a theatre. There was no sense in attending plays when he preferred to stay home in the evenings creating spreadsheets of profit and loss statements, or analysing a new potential investment. Lately he had been researching the way water was piped into the various bathhouses in town.

'It will do you good to see more of what Bath has to offer. You are always in a hurry. You need to slow your pace and enjoy the moment you are in.'

He had enjoyed every moment he was with her in the park and standing this close to her once again and breathing in the faint scent of roses that perfumed the air around her was more than a pleasant experience. Spending an evening in her company would not be a hardship. And Hart would be getting ready to go to London anyway. There wasn't more that Lane could do at the moment to further things along. His friend had been telling him to stop devoting all his attention to work. Hart's parting words to him had been 'go and find a woman.' He had never listened to that advice in the past. However, right now he was finding it hard to come up with a reason not to.

'I'll go.'

'Capital!' She adjusted her wrap while a smile brightened her face. 'I shall leave your name at the box office and instruct them to give you a token for my box. The performance will start at eight.' As she took a step back the faint scent of roses went with her. 'Enjoy the rest of your day, Mr Lane. I hope you find it improves.'

She had asked him to spend the evening with her. He couldn't deny that it already had.

Chapter Nine

The next afternoon Clara sat in the back garden of The Fountain Head Hotel across the table from her cousin Phillip Edwards, trying a new selection of bread that the hotel's cook had been interested in serving during breakfast. While Clara owned the hotel, it was Phillip who managed it for her and gave a face to the public of being the probable owner.

She moved in elevated social circles. One of her three nieces was a duchess. She herself had been married to the youngest son of an earl who had seen it as beneath him to own a lodging establishment and that was why when he was alive he never agreed with her that it was a wise investment when they had the funds. If word got out that she owned a hotel, she would be shunned by members of the *ton*, the very Society her family moved in, and she had no desire to bring any shame to those nieces whom she loved as if they were her own daughters. And when she was serving as chaperone for her unmarried niece, she would never have taken the chance of hurting Juliet's ability to make a strong match.

Phillip had agreed to run the hotel for her when she had purchased it not long after she became a widow and was free to buy the property she had long coveted. He was competent with her most valued investment and could keep her secret.

Two years ago, Clara had decided to turn the garden into an area where guests and local residents could go for a light breakfast to begin their day. The hotel mostly catered to bachelors since the families who were staying in Bath for an extended amount of time would rent houses. Bachelors didn't have cooks with them and she soon saw that they appreciated not having to travel far to break their fast after a late night out at one of the town's various entertainments. Serving breakfast had become a profitable venture and Clara was always looking for ways to improve upon it. Today, she was discussing her latest idea with Phillip.

'Gentlemen enjoy hearty meals,' she said needlessly to him as he sat across the table from her. 'So maybe we should offer them something more substantial than toast and tea.'

'This will give more work to the kitchen. We might need more staff.'

'Then we hire more staff.'

'There are already a number of places in town that serve a more substantial breakfast.'

'Yes, taking potential profits away from us. It doesn't make sense not to offer it on the menu. Yesterday morning, the Lower Assembly Room was filled with gentlemen coming in later in the morning after tending to their early morning business or going out for a ride. A good number of those men would enjoy a quieter, more refined experience.'

'I don't think it will bring the return in that you think it will.'

Clara picked up her cup and took a sip of the warm tea, which had cooled in her cup since they began this discussion. To those around them who knew them, it appeared to be a monthly family meal shared by the two cousins.

'But I disagree. We shall try it for a month. If in that time we find that it is not to our benefit, we change the menu back.'

His round face looked pinched as he stared across the table at her as if he were suffering from an aching head. 'Very well. Write up a menu and I'll discuss it with the cook.'

She could tell by his expression that he did not believe it would succeed. Even though the hotel was putting a good amount of money in her pocket every month, it was important to her to look for ways to make certain it remained a desirable place to stay. This hotel was everything to her.

The remainder of the day seemed to crawl by as she looked forward to heading to the theatre that night. Finally, at seven p.m., she entered her carriage with Harriet to see the opening-night performance of Sheridan's play.

'I have invited a few friends to join us tonight. It will give you an opportunity to meet some other people here in Bath.'

A flicker of nervous uncertainty crossed Harriet's face in the dim light of the rocking carriage. 'I hope you didn't go to any trouble for me. I know that my mother expressed an interest in meeting as many people as we can while we are here, but I am not of the same nature.'

'It was no trouble. I have asked Mr Lane to join us.'

Harriet's expression fell. 'I do not think Mr Lane likes me.'

'Nonsense. Mr Lane barely said two words to you.'

'That is my point. I don't believe I left him with a good impression. He might think I am too inquisitive, but the truth is I thought asking him about where he was from would be a good way to begin a conversation.'

'It is a fine way to begin a conversation. Don't let his gruff demeanour make you question your behaviour. He informed me that he had been having a trying morning. His reaction to our discussion had more to do with his troubles than our words.'

She hadn't seen the woman interact much with gentlemen during assemblies. Harriet would typically stand beside her sister while Ann received all the attention and Ann appeared quite comfortable talking with both gentlemen and ladies alike. Having Harriet converse with Mr Lane tonight, while she was with her, hopefully would help her practise feeling more at ease with gentlemen in the future.

And Mr Lane really did need to see more of Bath while he was here, so inviting him to join them for a lovely night out at the theatre was a benefit to him as well. It would be a pity if he returned to London without experiencing all the wonderful things Bath had to offer. If he enjoyed himself, he might recommend the town to his friends which would bring more people here and possibly to her hotel.

'You aren't just saying that to make me feel at ease in his presence tonight?'

'No, I am saying that because it is the truth. You will see. I am certain he will be more talkative this evening.'

At least she hoped he would be. If his day had gone as poorly as her day, then perhaps he would not be in the mood to chat with poor Harriet. 'It might be in our best interest to evaluate Mr Lane's disposition before trying to start a conversation with him.'

'And how are we to do that if we cannot speak with him?'

'There are other signs besides his speech that will be an indication.'

'Such as?'

'Harriet, can you tell when your father is out of sorts when he walks into a room?'

'Usually.'

'Well, most men are the same. Pay close attention to the line of his brow. One can typically tell a lot about a person by their eyes.'

Her friend looked down and picked at her pale blue silk glove. 'I think I will wait to say anything to him until I see how you proceed.'

'Very well, if it makes you feel more at ease, then follow my lead. I assure you, you will have no problems with the Dowager Duchess of Lyonsdale. She will be joining us as well and she is delightful.'

'A dowager duchess?' There was a distinct crack in Harriet's voice and her hands flew to her stomach. 'There really was no need to invite these people for my sake.'

'I assure you, she is lovely.'

'Maybe to people who have vouchers at Almack's, but my father is a barrister.'

'That's a very noble profession, Harriet.'

'Yes, but she is a duchess.'

'I would not invite people who I thought would make you feel uncomfortable.'

'Mr Lane already made me feel uncomfortable.'

'Yes, but he will be redeeming himself tonight. You will see.'

Harriet did not look at all convinced as she turned from Clara and stared out of the window of the rumbling carriage as they drove past houses silhouetted against the glow of the pink and blue evening sky.

It was particularly crowded at the theatre and Clara attributed it to being opening night for this production. As they made their way into her box, they found the Dowager Duchess was already seated in the front row with a young dark-haired gentleman whom Clara did not recognise. The Dowager turned as they entered the box and immediately the gentleman stood up. It was apparent from the way his formal black evening attire fitted his tall, slender frame that this was a man who had taken time with his appearance tonight and could afford well-made clothes. Although he was slender, his cheeks still possessed the round, smooth glow of someone who was not yet in the full maturity of his manhood and was probably only a few years past Harriet's nineteen years.

The Dowager stepped out from where she had been sitting and met them near the doorway. 'Thank you for the invitation to attend this evening's performance. It was such a nice surprise. I've always loved Sheridan.'

'I'm so glad you were able to join us. May I present Miss Collingswood to you. Miss Collingswood, this is Eleanor, the Dowager Duchess of Lyonsdale.'

Although Clara knew the woman was nervous, Harriet executed a graceful curtsy and waited politely for the Dowager to address her.

'It's lovely to make your acquaintance, Miss Collingswood. Mrs Sommersby has told me much about you and I am glad that we've been given an opportunity to meet. May I introduce you both to Mr Greeley. Mr Greeley, this is Mrs Sommersby and Miss Collingswood. Mr Greeley is the grandson of Sir Percy Fullerton, an old friend.'

Harriet seemed frozen in place as she watched Mr Greeley extend his greeting.

'Greeley, why don't you point out the new lights on the stage to Miss Collingswood that you were showing me earlier?' the Dowager said, arching her brow at him. 'He has assured me,

Miss Collingswood, they are a bit extraordinary. I cannot explain them myself, but he knows a lot about them. Apparently, this theatre was built almost twenty years ago and he knows one of the architects personally. Isn't that right?' She gave him an encouraging smile.

The poor man had been staring at Harriet and the Dowager's words seemed to bring him out of his stupor. 'Oh, yes. Mr Palmer was a family friend. He would tell me about building this theatre when I was a young boy. Hearing those stories helped develop my interest in architecture.'

Harriet was smiling a bit shyly at him. 'I like architecture as well, Mr Greeley. I am a great admirer of Mr Adam's work. I have a fondness for the classical designs.'

Apparently, her statement was met with approval from Mr Greeley, who was practically beaming. 'I've studied his work extensively. You have excellent taste, Miss Collingswood.'

'Greeley is an architect,' the Dowager interjected. 'And a fine one at that. He will be working on a number of follies on the grounds of Lyonsdale Hall later this year. Katrina, my grandson's wife, was very happy with his designs.'

'Oh, that sounds positively delightful,' Harriet exclaimed bringing her gloved hands together. From appearances, Mr Greeley might be the first architect that Miss Collingswood had ever met.

'What a wonderful project to be working on. Will they follow the classical designs or are you trying something else?'

'All resemble Greek or Roman temples except one. That one will look like a ruined abbey.'

Harriet's eyes lit up. 'Oh, how very Gothic.'

'Congratulations,' Clara said, tilting her head, trying to get his attention.

Mr Greeley barely looked away from Harriet for a minute to extend his 'thank you' to Clara. The Dowager nudged Clara's side and raised that brow of hers again. Apparently, she was very pleased with herself for her decision to invite the man.

'I believe Her Grace mentioned something about the lights here in the theatre.' With her hand, Harriet gestured to two seats in the front of the box.

That was quite a bold move for Harriet and it made Clara feel all warm inside as she watched the gentleman escort her friend over to the chairs that looked down at the red velvet curtain with gold trim that was closed on the stage.

To give them some privacy the Dowager took Clara by the arm and guided her away from the front of the box. 'I hope you do not mind that I invited Greeley to join me. He is a lovely young man and was the perfect escort for me. And it is so nice to have gentlemen about on evenings like this. They come in handy for fetching you a glass of wine and the like.'

'Is that why you did not want to accompany me in my carriage this evening?'

'It was.'

'I've invited a gentleman here tonight as well.' Now this could prove to be a bit awkward since Clara wasn't certain what she expected to happen between Harriet and Mr Lane.

'You have? Why did you not tell me?'

'I didn't think I needed to. I thought you were going to leave things up to me. He is the gentleman from out of town who we spoke about from the Pump Room. His name is Mr Lane.'

The Dowager brought her gloved hands together, eliciting a muffled clap. 'Capital! A girl should always have the option of choosing from more than one suitor.'

'I wouldn't exactly call him—'

'They do seem to be getting on rather well.' The Dowager motioned to Harriet and Mr Greeley who had their heads bent together in an animated discussion. 'Don't you think?'

'Well, yes, but I thought you were going to let me find her a suitor.'

'I told you I was bored here in Bath and needed something to occupy my time.' She dipped her chin into an almost coquettish look.

'I know what you're about. You want to see who is the better matchmaker.'

'That thought never crossed my mind.' Yet her expression told a different tale.

'What made you think Mr Greeley would be suitable for Miss Collingswood?'

'Have you not looked at him? My dear, he is a quite pleasing young man. Even at my advanced age I can see that.'

'Is that all he has to recommend him?'

'No. He has a charming manner, is affable, has a budding career as an architect and his father is a well-respected barrister who has presented cases before Parliament. That is a very well-respected position for a gentleman his age.'

'*Her* father is a barrister.'

The old woman tried to appear innocent. It wasn't working.

'You knew that.'

'You might have mentioned it the day we were sitting in your garden. You remember that day. Your dog seemed taken with the flowerpot.'

'Do not bring Humphrey into this discussion. I see that look in your eyes. You had every intention of making this a competition.'

'As I said, I was bored and a competition will make this more exciting. Now tell me about your Mr Lane.'

'He is the blond-haired gentleman we spoke to

by the fountain. The one you suggested might be a good match for her.'

'The one who was reluctant to drink the water.'

'That's him.'

'The one I caught watching you a number of times while we stood around the fountain?'

Just as he was watching her yesterday during breakfast…

'So you said.'

'The one you also seemed to study that day.'

Clara looked down and tugged her white-silk glove above her elbow. 'I don't believe that is exactly accurate.'

'The one with the strong set of shoulders and square jaw.'

'I hadn't realised you yourself had studied him that closely.'

'I had. And you invited him here…for Miss Collingswood.'

'I saw him yesterday in the Lower Assembly Room during breakfast. I was inspired.' That inspiration had more to do with giving Harriet opportunities to feel comfortable conversing with a gentleman than it did with arranging a courtship.

'I see. Well, we will have to wait and see which one she prefers.'

From the time she was a young girl, Clara had had a competitive streak. It was not her finest quality to be sure, but it was a part of her that would surface every now and then. And right now that part of her nature was screaming that she was a better matchmaker.

Looking over at Harriet, she found her listening intently to what Mr Greeley was saying while their heads were lowered close to one another. She looked very comfortable and happy with him. Less than an hour ago she looked as if she had wanted to jump out of the carriage when Clara mentioned that she would be seeing Mr Lane again.

If she were to seriously propose Mr Lane as a potential suitor, she needed to know far more about him than she already did. She knew nothing of his background. She didn't know where he lived, aside from London, or anything about his family. He was a businessman, but what kind of business was he involved in? And she still needed to find a way to repair the damage he had done with his brusque manner yesterday.

Clara did not like losing and she did have a skill for matching up suitable partners. Mr Lane was handsome, at times charming, and she knew he hid a wonderful dry sense of humour. She got the impression he was an intelligent man. And while he might not be a gentleman who favoured the very latest fashion, the cut of his clothes showed off his athletic form and she could tell they were well made. And he was just the right height for a man. Not overly tall and not diminutive either. He would make an ideal suitor…for Harriet.

'The performance is about to start. Are you sure he's coming?'

'He said he would be here.'

One thing she didn't know about him was if he was punctual—or if he was a man of his word.

Chapter Ten

Lane was not fond of crowds. But he had given his word to Mrs Sommersby that he would be here and he never went back on his word. However, the next time someone invited him out to a social engagement, he would find a reason to decline. It was moments like this that he was reminded why he preferred to stay in at night. He had a much better time obsessing over his business ventures.

Tonight, for example, he could have been relaxing in his office at the coffee house and drinking some fine Madeira while he read the profit and loss statement for the racing stables he owned with Hart in York. Just because he was consumed with the idea of building a spa here in Bath didn't mean he could afford to neglect his other ventures. They needed his attention as well. He wouldn't risk handing over complete control of these businesses to someone else and take the chance that they might run them into the ground.

He grew up having nothing to call his own. He would never allow that to happen again. That's why he was very selective about where he chose to invest his time and money.

But now, instead of scrutinising the expenses of the stables, he was making his way up the stairs to Mrs Sommersby's box to see a play that would probably bore him so much he would fall asleep in the middle of it. Why in the world did he ever agree to this?

The one saving grace in coming here tonight was that he would be spending the evening alone with Mrs Sommersby. At least that was what he thought until he entered her box in the theatre.

Standing next to Mrs Sommersby, only a few feet from him, was the woman he had spoken to at the Pump Room days before. She was about the same height as Mrs Sommersby—however, the large white plume in her turban reached at least six inches higher. Considering she was a woman with such an elevated title, he was surprised that she gave him a friendly smile while he stood frozen in the doorway.

Mrs Sommersby, on the other hand, appeared almost relieved to see him and took a step closer. 'Mr Lane, I'm so glad you are here. I hope you had no trouble getting the token from the box office.'

This was not what he expected—none of it.

If it weren't poor form to turn on his heels and leave, he would have been thinking of an excuse. 'It was no trouble at all.'

She turned briefly towards the Duchess. 'This is Mr Lane. You may recall speaking with him in the Pump Room a few days ago by the fountain. Mr Lane, may I present Eleanor, the Dowager Duchess of Lyonsdale.'

Lyonsdale? The very name sent an uneasy tingle up his spine. Her grandson knew of his background. He knew that Lane was an unwanted bastard. If she knew that Lane was a business associate of her grandson, she might mention she'd met him. Suppose Lyonsdale told her of Lane's background. She might decide to share that information with Mrs Sommersby.

There was something about Mrs Sommersby that took him away from obsessing about his work and relieved some of the pressure he felt on a daily basis. While he knew he should be home reading that report, he found his chest felt lighter when she was around—and he liked that. The idea that she might cut all ties with him should she find out that he was born on the other side of the blanket, probably to a servant girl, made his stomach drop. His pride had already been dented this week by his disagreement with Lyonsdale. He wasn't about to take another blow. The Dowager didn't need to know that he knew her grandson.

While Lane lowered his head in a respectable bow, he spotted a man and a woman sitting in two of the chairs in the front row of the box. How was it possible that he had assumed he would be spending the evening alone with Mrs Sommersby and she had an entirely different evening planned? He tried to recall her exact words when she invited him to join her tonight, but couldn't.

'It is a pleasure to formally make your acquaintance, Mr Lane,' the Dowager said with a warm smile, reminding him how surprisingly affable she had been when they stood around the fountain. 'I hope you found the water you drank to be beneficial in some way.'

'My morning at the spa was very beneficial. Thank you.'

'Capital! You should try bathing in it. It can be very restorative. Isn't that right?' she said, turning to Mrs Sommersby.

'I've found it to be.'

Once more the image of Mrs Sommersby in the hot spring bath popped into his mind and once more he wished he was spending the evening alone with her.

The Dowager took a step back. 'If you two will excuse me, I think I'll take my seat. The production should begin shortly.'

As the older woman walked to the front of the box, Mrs Sommersby moved closer to him.

'Shall I be wary of your disposition tonight? Your brow is all wrinkled.' She waved her hand in the direction of his face and he consciously relaxed the muscles in his forehead.

'My disposition is fine.'

'So you say, but I am not quite sure I believe you.'

He couldn't admit all the thoughts going through his head. He would sound like a love-struck fool to admit he was disappointed they were not going to be alone together. 'You'll have to trust me.'

She narrowed those amber-coloured eyes at him and her pert nose seemed to twitch. 'Very well. Time will tell if that is a wise decision. Let me introduce you to Mr Greeley. He's a guest of the Dowager's. Then you can say hello to Miss Collingswood. Just please don't frighten the girl.'

'I never frighten people.'

'I think you underestimate your abilities.'

After he shook the young gentleman's hand in a firm grasp, he could see how wide Miss Collingswood's eyes were as she waited for him to address her before she glanced quickly at Mrs Sommersby. She had to be about twenty years of age and looked like the ideal debutante with her dewy skin, white muslin gown and the pale blue satin ribbon in her red hair. Her appearance was a sharp contrast to the sophisticated and alluring look of Mrs Sommersby, who was wearing a deep blue satin gown that hugged the curves of her breasts and showed a good amount of her décolletage with the low-cut neckline of the gown.

Thankfully, Miss Collingswood was tucked into the corner beside Mr Greeley in the last seat in the row, so he didn't have to worry that anyone was considering him as a potential suitor for her. Over the years he had come to realise that there were those people who assumed, because he was a bachelor, that he was looking for a wife. He had been abandoned once in his life by a woman. He was not eager to put himself in a situation where it could happen again. At seven and thirty he had become very skilled at avoiding the matchmaking mothers who valued his wealth over the circumstances of his birth.

As they went to sit down, it was Mrs Sommersby's turn to wrinkle her brow when she took note that the two vacant chairs were on the other side of the Dowager. 'We could sit behind Miss Collingswood and Mr Greeley,' she offered.

'Or we could sit in the front row and have a better view of the stage.'

'Oh, quite right. I just thought this might be more conducive to conversation.'

'Do you frequently talk during a performance?'

'Well, no. Do you?'

'I can't recall the last time I went to the theatre, but I doubt I spent much time talking.'

'Now that I can believe,' she replied over her shoulder in a teasing tone as she made her way to the chair beside the Dowager.

Just as Lane took his seat next to her, the red-velvet curtain on the stage came up. With everyone's attention fixed on the actors, Lane closed his eyes and hoped that his head wouldn't bob if he nodded off to sleep. He had been up well before sunrise today, observing the delivery process of the coffee and sugar at the coffee house and reviewing with his manager the amounts ordered. No matter what type of business they purchased, Lane always saw to it that he knew everything he could about it.

'I didn't invite you here tonight so you could fall asleep beside me.'

The air around him had the faintest scent of roses and the warm breath of her whisper caressed his cheek. How he wished he could stay like this to savour the sensation.

'I know you are not asleep, sir.'

'I never said I was.' Just to see what she would do, he kept his eyes closed.

'You will miss the play if you continue to do that.'

'I was content to listen to it, but there appears to be a persistent buzzing in my ear.'

He peeked at her out of one eye and felt satisfaction when she let out an exasperated breath.

'You are impossible, Mr Lane.'

The sound of her voice was replaced by those of the actors on the stage and, instead of being lulled to sleep, Lane found he wanted not only to hear but to see what was going on. The story was a comedy of manners about a courtship of a young woman in which a suitor pretended to be someone he was not. There were times Lane pretended to be a gentleman from a respectable household, as he was doing right now with Mrs Sommersby—only *he* wasn't attempting to court her. Mr Greeley, however, appeared to be besotted by Miss Collingswood.

Because the box was located so close to the stage, Lane had to look past the profile of Mrs Sommersby to see it and his gaze would periodically shift from the actors to Mr Greeley, who was watching the animated reactions of Miss Collingswood.

'I'm glad to see you've not fallen asleep,' Mrs Sommersby said after a time, low enough for only him to hear. 'She really is a lovely woman.'

'Who?'

'Miss Collingswood.'

'Greeley seems to think so. Are they engaged?'

'Greeley and Miss Collingswood? No, they

just met this evening. I don't even know if she likes him.'

'Ah, so it truly is a matter of art imitating life. Well, you have nothing to fear. You seem to have made a good match.'

Her eyes widened as she brought her fan up to her chest. 'You misunderstand. I am not trying to foster a match between them.'

None of the women he knew were matchmakers. At least he hadn't witnessed any attempting such a feat. And if they did, he doubted they would have confessed as much to him.

'Are you saying I'm Mrs Malapropism in this scenario?' she continued with low indignation. 'The one who in that scene was just accused of being an old weather-beaten she-dragon guarding her charge? The one who was accused of being vain with coarse features? The one who uses words incorrectly?' Her voice was low, but sharp, and there was a distinct possibility she was about to hit him with her fan.

Although they were in a crowded theatre, it felt inexplicably as if they were all alone. He leaned his head close to hers and she did not back away. 'You are far too young to be accused of being old and weather-beaten.'

'But I am still a vain she-dragon with coarse features? That makes it all so much better.' She rolled her eyes at him before snapping open her fan so sharply that he had to lean back or it might have struck his nose.

'I assure you that no one would accuse you of any of those things.'

'I believe, Mr Lane, that I prefer you when you say very little.' There was a teasing lilt to her voice that he was growing accustomed to.

She focused her attention back on the stage and he shifted in his chair so that he was resting his elbow on the left armrest, mere inches away from her torso and her very shapely breast. They stayed that way for what felt like an hour, until the fan that had been resting on her lap slipped to the floor when she moved her leg.

Instinctively he bent to pick it up just as she lowered her arm to the floor. The abruptness of the movement made him stop—and their cheeks almost brushed against one another. The warmth from her skin was tangible and he didn't want to move away. She turned to look at him and her gaze slid to his lips, which were now aching to brush against hers. Tucked behind the low wall of the box, they had more privacy sitting where they were than most people in the theatre. Just a few more inches and he could kiss her. Just a few more inches and he would be able to see if her lips really were as soft as they looked. No one would even be able to see them.

A loud burst of applause rang out around them, causing both of them to jerk apart. The moment was lost—and the realisation that the Dowager was just on the other side of Mrs Sommersby struck him.

'What a lovely performance,' she declared, turning to them both. 'I cannot believe we are already at the interval. I didn't even need wine to get through it.' The wrinkles on her brow deepened. 'What are you two doing down there?'

They both straightened up and thankfully Mrs Sommersby had the fan in her hand. He had forgotten all about it.

'My fan had fallen.' As if the Dowager would not have believed her, she held it up to show her for good measure. 'The production has been wonderful so far.'

The Dowager shifted her attention between the two of them before settling on Lane. 'And are you enjoying it?'

He tried to swallow away the dryness in his mouth. 'Quite, thank you.' It would have been more enjoyable if his moment with Mrs Sommersby hadn't been interrupted and even more so if they had been alone. It was hard to stop imagining her soft lips against his.

'Oh, it is simply a wonderful play,' Miss Collingswood exclaimed, practically jumping into the seats behind them with Mr Greeley. 'Don't you agree, Mrs Sommersby? Thank you for asking me to join you here tonight. I am so thrilled that I did not have to miss it.'

'I'm glad that tonight has brought you so much joy,' Mrs Sommersby replied with what almost appeared to be a pleased maternal expression.

'And you, Mr Greeley,' the Dowager addressed the man who was younger than Lane. 'Are you enjoying the play?'

'Yes, Your Grace. Mr Sheridan has done a fine job capturing the foibles of courtship.'

'Let us hope all courtships aren't like that,' she replied. 'I would like to believe that most people are not filled with artifice.'

'But don't you think most are, in some way?' Lane chimed in.

Mrs Sommersby looked as if she were studying him. 'I suppose. People tend to show only the best of themselves in the beginning, not wanting to do anything that will push the other person away.'

'But is that truly artifice,' the Dowager asked, 'or is it simply being on your best behaviour?'

'I think it might be more. Everyone has skeletons in their closets,' he replied. 'Some are better at hiding them than others.'

Mrs Sommersby's gaze ran up his torso and settled on his face. 'And what skeletons are you hiding, Mr Lane?'

He wondered if she liked what she saw. 'I fall asleep at the theatre.'

'But you did not do so during this performance so far.'

'Maybe I'm practising artifice.'

'Hmmm. Falling asleep at the theatre is a horrible trait. You made a wise decision to hide it.' She shook out her fan and waved it near her neck.

Miss Collingswood's eyes widened as she turned to him. 'Do you truly fall asleep in the theatre, Mr Lane? I can't imagine doing so. The building, the costumes, the orchestra—it is all so thrilling.'

'I have not attended the theatre enough to know for certain. I surmise it has more to do with the quality of the performance.'

Her features softened as she nodded slowly while keeping her eyes on him. If he had frightened her the other day, she seemed to have overcome her fear now.

Mr Greeley leaned forward a bit, obstructing Lane's view of Miss Collingswood. 'I find living an honest life is one of the most noble things you can do.'

His comment was given rather abruptly and it took Lane a moment to remember that they had been discussing artifice. 'Honest in what way?'

'Honest in the eyes of God and the church.'

'But would you say we are being dishonest

when we do not reveal our foibles to the people we meet?'

Mr Greeley looked a bit confused by the question.

'I think what Mr Lane means,' Clara interrupted, 'is if you have a habit of picking your teeth with your fork, should you disclose that to Miss Collingswood now for the sake of honesty or wait until a later date when you are confident that she has affection for you?'

Mr Greeley looked nervously at Miss Collingswood as if it had been revealed to the entire theatre that the man did pick his teeth with his fork.

The orchestra struck up a few chords, letting the people milling about in the corridors and visiting other boxes know that the performance was about to resume, saving Mr Greeley from continuing the conversation. The noise in the theatre grew louder with the sounds of people returning to their seats and as the young couple moved back to their chairs, Lane exchanged a small smile with Mrs Sommersby.

'One has to wonder if Mr Greeley does indeed pick his teeth with a fork,' she said low enough so only he could hear her behind her fan.

'With his truly honourable nature, he is probably confessing it to her as we speak.'

They both leaned out to see past the Dowager and watched the couple deep in conversation. Whatever they were discussing didn't seem to bother Miss Collingswood since she still appeared to be in very good spirits.

The Dowager waved her gloved hand at Lane and Mrs Sommersby. The diamonds in her substantial bracelet sparkled in the candlelight. 'Leave them alone, you two. We all have skeletons as Mr Lane has said.'

'Yes, but mine do not have cutlery,' he replied, sitting back in his chair and settling in, missing the amused expressions the ladies shared.

Chapter Eleven

Sitting this close to Mr Lane, Clara was able to smell the light scent of his cologne and for the past hour she realised that she liked the way he smelled. And she liked how he made her feel. They shared a similar sense of humour and he had a wonderful way of making her smile when she least expected it. And she felt comfortable with him, as you did with someone who you'd been friends with for a long time, which made no sense since they barely knew one another. Yet all of that had nothing to do with why her heart seemed to beat a bit faster when he was around.

A short while ago she actually thought he was going to kiss her. When they both reached for her fan after it had fallen to the floor, their faces were so close together she could feel the exhale of his breath skim across her lips. Foolishly, she felt her body lean closer towards him, as if they weren't in a very public theatre with her friend sitting on her other side. She didn't want another husband and she didn't want the complications that would arise in her life if she took a lover. But she had desperately wanted to kiss Mr Lane.

She settled into her chair, still trying to imagine what kissing him would have felt like when her arm accidently brushed against his rather solid one, encased in his black tailcoat. Their eyes held for a moment before she looked down and brushed out the wrinkles from her skirt and opened her fan, hoping to cool the flush spreading throughout her body from that one spot on her arm where his body had touched hers.

He looked very handsome in his formal black evening attire. The jacket and trousers were cut well, showing off his broad shoulders and well-defined form. His cravat had a nice fall to it and his cheeks and jaw were so smooth they must have been freshly shaven. One thing that she found herself continually drawn to was this commanding presence he had about him that led her to believe that he was the type of gentleman who faced his problems head on and would not run away from them. From her marriage, she was more accustomed to the uneasy feeling she got around a gentleman who would run. Her late husband, God rest his soul, had frequently hid from their creditors. That had forced Clara to be the one to try to placate the shopkeepers in town during those times when they were short on funds to settle their bills. She was the one who made sure they weren't thrown in debtors' prison. What would her life have been like had she married a man like Mr Lane?

She really didn't know anything about him. Perhaps he wasn't as financially solvent as she would have liked to believe. Over the years she had helped to encourage the courtships of a number of women and she had developed a keen sense for how to analyse a person. Lowering her eyelids, she took note of the condition of his sleeve and the fact that it was not threadbare. The cuff of his linen shirt that peeked out from the cuff of his coat was pure white, telling her that he was both clean and financially solvent enough to pay someone to have his clothes washed. He wore no ring on his hand or stickpin in his cravat. His shoes, however, had been buffed to a high shine and, if she had to wager, she'd say they were an expensive pair.

Just as the curtain on the stage was going up, she leaned her head towards his and the topaz stones in her earring brushed against her shoulder. 'How did you arrive at the theatre tonight?' she whispered.

'My carriage.'

'Yours?'

His attention moved from the stage to her. 'Yes, people do own them. I did try one of those sedan chairs your town is so fond of, but I could not abide having two men carry me around in it so I decided to take my carriage tonight.'

When Harriet had asked him where he was from when they saw him at breakfast, he'd said he was from London. Having a London town house of her own, she knew that keeping a carriage there was very expensive. If he had one, then he was most probably doing well for himself.

'Did your family take you to the theatre when you were younger?' she asked, wanting to imagine what he was like years ago.

Once more he looked over at her and shook his head no. Then his eyes narrowed. 'I thought you said you do not talk during performances.'

'I don't.'

'You are now.'

'I didn't realise you were so attentive to the production.'

'Well, you were the one who told me not to fall asleep. You can blame yourself.'

'Shh.'

The hush came from the Dowager, making Clara feel as though she was younger than Harriet.

There were so many questions she suddenly

wanted answers to. There were so many things she did not know. And, oh, how she wished she could ask him about all of them. However, if there was one thing she knew for certain, it was that Mr Lane did not appear to be a gentleman who liked talking about himself.

They sat side by side and watched the remainder of the play together. Occasionally, they would share a smile over something that was happening on the stage. And at times she felt acutely aware of his body so close to hers, which would prompt her to fan herself and hope the flush she was feeling was not that noticeable. When the curtain went down one final time, she leaned her shoulder towards his, wondering if he regretted accepting her invitation this evening. 'Are you glad that you stayed awake tonight?'

'Surprisingly, I am.'

'And would you agree that coming here tonight was a better way to spend your evening than the way you had planned to spend it?'

He looked as if he were actually trying to determine if it were—which felt rather insulting—and made her very curious.

'What was it that you were planning on doing tonight?'

'I was going to review a business report.'

'Ah, business. The mysterious thing that keeps

you so busy and has prevented you from enjoying your time here. What was the report about?'

They stood up to join the rest of their party by the door to the box.

'It was a profit and loss statement on a stable that I own. I had planned to review all the figures on the facility tonight.'

She appreciated the fact that he was specific and did not oversimplify his answer to her because she was a woman, which some men would have done. 'You own a stable?'

'Two, actually. Mainly for racehorses.'

That was not what she was expecting. She wasn't sure what kind of business she imagined him to be in, but he seemed much too staid to be involved in racing. That seemed more of a business that a man about town would be involved in. But what did she really know of him?

As the small party of five waited by the door to the box for the crowds to lessen so they wouldn't be jostled about on their way down the stairs, Clara saw Harriet sneak occasional glances at Mr Lane. The fourth time her eyes shifted his way, they stayed there and when he looked her way, her eyes widened momentarily, knowing she had been caught.

'Did you enjoy the play tonight, Mr Lane?'

'I did. Thank you. Did you?' Thankfully he exhibited no signs of his previous gruff demeanour with her. In fact, he appeared to be rather pleasant in his response.

'Oh, I did. I'm glad that you were able to join us.'

'As am I.' Although he wasn't giving her a full smile, the corners of his mouth were tipping up and there were small creases in the corners of his eyes. His gaze skirted past Clara and settled on the Dowager. 'Your Grace, might I have the honour of offering you my arm on our way to the carriages?'

'That's very kind of you, Mr Lane. Mr Greeley accompanied me to the theatre tonight. I will give him a reprieve of spending more time with me until my carriage arrives. Then he will be forced to endure my chatter all the way home.' She was watching Mr Greeley and Harriet with marked interest, which reminded Clara about the woman's challenge to see who would find the more desirable suitor for the young woman.

'I assure you it will be my pleasure to ride back with you,' Mr Greeley replied with a tip of his head before turning to Clara. 'Mrs Sommersby, Miss Collingswood, might I have the honour of escorting you both outside?'

Harriet took his right arm, leaving Clara with his left. The staircase was wide enough to accommodate the three of them as they made their descent, but when they reached the door, Clara let go of his arm so they could fit through the door to the outside. She threaded both her hands through the braided handle of her reticule as they waited on the pavement for the three carriages to arrive.

The Dowager's carriage arrived first and, after she bade them a safe trip home, Clara stood alone outside with Harriet and Mr Lane. It appeared they were some of the last to leave the theatre since there was only one other small group of people standing about twenty feet from them. The yellow glow from the lights inside the building shone on to the narrow strip of pavement they were standing on, making it easier for them to see each other in the darkness that surrounded them.

'Will it be a far drive for you, Mr Lane?' Harriet enquired, seeming to have completely lost her trepidation about the gentleman.

'Not too far.' He stuffed his hands in the pockets of his coat. 'Will you have a far drive ahead of you?'

'My family is staying next door to Mrs Sommersby. It should not take us long before we are home.'

Mr Lane's carriage pulled alongside the pavement before Clara's and he offered to wait with them until her carriage arrived, but Clara could see her driver had just turned down the street. 'There is no need to wait. Our driver is right there.' She gestured towards her carriage as the door to his was opened for him.

'I insist. I will not take the chance of anything happening to either of you.'

She pointed yet again to the carriage rolling up their street. 'It is right there.'

'Then I won't have long to wait with you.'

When her carriage pulled behind his, he helped them both inside. First, he assisted Harriet, then he took Clara's hand. The mere touch through his glove sent a heated shiver up her spine and she felt the loss when he let go. Through the carriage window she surreptitiously watched him walk away in the golden light from the theatre windows.

While the carriage rocked along the cobblestone road up to the Royal Crescent, Clara eyed Harriet, who was looking out her side of the window.

'I assume by that smile, Harriet, that you enjoyed yourself this evening.'

Her friend turned back to her and even in the dim light of the carriage lantern she could see the young woman's eyes were shining. 'Oh, I did. Very much.' She looked down at her gloves and back up at Clara. 'You were right. Mr Lane is a lovely man. I am so glad you asked him to join us.'

'You are?'

'Yes. I tried not to make too much of a spectacle of myself when I spoke with him. You don't think I did, do you?'

How was it that she was speaking of Mr Lane when Mr Greeley had appeared to have also captured her attention? 'You comported yourself very well. So, you are fond of Mr Lane?'

'I am. I think he is a fine man.'

'I agree.'

'And very handsome.'

What? 'You do? Think he is handsome, that is?'

'Yes. Don't you?'

'Well, yes I suppose.'

'You suppose?' Harriet's eyebrows rose. 'He has such well-defined features, unmarked skin and such a strong square jaw. And that hair of his appears to be so thick you could start to comb your fingers through it and not finish until the next day. Oh, and have I mentioned that he has a very fine form…if one was to notice such things.'

'I truly did not look to see.' Which was a lie. Of course she'd noticed what a fine specimen of a man he was. It was hard not to when she was sitting close beside him and when she was close enough to kiss him. 'Tell me your thoughts on Mr Greeley.'

'Mr Greeley is a lovely man,' she replied with a carefree wave of her hand. 'I'm not saying he is not, I just think that a woman would be lucky to marry a man like Mr Lane.' She tilted her head and looked at Clara as if she were waiting for her reaction.

The distant cry of the night watchman carried through the carriage with an 'all is well.' It was well, wasn't it? She had considered matching Harriet with Mr Lane. She was even challenged to do so by the Dowager. And now it appeared it would be no problem at all to convince Harriet to consider him. That should have made her feel good. She should be delighted and relieved that Harriet found him handsome.

Clara looked out into the darkened night and her gaze roamed over the windows of the terraced town houses now glowing with candlelight. She silently reminded herself that she had been married before and had no desire to give up her autonomy to marry again. Harriet had never been married and she probably never would be if they left it up to her mother to make an arrangement. A match between Mr Lane and Harriet was a far better thing than it would be for Clara to simply know what his kisses felt like. She had married for love and discovered that the men you could fall in love with weren't always the best men to marry. Not that she even felt the slightest bit of love for Mr Lane, but she knew enough now that she was certain no good could come from letting her emotions cloud her judgement. It was time she returned to being practical.

She adjusted her hands on her lap. 'It would be lovely to see Mr Lane again. He proved to be an entertaining companion tonight. Wouldn't you agree?'

'Very much so.'

'I do wish there was a way to see him again,' she mused out loud, 'unfortunately, I have no idea how to reach him. Each time we've met, it has been a bit of serendipity.'

'I heard him mention to Mr Greeley that he has started taking morning walks through Sydney Gardens.'

'He did?'

'Yes, while we were waiting for the carriages. It must have been when you were speaking with Her Grace.'

He was going there in the morning? They had met in the wooded area at the edge of the lawn across from the Crescent. For the days that followed she had found herself scanning the faces of the gentlemen she would pass while walking Humphrey there, wondering if she would see him again. And all this time he was going to Sydney Gardens? She certainly had not left an impression on him if that was where he was going. If he'd had a desire to see her again, he would have made certain to walk near the Crescent. Not that it mattered. She was not looking for a gentleman of her own and, even if she were, she was too old for him anyway. A gentleman as young as Mr Lane would want a family. That was something she could not give him.

For Harriet's sake, she should try to locate him and find a way to bring them together again. This time Harriet should have an opportunity to spend time with him without Mr Greeley there to muddy the waters.

'I could take Humphrey for a walk in Sydney Gardens tomorrow on the chance that he might be there,' she offered. 'He did seem to enjoy himself this evening. I don't think he would mind if I invited him to something else.'

Harriet sat up taller. 'I think you should.' She really was more attracted to him than Clara had thought.

Just the idea of seeing him again had her opening up her fan. She would have to approach this delicately. If possible, she needed to find something that she could do with Harriet that did not involve her family. The last thing she wanted was for her mother to throw her sister Ann in his path which might have Harriet retreating back into her shell.

There was still more she needed to find out about him before she could recommend him to Mr and Mrs Collingswood. If she needed to spend more time with him to do that, she would find the time for Harriet's sake, though, she didn't want Mr Lane to feel like a hunted man. There was no reason he should think of her as Mrs Malapropism from the play. She was no she-dragon and she didn't want him to see her that way. But the way she did wish he would see her would not help Harriet.

Chapter Twelve

The desire to remain in bed after the sun came up was a new one for Lane. When he was a child, he would be woken up at seven each morning to have enough time to dress and make it down to the dining hall for breakfast. Even now, as an adult, he never slept past six.

But this morning as he lay in his bed in his room in The Fountain Head Hotel and watched the sky change colour outside his window, going from inky black to orange streaked with red, he rested his head in the crook of his arm and thought again about last night. And those thoughts were making him want to remain in bed for as long as he could.

The image of Mrs Sommersby was fresh in his mind. He could still picture her intelligent eyes and amused expression as she sat beside him in her deep blue satin gown that cradled her breasts and skimmed along the rest of her body. The soft scent of roses still somehow seemed to linger in his nose and, if he closed his eyes, he could imagine the puff of her soft, warm breath near his ear that he had felt each time she would lean over to whisper to him.

She had asked if his family had ever brought him to the theatre. It never occurred to him that families would do such things together. Over the years he realised it was best not to think about what families did. He never knew his father or his mother. He had been left at the Foundling Hospital when he was a small infant.

As was their custom with the orphan babies, he was sent to spend the first five years of his life being raised by a wet nurse and her family in the country before he was ripped from that happy existence to be returned to live out the rest of his youth in London at the Hospital. The Hatwells had been very nice to him. But he still could recall the day he called Mrs Hatwell 'mother' and she informed him that she was not his mother. When he had asked where his mother was, she ignored his question and asked him to help her make a trifle. When he asked a few more times, the same thing happened. In time, he stopped asking.

He did eventually get an answer, though, when he was returned to the Hospital. One of the older boys told him that Lane's mother must have been a whore who had let a man rut between her legs and he never bothered to marry her. His father had never wanted his mother and his mother had not wanted him. It was the first time in his life that he heard the word bastard, but it wasn't the last. How he had hated that boy.

He had no reference for how fathers behaved with their children, save for the few instances when he was around his friends who had children. But for the first time in his life, he thought about what kind of father he would be—and what kind of mother Mrs Sommersby would make.

He saw how she looked out for Miss Collingswood. He saw how she would periodically study the young woman in a way that made him think she wanted to be sure the girl was comfortable and enjoying herself. He imagined that was what a mother would do. And he believed she would most likely be a good one.

As he rolled on to his back, the soft white sheets brushed across his bare legs. Taking a deep breath, he stared up at the blue-and-brown-striped bed hangings and wondered what kind of room Mrs Sommersby slept in. Was she still asleep or was she lying on her back right now, staring up at her own bed hangings in the way he was staring up at his?

Pushing his palms into his eyes, he rubbed away his mawkish pondering, wondering what

bit of witchcraft had turned him into a school-
boy with his first taste of passion. Not that he had
tasted anything of Mrs Sommersby—but every
fibre of his being had wished he had. When he
thought about how close he had come to kissing
her last night, he let out a frustrated groan.

A desperate need for her pulsed through him
and he threw his pillow across the room. Whatever it took, he was going to figure out a way to
find Mrs Sommersby and when he did he was
going to kiss her. He had seen the passion in her
eyes. He had felt her uneven breathing on his skin.
It was inevitable.

Once more he rested his head on his arm. This
time instead of imagining what she was doing at
that very moment, he thought more about what he
would like to do to her the next time he saw her.

Less than two hours later Lane was sitting
downstairs in the walled garden of The Fountain Head Hotel, drinking coffee at one of the
round tables while he read the hotel's most recent edition of several newspapers. He couldn't
spend all his time at the coffee house watching
over Mr Sanderson's shoulder. His manager was
a hard-working man and it was imperative that
there was a position for him in the new spa. Just
because Lane decided to change the direction of

the business it shouldn't mean that his employees would be out of work.

Ripping off a piece of the Sally Lunn bun that was on his plate, he let his attention wander around the garden that was cast in the soft light of a cloudy morning. Whoever had thought of having breakfast available outside on days when the weather was pleasant really understood the needs of travellers. He only wished they served heartier fare since he was rather hungry this morning and his coffee and this bun were not going to be enough.

He glanced down at the untouched edition of the *Chronicle* with little interest and then surveyed the small skirted tables that were around him on the large gravel-covered square in the centre of the garden. Looking past the nicely dressed gentlemen, eating and reading their papers, his gaze settled on the few women who were also in attendance, all of them with a gentleman by their side. None of them was Mrs Sommersby. Even the pale pink and red roses that lined the garden reminded him of her. It was a good thing it was not Wednesday because if it had been he knew he would have found some excuse to go to the Lower Assembly Room for breakfast to see if he might spot her.

He needed to focus. And not on Mrs Sommersby. He should be receiving word any day now from Hart letting him know if they had secured enough money to purchase this hotel. When that happened, he needed to be ready to negotiate a reasonable sum for it. To do that, he needed to find out everything he could about the owner.

Once more his gaze trailed over the rose bushes in the distance and he took a deep breath to see if the scent lingered in the air. All he could smell was coffee. When he owned this hotel, he would have to find a way to utilise this garden in some way at the spa. And he would keep the rose bushes.

'Is everything to your liking, sir?' his waiter asked, stopping at the side of his table. 'Would you care for some more coffee?' His youthful exuberance that accompanied the offer was a contrast to the unusual languid feeling that Lane was experiencing this morning.

'Yes, thank you, Jack.'

The waiter returned with the pot in his hand and proceeded to pour more of the steaming dark liquid into Lane's cup.

'Jack, how long have you been employed here?'

The hand that had just finished pouring the coffee stilled above Lane's cup for a moment before Jack pulled it in closer to his body. 'About five years, sir.' His eyes shifted to another table as if he could not wait to leave Lane's side. Lane had encountered rude patrons in his life and re-

alised that Jack must have as well. If he had been
working here for five years, he must have started
when he was about fifteen by the looks of him.

'And if I wanted to compliment the owner of
this fine hotel on the service you have been pro-
viding me with during my stay, who might I direct that information to?'

A look of relief crossed Jack's face and his
shoulders relaxed. 'Mr Edwards is the manager.
He would be the one.' A look of appreciation replaced his former anxious expression.

'I see. I've met Mr Edwards. So, he owns the
hotel as well as manages it?'

A shrug from Jack was his answer. 'I would assume so. He makes all the decisions around here.'

'Of course, and how long has Mr Edwards
been here?'

'As long as I've been. I've heard he is from
Bath, though, so perhaps a long time.'

'You did not grow up here?'

'Me? No, sir. I'm from London.'

'London? What brings a fine man like you to
Bath all the way from London?'

'I was introduced to Mr Edward's cousin in
London. She said I might enjoy living in Bath
and that she knew her cousin could use some help
here at the hotel. She was the one who brought
me here.'

'That was very kind of her.'

'She's a very nice lady. One of the finest I know.' He gave a brisk nod of his straw-coloured head for further emphasis.

'I've been admiring this garden. I cannot recall staying in a hotel or inn that serves breakfast outside like this. It's quite nice on days like today. I wonder if Mrs Edwards helped him design this. There seems to be a woman's touch about.' That was one way to find out if the man was married. The needs of his family could be a point in the negotiations.

'There is no Mrs Edwards.'

'He's not married?'

'No, sir. This was Mr Edwards's idea to serve breakfast out here. We started this last summer. I like it better than serving in the dining room. The tables are further apart out here and I don't have to worry about tripping over someone's foot.'

'Yes, I can see how that would be a concern. Well, you're doing a fine job and I'll be sure to let Mr Edwards know.'

'Thank you, sir,' he said with a beaming smile and a bow of his head, before turning to check on the next table.

That bit of information on Mr Edwards only scratched the surface. He would try to find out more about the man from Mr Sanderson. There had to be a way to do it discreetly without revealing his plan to acquire the property. He had been trying to keep the discovery of the spring to only a very few people. The last thing he wanted was for the owner of the hotel to find out about the spring and then create a spa on their property first. The hotel had more land, they could offer more than they currently did.

His gaze dropped to the *Chronicle* that was in front of him. Could he be lucky enough to glean some additional information on Mr Edwards from the local paper?

What his eye did land on was a mention of a *'widowed Mrs S. who, Tuesday of last, had been at a ball in the Upper Assembly Rooms, speaking with a new friend, and who might be testing her famous matchmaking skills once again.'*

Thoughts of Mrs Sommersby with Miss Collingswood popped into his head. She had to be the woman they were referring to. How many widows were in town with the last initial of 'S'? Well, how many of them were fond of matchmaking—even if they didn't like to admit it? In fact, he would bet fifty pounds that she was indeed the woman who was mentioned.

He hadn't been to a ball in years. He wasn't very fond of dancing and if he wanted to play cards he could do that at his club. So why was he trying to picture her moving through the Upper Assembly Rooms with Miss Collingswood at her side in some tempting ball gown that would highlight the curves of her body and shimmer in the candlelight as she walked? He still wanted to kiss her. He still wanted to feel the soft skin of her neck while he held her there as he deepened his kiss. And he still wondered if a kiss might lead to something more.

It took some time before the words on the paper before him came back into focus.

The only thing, short of going back up to his room, that would help settle his frustrated state was a good brisk walk in the fresh air. Hopefully it would set his mind and body at ease. Just the thought of walking near the Crescent again, where he had seen Mrs Sommersby a few days before with her dog behind a hedgerow, set his heart pounding.

He needed to be able to focus on work today. He had reports about the stable to go over. He'd never be able to do that if he ran into Mrs Sommersby. Today, he'd return to the meandering pathways of Sydney Gardens. That pleasure garden was closer to his current location anyway so he wouldn't have to be gone long. He could spend an hour there and then begin his day. It would be much later than usual when he entered his office, but at least he would be getting some work done.

Chapter Thirteen

As Lane walked through the gates of Sydney Gardens, he was tempted to turn around and head to the wooded space near the Royal Crescent. The muscle by his jaw started to twitch as he checked the time on his watch. It was far later than it should have been. This is what he got for spending hours daydreaming about a woman. He was already behind in his work. Today, he would only have an hour to walk through the gardens.

He took a deep breath of the clean air, taking in the smell of the expanse of grass that stretched out ahead of him that formed the bowling green. One of the things he liked best about being here was that the air smelled better in Bath than it did in London. This had been the fourth time he had walked the pathways of Sydney Gardens and he knew for certain that he would be coming back to this picturesque location each time he returned to Bath to check on his property.

Shoving his hands into the pockets of his coat, he took off at a brisk pace down one of the serpentine walks on his way to the pathway that ran alongside the canal. He strode under the leafy bowers past alcoves tucked away where one could sit on a warm day on the wooden benches. Nannies and mothers strolled past him with babies and small children by their sides, some of those children rolling hoops with sticks. Others were chasing after one another in games of touch tap.

His previous visits to this garden had been much earlier in the morning and the occupants had been gentlemen like himself or the occasional fashionably dressed couple. But at this time of day, the garden seemed to be filled with children. He recalled being a boy with a lot of energy who was forced to repress it to sit still in class and throughout liturgical sermons. How he would have loved a park this large to run around in with his friends when he was small. The grounds of the Foundling Hospital were their playing field and it could not compare to the features in this garden with all the places you could hide in.

As he made his way down the pathway, he was still trying to recall all the games he and his friends had played when he heard the yapping sound of a dog not far behind him. While he tipped his hat to a gentleman strolling in the opposite direction, he was startled when he almost tripped over a small black and brown dog that was now barking up at him, mere inches from the tips of his boots.

It resembled Mrs Sommersby's Cavalier King Charles spaniel. He tried to recall that dog's name as he squatted down and rubbed the small pup behind its long black ears. The dog looked as if it were dressed as a highwayman because his big dark eyes were outlined in light brown fur that resembled a mask. Mrs Sommersby's dog had similar markings from what he could remember. The dog's eyes closed in bliss when Lane rubbed its neck. The moment Lane stopped scratching him, the dog poked at him with his small shiny nose.

'I see. You like that, do you?' He took off his gloves, draped them over his thigh and went back to scratching the soft fur under the dog's chin. As he did so, he looked around and tried to see if anyone was searching for it. 'You couldn't have got in here by yourself. Where's your owner?'

With small yaps, the dog appeared to try to explain.

'You've run off, haven't you? You do remind me of another dog here in Bath. Do you have a brother? Perhaps a very young uncle?'

The dog barked this time—a louder sound which carried on the breeze that was rustling the leaves on the branches above them.

'Humphrey!' The name was called out from somewhere behind him.

Lane's heart skipped a beat. 'It *is* you,' he said to the small dog that was now balancing himself up on his hind legs with his paws resting on Lane's knee. 'Tell me you have not got Mrs Sommersby caught up in some bit of shrubbery again.'

He turned his head, following the sound of her voice, but he didn't see her.

'Humphrey!' she called out again.

'He's over here!' Holding the pup firmly, he began to pat its back. 'Now you stay right where you are. Don't you try running off again until your mistress gets here. I doubt she wants to have to chase you around this park today.'

'No, she does not.'

The sound of her breathless voice behind him made him smile since there were a few times he had contemplated how she would sound after a vigorous bout of sex.

'Mr Lane!' Her eyes shifted from him and widened when she spotted her dog.

'Mrs Sommersby.'

'Oh, dear Heavens… Humphrey, what are you doing?' There was a hint of panic in her voice as she stood holding the dog's red leash in her white gloved hand, looking at her dog as if she wanted to scoop him up immediately and run.

'He's just getting his ears scratched.'

'Oh.' She tilted her head to get a better view of the little scamp and looked somewhat relieved. 'How did you find him?'

'I didn't. He found me.'

'I'm sorry if he is being a nuisance.'

Lane picked Humphrey up and he cradled him in his arms. As a reward for all that scratching, he received a series of kisses from Humphrey on his chin.

'I've found him, Harriet,' she called over her shoulder, giving Lane a few moments to run his gaze over her body.

'What did he do this time?'

'I went to adjust his lead and before I could stop him, he slipped out and took off down the path.'

'You really do need to train him to listen to your commands.'

'I've been trying. Just when he masters one command, he proceeds to discover another way to get me to question the reason I'd decided to keep him.'

'There are only a few commands you need to teach him. If you can manage those, you can address any behaviour that he learns.'

'You make it sound so easy. No matter what I try, he never listens to me when I tell him to stop. If only I could pay you to train him.'

Humphrey looked between them, then tilted his head.

Lane took a step closer. 'Perhaps I would do it without monetary compensation.' The air around them grew thick and the sound of his heartbeat grew louder in his ears.

She licked her lips and swallowed. 'How I wish you were serious.'

'What makes you believe that I'm not?'

They were less than two feet apart. Between them, Humphrey began to wriggle in his arms and leaned out to lick Mrs Sommersby on her cheek.

'Do not think to charm me with kisses, you rascal. They have no effect on me.' But even as she said it, she reached out and rubbed the dog's little head.

From behind Mrs Sommersby he saw Miss Collingswood making her way towards them and he held up his hand in a greeting.

'Mr Lane! Imagine seeing you in this park. How did you find Humphrey?'

He gave her a friendly smile. 'He seems to have found me.' He turned back to Mrs Sommersby. 'It never occurred to me that it was him when he ran up to me. This garden is far from where I saw you walking him last.'

She lifted Humphrey out of his arms and took a step back. She even started to rock the pup in her arms the way he had seen a mother in the garden not long ago rock a fussy infant. Humphrey continued to lick her face. 'I've taken it upon myself to show Miss Collingswood more of Bath and it's a lovely place to spend a pleasant day such as this.' Her brow furrowed and she glanced quickly at her friend before meeting him in the eye. 'I've been here before. In fact, I come here often. It isn't so rare that I would be here today...with Miss Collingswood.'

'And with Humphrey.' He felt the need to add that since she had felt the need to explain how often she went on walks here.

Her gaze shifted to the expanse of lawn beside the pathway. 'Of course. I wouldn't leave him home. He loves it here.'

'Where does he like to go?'

'Pardon?'

'Where does Humphrey like to walk when you are here? He obviously has very definite opinions on what he likes to do and where he likes to go. Have you noticed if he favours one particular area of the garden?'

She scratched her neck. 'No. I haven't noticed.'

'Where do you like to walk, Mr Lane?' Miss Collingswood asked, stepping up to Mrs Sommersby's side and rubbing Humphrey's back.

'I haven't had the opportunity to explore the

entire garden as of yet, but I have enjoyed walking along the pathway beside the canal.'

'That sounds lovely. Mrs Sommersby was planning on bringing Humphrey here this morning and she was kind enough to ask if I wanted to accompany her. That's why we are here. Humphrey needed a walk.'

These women seemed to feel a need to explain how they had wound up here in the park today. From the corner of his eye he could see Mrs Sommersby watching them as she snuggled her dog.

'Where were you heading just now? Were you going towards the canal?' Miss Collingswood asked.

'I wanted to see the labyrinth.' He would have much preferred to be alone with Mrs Sommersby in one of the secluded spots in the maze, but if his only chance at spending time in her company today was with Miss Collingswood then he would take what he could get. And the young woman, he was discovering, was not horrible company. 'Would you ladies care to join me during my brief walk?'

He had come here to forget her. Now, if she declined his invitation, he would be spending the remainder of his day wondering where in the garden she had gone and what she had done.

'How long do you intend to walk?' Mrs Sommersby asked, shifting her wriggling puppy in her arms.

He took out his watch from his waistcoat pocket to check. 'Another half an hour.'

Chapter Fourteen

Clara reminded herself that the reason they were in Sydney Gardens this morning was because they had hoped to see Mr Lane. But now that they had seen him and she had looked into his eyes, she wasn't sure that she wanted to see if there was a spark between him and Harriet. She shifted her gaze to her young friend and the contained excitement in Harriet's eyes spoke volumes about her interest in the man. Clara looked back at Mr Lane and found him studying her. Did he suspect what she was up to? The leaves around them rustled as the soft breeze grew stronger.

'We would love to join you, Mr Lane.' The words were spoken on an exhale as if she needed to push them out of her body. 'Thank you for the kind invitation.'

'It's my pleasure.'

'Hopefully, Humphrey will not slow us down too much. He can be easily distracted.' She placed her dog down on the path and secured the lead to his collar. 'Be a good boy, will you?'

The three of them began their stroll along the pathway and she almost had to tug Harriet to walk in the middle of them. Sometimes she forgot that Harriet wasn't always comfortable in the company of gentlemen.

As they strolled in and out of the patches of muted sunlight that shone on to the path through the leaves above them, their conversation drifted from last night's performance of *The Rivals* to the fact that she had missed her daily morning visit to the spa.

Miss Collingswood's brows drew together. 'Do you truly go every morning?'

'I do. I've been doing that for more years than I can remember.'

'But why?'

'Years ago, I went for my health. Now I suppose I go more out of habit than anything else. Bathing in the waters of the spa is wonderful. There is nothing like being submerged in all that hot water.'

Early on in her marriage she had lost a child before she could carry it to full term. She had been advised that bathing in the water could strengthen her womb, so they had moved to Bath from London and she went to the spa every day. She lost two more children after that, in much the same way as the first. After they had buried the third infant that came from her body before it was ready, Robert said that they should stop trying. He loved her too much to lose her and was afraid she would bleed out and die if it happened again. Clara had continued to go to the spa even after that in the hope that some day he might change his mind. He never did and eventually they left Bath and moved back to London. But even when she returned after he died, she still continued to bathe in the spa. Old habits were hard to break. Even those that didn't make sense any more.

'How often do you take the thermal baths?' Mr Lane asked as she stopped to let Humphrey sniff a particular tree.

'Every Tuesday and Thursday barring extenuating circumstances. Soaking in the hot water for long bouts of time can relieve any soreness you might have. It feels wonderful. Have you tried it yet, Mr Lane? You had been at the spa the day we met.'

His eyes were on her and yet he didn't respond. It almost appeared as if he hadn't heard her until he eventually shook his head. 'I've not taken a bath in any of the spas here yet. The only baths I've taken have been in my room at my hotel.'

She gave a tug to Humphrey's leash, coaxing him to continue walking. 'It's a very different experience. The lovely thing about bathing in the spa is that not only do you have enough room to stretch out under the water, but you never need to concern yourself that the water will cool down. The water remains hot.'

'That sounds heavenly,' Miss Collingswood chimed in. 'And you say you go on Tuesdays and Thursdays?'

'Most weeks I do, but this morning all I wanted to do was remain in bed.'

Mr Lane stopped walking and stared at her. 'What time did you finally rise this morning?'

What an odd question to ask. 'I believe it was around eight.' He didn't need to know he was the reason she had got out of bed so late. Neither Mr Lane nor Harriet should have any idea she had been daydreaming about him this morning, thinking about the time she had spent sitting close beside him last night and replaying their conversations over and over in her mind.

He continued to walk, coming up alongside of her this time. 'I was not able to get out of bed this morning either. I'm usually up before the sun, but this morning I didn't rise until closer to eight as well.'

It would be wonderful to believe that he had been thinking about her this morning, but, knowing Mr Lane, she guessed his mind was probably on business.

'Spending a late night out can truly make it hard to rise the next morning.'

Harriet's innocent comment as they strolled behind Humphrey made Mr Lane utter the funniest combination of a laugh and a cough before he caught himself and cleared his throat. Clara caught his eye and he quickly looked away. She tried to suppress a smile, knowing where his mind had gone.

Harriet slipped away from them and walked over towards a flowerbed at the side of the path and bent to smell some of the roses. Clara's eyes met his and they held for a few moments before he stepped closer to her. Their arms were almost touching. If she lifted a finger, she would be able to caress his and through her clothes it felt as if she could feel the heat radiating from his body.

Once more she imagined his mouth on hers. She wanted to kiss him. She wanted him to kiss her. And when his gaze dropped to her lips, she was thinking that maybe he wanted to kiss her, too.

The sound of two women chattering and moving around them on the gravel path was enough to break the spell and she looked over at her friend, who was still smelling the rose bushes.

'That's a Celsiana Damask rose,' she called to Harriet while she adjusted her grip on Humphrey's leash, needing something to do and say that would keep her focus away from Mr Lane's mouth.

'It's so fragrant,' Harriet replied, leaning in again to sniff it once more.

'They use the petals to make perfume.'

'I'm not surprised that you know that.' His deep voice, not far from her ear, had broken her forced concentration on Harriet and sent a wonderful tingle up her spine. Did he have any idea of the effect he had on her?

'Why do you say that?'

'You smell like them.' The heat from his whispered breath caressed her neck.

How she wished she could grab him by the collar and press their lips together. She wanted to kiss him. Right there. Right now. On this garden path. 'Is that your polite way of telling me that I wear far too much perfume?' There, that sounded composed.

'Not at all. I like how you smell. It reminds me of being out in the garden on warm summer days.'

And now she was thinking about being in his arms in a walled garden away from prying eyes on a warm summer day. The leash around Clara's hand pulled against her skin and she realised that Humphrey was straining to get closer to Harriet. 'Pardon me.' She gave him an apologetic smile before letting Humphrey lead her over to Harriet. 'Won't you join us?' she called back to him.

Mr Lane remained on the pathway and shook his head. It felt as if he was half a world away from her as he stuffed his hands into his pockets. Humphrey went to eat one of the roses and she pulled him back before he found his snout covered in thorns.

'Come on, you. Back on the path you go.'

She walked back with Harriet and found Mr Lane's focus was now on her dog.

'I need to go,' he said, keeping his eyes on Humphrey.

What? Now? I don't want you to leave now.

'Oh, of course.'

'But we haven't done the labyrinth.' The tone in Harriet's voice matched her confused expression. 'We are here now. It's just over there,' she said, gesturing to the large thick wall of privet hedgerow that formed the outside of the maze.

'There isn't enough time.'

'We can walk with you back to the gate.' At least Harriet wasn't pleading, which is how it probably would have come out if Clara had said it. But when he shook his head, it felt as if she could hardly breathe.

If she had kissed him, would he have stayed?

'That's not necessary. Enjoy the gardens, ladies.' Before either of them could reply he turned and walked away from them with the sound of the gravel crunching under his shiny boots.

'Wait!' she called out after him rather inelegantly and shoved Humphrey's leash into Harriet's hand.

He stopped and slowly turned around as she walked quickly towards him. When she reached him, she realised Harriet had stayed behind.

'You offered to help me train my dog.'

A small smile was playing at the corners of his lips. 'I did, didn't I.'

'You did. I even recall you offering to do so for free.'

Raising his eyes skywards as if he was trying to recall making that offer, he folded his arms. 'Are you sure that's what I said?'

'I am.' Their eyes met again and she was so glad she had stopped him from walking away. 'Will you help me?'

He shoved his hands back into his pockets and lowered his head. 'I can't.'

'Why not?'

'We want different things. It's best if we part ways.'

'What things? What do you want?'

He stepped closer. Since he was taller than she was and they were standing so close it was as if she was almost about to be wrapped in his arms before he lowered his voice so only she could hear. 'I want to kiss you. And you want to match me with Miss Collingswood.'

All she heard was that he wanted to kiss her.

He glanced past her shoulder before looking back down at her. If Harriet was coming their way with Humphrey, she couldn't tell by his expression. 'I am not the kind of man one recommends to a young lady. You should know that. And more to the point, I still want to kiss you. Even now.' His low voice rumbled through her body and she wanted to lean into him. 'That's why I am leaving.'

'I wish you would stay.'

'I know, but for all the wrong reasons.'

'How do you know that?'

His eyes narrowed on her for a few heartbeats and he placed his lips by her ear. 'The next time I see you, I'm going to kiss you. You want me to. I've seen it in your eyes.'

When he lifted his head away from hers, the air slapped her neck where it had been warmed by his breath. Clara opened her mouth to reply, but she couldn't think of any way to respond. Suddenly she felt Harriet's presence at her side and Humphrey jumped up on Mr Lane's leg.

He rubbed Humphrey's neck before he tipped the brim of his hat at her and walked away. She hadn't given him her address. They hadn't made any arrangements to see one another again. But deep inside she had no doubt that the next time she ran into him, he would make good on his promise.

* * *

The ride back to the Royal Crescent had been particularly quiet and Clara had spent most of it keeping an eye on Humphrey so that he didn't jump out of the window from her lap. She didn't want to look at Harriet. She couldn't face the girl, knowing that Harriet liked Mr Lane.

It was Harriet who finally broke the silence that stretched between them over the sound of the rolling carriage wheels on the cobblestone streets.

'I am glad you went after him. His departure was so abrupt that it was unsettling.'

Something outside the carriage must have caught Humphrey's attention since he lifted his paws to the carriage window and let out a series of barks. 'Humphrey, shush.' He adjusted his hind legs on the jonquil fabric in her lap and barked at the window again.

'Did he explain why he needed to leave so quickly?'

'He had business to attend to.'

'And that is all?' Harriet didn't sound as if she believed her.

It had become apparent that Harriet was attracted to Mr Lane. Clara could tell that the moment they left the theatre last night when she came up with this plan on how to find him. She didn't have the heart to crush Harriet's hopes. Perhaps she should begin championing Mr Greeley.

'Why are you so quiet?' Harriet took Clara's hand in a comforting gesture that under the circumstances felt like a punch in the chest. 'I hope he didn't say anything to upset you.'

'No. He didn't.' Clara kept her eyes on Humphrey, not wanting to see Harriet's concern for her. The young woman was truly lovely and had been ignored by men who were only interested in her sister. How could Clara put her through the same pain as well?

'Please don't worry, Clara. I'm certain he likes you. I can see it in the way he looks at you. I'm sure his leaving so abruptly had nothing to do with you.'

Clara's eyes snapped to Harriet. 'Me?'

'Yes. I hope I didn't do anything to cause him to leave. I wasn't certain how long I should stay behind when you went after him, but Humphrey kept pulling on the leash to go to you and I was afraid if I waited too long he might find a way to get loose again.'

'I don't understand. Harriet, you like Mr Lane.'

'I do. I like him very much.'

'You were the one who suggested we search for him today.'

'Yes…'

None of this was making any sense.

Suddenly Harriet's mouth opened and she looked as if she understood more of what was happening than Clara did. 'Oh, you don't think I have designs on Mr Lane for myself? He is positively ancient.' As if she realised what she had said and how it would have related to Clara's age, she looked down at her hands on her lap. 'I don't mean ancient exactly. What I mean is that Mr Lane is too old for me.' She looked back up at her. 'I like him well enough and he is attentive to me even though I can tell he just wants to keep staring at you. None of my sister's suitors shows me that courtesy. Maybe that comes with age. I mean… I think he is perfect for you.'

'For me? He is too young for me.'

'That's not possible. You two are probably the same age.'

'No, Harriet, we aren't. I think Mr Lane is almost ten years younger than I am.'

'That can't be. Are you certain you know what his age is?'

'I am fairly certain.'

'Well, it doesn't matter. I still think you are perfect for one another.'

'I'm sure many people here in Bath would disagree.'

'I doubt Mr Lane would. When will you see him again?'

Clara shrugged with the words he whispered to her still echoing in her mind. *'The next time I see you, I'm going to kiss you.'* It would be a long time before she forgot those words.

'Do you know where he is staying?' Harriet asked. 'I thought I heard him mention The Fountain Head Hotel in town.'

'He did. You seem to have developed a habit of paying close attention to what Mr Lane says.'

'When you don't talk very much, you learn to listen well when it matters. Are you going to see him again?'

'He hasn't arranged anything, if that is what you are asking. But I do have a feeling that I will be seeing him again.'

The question was, how soon?

Chapter Fifteen

When he arrived back at the coffee house, Lane was still incredibly frustrated by his encounter with Mrs Sommersby. He had been excited to see her in the park, yet it was becoming harder and harder to be in her presence without touching her.

When she had moved away from him on the path and went down to Miss Collingswood, who was admiring the flower beds, Lane realised she was trying to bring attention to her friend—the very friend that the Dowager was attempting to match with Mr Greeley. He liked the girl well enough, but she was too young for him and she didn't make him feel anything close to the things Mrs Sommersby did. No one in recent memory made him feel the things Mrs Sommersby did. She stimulated both his mind and body.

Even now when she wasn't in front of him, he wanted to kiss her with every fibre of his being—and he could tell there was a part of her that wanted him to. They had come too close to kissing, too many times, for him to misunderstand that look in her eyes.

Thinking about her was doing him no good. He needed to concentrate on work. He needed to stop thinking about how much he loved the way she smelled...and talked...and would fit so perfectly in his arms if he ever got the chance to hold her.

He needed to spend the day locked in his office, alone, reviewing those books from the stable. But as he walked down the dark corridor at the back of the shop and opened the door to his office, his plans fell apart when he spotted the Earl of Hartwick reclining back in Lane's desk chair, with his booted feet on Lane's large oak desk.

Lane blinked to make sure he wasn't imagining it. 'What are you doing here?'

'I would think that was fairly obvious,' Hart said, lowering his feet and sitting forward so his forearms were resting on the surface of the desk. 'Where the hell have you been? It's almost noon.'

'I've been out.' Lane pointed behind him with his thumb in the event Hart didn't know where the front door to the coffee house was.

'Why? You never go out. I was beginning to think you must be in a ditch somewhere with your throat cut...probably clutching profit and loss statements with your dying breath.' His voice was rough with anxiety as he grabbed the papers from the desk that Lane had intended to review today.

'Well, as you can see my throat is fine—however, those papers aren't. If you keep crushing them in your fist, I might have the devil of a time reading them when you are through.'

As Hart dropped the papers on the desk, his sharp blue eyes became hooded like a hawk. 'I looked for that handy analysis you love to do, but didn't see it, so I thought I'd take a crack at recalculating the numbers myself.'

'Any luck?'

'No. I was too worried about you to concentrate. Sanderson didn't know where you were. He said you were always here by eight. We even went to your room at the hotel, you know, to look for you.'

'We?'

There was a small nudge at Lane's back, moving him slightly forward from where he stood in the doorway.

'Yes, I'm here as well. Hart brought me in through the back door.'

It was Hart's wife, Sarah, standing behind him, holding two cups of coffee. Lane stepped inside, allowing her to pass so she could put the cups down on his desk.

'You just walked past me, you know. I was out

in the corridor, waiting for these cups, and I said hello, but you walked on by.'

'Where?'

'Out there.'

'I did?'

'You did.'

Hart openly studied Lane as he took his cup. 'What has got into you?'

'Nothing. Now get out of my chair and leave me alone. I have work to do.'

Lane just needed to focus. Having Hart and Sarah here would only serve as a distraction. Hart stood and switched places with him, as his friend exchanged looks with his wife.

'You're really not going to ask me.' Disbelief was in Hart's voice.

It took Lane a minute before the realisation of why Hart was here struck him like a brick.

'You know. You have news about the money.' He couldn't say it fast enough.

'Well, it's about time. Yes, I have news. We have come all the way from London to tell you that I have found an investor in this venture of ours.'

The weight that Lane had been carrying around in his chest was suddenly gone and he threw his head back and closed his eyes in relief. 'Thank God! Who is it? Do I know the gentleman?'

'It's Lord Musgrove.'

'I don't know anything about him.'

'Well, he didn't know anything about you either, so the field is even. He has agreed to fund this endeavour of yours, but he wants to see for himself what he will be investing in.'

'He's coming here?'

'Yes, he should arrive shortly and, if all goes as planned, we will be signing a contract with the man and getting the money we need to purchase and rebuild that hotel.'

Soon, he would show Lord Musgrove just how profitable this spa was going to be and he would finally be able to make an offer on the hotel next door. His vision was finally going to happen.

He let out a long breath and rubbed his eyes with the palms of his hands.

'Something is different about you,' Hart commented before taking a sip from his cup. 'I can't quite put my finger on what it is, but there definitely is something different about you. Where were you this morning?'

'I told you I was out. I went for a walk in Sydney Gardens. It's this pleasure garden I discovered not far from here.'

'You were walking in a pleasure garden all this time?' He raised his cup to his lips and took a slow sip, studying Lane over the rim of porcelain. 'That's all you have to say? You aren't going to ask me fifty things about Musgrove in the span of thirty seconds?'

'It's a woman.' Sarah's brown eyes narrowed on him as she tapped her finger on her lips.

'No.' There was a definitive sound to Hart's word, until he glanced between Lane and his wife and then looked at the wrinkled papers on the desk. 'Oh, hell, you're right. It is a woman. I never thought I'd see the day.'

If Lane rubbed his brow hard enough, could he make these two disappear from his sight?

'Well, I for one think it's a good thing.' The warm, friendly smile Sarah gave him matched the tone of her voice. 'Everyone should have a special someone.'

Hart sat on the corner of the desk with even more of a bemused expression. 'I'm not disagreeing. It is a good idea. Tell us about her.'

'Why don't you tell me about Lord Musgrove instead?'

'Because at the moment you couldn't give a damn about Lord Musgrove and you know it.'

The smile on Sarah's face widened. 'This is why you walked past me and didn't see me, even though you looked right at me. You were thinking of your lady friend.'

'Lane has a lady friend.' The sing-song voice that Hart used made Lane want to punch him.

'Are you twelve?'

'It wouldn't be the first time I've been accused of being that age. Now tell us about her.'

'There isn't anything to tell. I have met a woman. We are friends. That is all there is to it.'

Hart adjusted his seat on the desk. 'There has to be more.'

'There isn't.'

His friends exchanged a look, which was never a good sign. His relationship with Mrs Sommersby was complicated enough. A change of subject was in order.

'Tell me about Lord Musgrove. How did you meet?'

'Andrew Pearce introduced us. So where did you meet this woman?'

'At the spa. Did Lord Musgrove indicate how much he was willing to invest?'

'Everything we need. He is interested in diversifying outside his tobacco interests. Were you bathing when you met her at the spa?'

Sarah swatted him on his shoulder.

'I'm simply trying to fill in the details so I understand how this woman could possibly bring my friend into such a state that he forgot to analyse a profit and loss statement. This is unprecedented.'

'I didn't forget.'

'Forgive me, you had better things to do.'

'No...yes...will you two leave me be so I can look at these figures in peace?'

'Come with me, Sarah. We will leave Lane to pretend he is working when we know he will be pining for his…oh, what was the word?'

'His friend,' Sarah replied with a laugh.

'Oh, yes, his friend. I will inform you when Lord Musgrove arrives. In the meantime, we are staying with Lyonsdale at Number Twelve on the Royal Crescent. Send word to his home if you need anything.'

What he needed was Mrs Sommersby. He couldn't call on her. He didn't know where she lived. If he wanted to see her again, he would have to go to a place he knew she would be. When they met at the park by the Crescent that day, she had mentioned various entertainments in town that she thought he might enjoy. Then he recalled seeing her name in the *Chronicle* that morning.

'Do you dance, Sarah?'

His friend's wife paused by the door and appeared very pleased with his question. 'I do.'

'I might be in need of your help, if you are so inclined. I think there is a chance I will need to polish up on my skills. They are probably a bit rusty.'

'It would be my pleasure, Lane. I am happy to help in any way I can.' She scrunched her shoulders up towards her ears in excitement and gave him one last bright smile before closing the door behind her.

Chapter Sixteen

Clara stood on the edge of the dance floor in the large ballroom of the Upper Assembly Rooms with the Dowager Duchess watching Harriet fade into the woodwork as her sister Ann took centre stage among a group of young gentlemen.

She looked over at the Dowager standing beside her and tried not to frown. 'I thought you were going to invite Mr Greeley this evening.'

'The man was called out of town on a family matter.'

'Well, that's unfortunate. If she wasn't an unmarried young woman, I'd take her with me into the card room.'

'If she wasn't an unmarried woman, you wouldn't have to. And where is your Mr Lane this evening?'

'He is not *my* Mr Lane and I have no idea.' She hadn't seen or heard from him for days and was beginning to wonder if he, too, had been called out of town.

'Pity. There was something about that man I liked.'

There was a lot about him that she had liked as well—more than she would care to admit, even to herself. She couldn't trust herself when it came to men. She had married for love and it had turned into a disaster. It was probably smarter to keep her distance from him anyway.

'Well, if those gentlemen are not here this evening then we should take it upon ourselves to look for additional gentlemen to throw at Miss Collingswood,' the Dowager said, scanning the groups of people around them.

'I don't know if Mr and Mrs Collingswood would appreciate us throwing men at their daughter.'

'Nonsense. They want to see her wed. We want to help facilitate that. There could be another gentleman here that she might like. Although I do think Greeley is perfect for her.'

'Are you suggesting that we split up and search this room?'

'Are you mad? I am too old to walk around and search for anything. At my age, the best course of action is to survey the selection from right where we are standing.'

Clara's gaze travelled over the room—at least

what could be seen of it from where they were standing. On the dance floor ladies and gentlemen moved to the music that drifted down around them from the orchestra that played on the other side of the ballroom. And there were groups of people standing along the edges of the dance floor and sitting on the benches behind them. There were so many gentlemen in formal black attire with black breeches, white stockings and black shoes that they all blended into one. She was about ready to turn back to the Dowager when her eye caught the friendly nod of Mr Charles Whelby.

It had been four years since she had been introduced to Mr Whelby in this very Assembly Room, shortly after she had returned to Bath after staying for months in Paris with her niece Juliet. In that time, the gentleman who owned an estate just outside Bath and visited the city frequently had become a friend. He made his way through the crowd to her, looking completely unruffled in his impeccable evening attire.

'I didn't know you had returned from London.'

He rose from his bow with a sparkle in his grey-blue eyes. 'If I knew you would be missing me that much, I would have called on you directly after we crossed the river.'

'I always miss you when you are gone. I become completely despondent. It is remarked upon by all who see me and is written about extensively in the *Chronicle*,' she replied with excessive dramatic inflection and let out a long sigh.

'I've told you there is a remedy for that, but you refuse to marry me, so it appears, until you do, you will find your name in the papers with some regularity.'

Shaking out her fan, she hid her smile from him, but knew by his expression that he saw the merriment in her eyes. Glancing at the Dowager, she saw Eleanor was watching their exchange with marked attention. 'Your Grace, may I introduce you to Mr Charles Whelby? Mr Whelby is a friend and terrible tease. Mr Whelby, may I present Eleanor, the Dowager Duchess of Lyonsdale?'

'Your Grace, it is an honour to make your acquaintance.' In the candlelight from the five enormous cut-glass chandeliers hanging high above the room, the small diamond stickpin in his cravat winked at them as he bowed.

'Did I hear you have recently come from London, sir?'

'I have, Your Grace.'

'I am quite fond of London and spend most of the year there myself. Most people my age prefer the countryside. I find no comfort in being left with such a restricted number of companions.'

'Well, one can never accuse Bath of being a

city with restricted company,' he replied. 'Here the company can change from day to day.'

'That is true. It's one of the reasons I agreed to spend a month here.'

Clara fluttered her fan near her chest. 'Another is that she probably has matched every available female of her acquaintance in London and needed to expanded her circle of unwed women.'

'There are worse things I have been accused of. Which leads me to ask after your marital state, Mr Whelby.'

'Shameless. She is shameless.'

The Dowager ignored Clara's comment, which was of no surprise. When she had matchmaking on her mind, she was relentless. 'I take it you are unwed.'

'I am,' he replied, appearing as if he was trying not to smile at the boldness of the woman. 'I had asked Mrs Sommersby to marry me, but she refused.'

She would never marry again and place her future in the hands of a husband. No man would relinquish his investment decision-making to his wife. Men were too proud for that. And she was too smart now to turn over control of her future to someone else. That feeling of panic was rising again and she reminded herself once more that she was fine. No one was ever going to force her to marry.

The Dowager looked at him with a sympathetic smile.

'Oh, do not feel sorry for him. What Mr Whelby has forgotten to mention is how that proposal occurred.'

'It was given in earnest.' He appeared affronted, but she knew him better.

'He had come down with a particularly bad cold and wanted someone to nurse him back to health.'

'As a wife would do,' he explained in his defence, adjusting the cuff on his impeccably cut tailcoat with his head bent down so all she could see was his very close-cropped brown hair that was just starting to turn grey.

'Well, since you will not be marrying Mrs Sommersby, perhaps we might interest you in meeting another lady?'

'She is not a fine pair of embroidered gloves that you can offer like that,' Clara said, chastising her outspoken friend.

The Dowager waved her pink-gloved hand at her. 'I didn't say that she was—however, I find being direct is the best course of action. This way no one can misconstrue your meaning.'

'I don't believe anyone could ever misconstrue your meaning.'

'Which has served me well in life and why I am so good at determining which people should be together.' She turned her attention back to Charles. 'Mr Whelby, if you would care to meet a lovely young woman who is in attendance tonight, please let me know.'

'I will, should I decide to expand my social circle.' Once more he seemed amused by the Dowager's directness. It was amazing that he hadn't made an excuse to run away by now.

'Capital. Please do. Now, if you will both excuse me, I think I will go and save that girl from boredom.' She walked slowly away from them towards Harriet. Clara couldn't imagine what the woman did to relieve boredom in a ballroom and she wasn't certain it would be good for her to find out.

'What a very unusual woman,' Charles said, following the Dowager's progress across the room with his eyes. 'Which is the woman she is championing?'

'The one with the red hair in the long-sleeved, white-muslin gown and the blue ribbon in her hair.'

'Ah, I see now.' His attention was fixed on Harriet. 'Well, the girl is fortunate to have someone looking out for her future.'

'She is a lovely woman who is overshadowed by her younger sister.'

'Well, I can see why. The sister is a diamond of the first water.'

Clara looked across at Ann in a white muslin gown similar to Harriet's, but with one pale pink satin ribbon under her breasts and another woven through the curls in her blonde hair. She was addressing her very attentive suitors in a lively manner and ignoring her sister's obvious discomfort.

'You really think the sister is that stunning?' she asked.

'Of course. Don't you? It's no surprise all the young bucks are flocking around her with those looks…and she appears quite charming.' He nodded towards the group with his head and let his gaze linger on them.

Clara turned to watch them as well. 'But you can't hear what she is saying. How do you know she is charming?'

'Watch the way she smiles. Look at the way she engages each of the men.'

'But what about her sister?'

'What about the girl?'

'The younger one is doing nothing to make it easy for her to join in the conversation. She is not engaging with *her*.'

He shrugged. 'If the sister wanted to contribute to what was being discussed, she would join in, instead of standing back the way she is.'

It wasn't that easy. She knew that from experience. She knew what it was like to stand beside a sister that men wanted and they barely noticed you at all, even though you were less than two feet from her. She knew what it was like when you tried to join in a conversation and the people around you didn't even acknowledge what you said. It was as though you were invisible. Eventually you stopped contributing. Being invisible was so much easier on your soul when you were the one who decided it was how you wanted to be.

Charles's attention remained on the little group. 'Who are they?'

'They are the Collingswood sisters. Their family is leasing the house next door.'

'On the Crescent?' His brows rose as he nodded his head in approval of the fashionable address. 'They must have deep pockets. What of the father?'

'He is a barrister who has presented his cases before Parliament and the son of a baron.'

Charles was casting an appraising gaze over Harriet and Ann. 'Neither are spoken for?'

'No. I know the blonde has had numerous offers, but has not found a gentleman that suits her fancy.'

His eyes remained on the small party a bit longer before finally returning his attention to Clara. 'Well, we could stand here for the rest of the night watching your friend, or we could dance. I think we should dance.'

Since the Dowager was going over to Harriet,

Clara was certain she would find a way to make the girl feel appreciated. She looked back up at Charles. 'Are you asking me to dance?'

'Would you like me to?'

He had a habit of doing that—of posing a situation and then making her feel in the end that somehow it was her idea because she would be the one doing the asking.

'Yes, Charles. Why don't you ask me to dance?'

'Mrs Sommersby, would you do me the pleasure of dancing with me…if your card is free, that is?'

She looked at the white silk of her glove on her empty right palm. 'You are in luck, Mr Whelby. It seems that I have the next dance free.' Women of her age weren't asked to dance as frequently as the younger women were. Each time she was asked, it felt like a treat.

He held out his arm and escorted her to the dance floor where they took their places. When the dance began, Charles took her hand in his. 'I knew I would see you here,' he said. 'You're quite predictable, you know.'

'How very boring of me. Next week I will shock you and I will not be in attendance.'

'You'll pass the time attending another private ball and staying out much later than one should, I'm certain of it.'

'Perhaps I will shock you and simply remain at home.'

'On an evening when entertainments are offered? That would shock me.'

They separated with the movement of the dance and, as they did, she had the oddest sensation that someone was watching her. As she scanned the crowd of well-dressed ladies and gentlemen, she knew she was being foolish and was proven so when she didn't make eye contact with anyone.

They came back together once more in the movement and he narrowed his eyes on her. 'Is anything wrong?'

'No, it's nothing. What have you been doing with yourself since you've been back avoiding me?'

They separated once again.

'Well, let's see. I've been reading all my correspondence that has piled up on my desk. Oh, and I had breakfast in the garden at The Fountain Head while I met with your cousin, Phillip.' Charles was one of only a small handful of people who knew she owned the hotel. 'Apparently, more and more people from Bath have taken to having breakfast in the garden lately. Friends are telling friends. Which is good news for the owner.'

'I'm sure the owner is quite pleased. Did you

enjoy their new offerings for breakfast?' she asked as he came up once again at her side.

'There wasn't anything that was new since the last time I was there.'

They separated once more and anger started to rise up inside her. She had specifically told Phillip she wanted to expand the menu and he had agreed he would. It was times like this when she regretted having her cousin manage the establishment. Perhaps if they weren't related she would have a manager who did not see fit to go against her wishes.

'You are certain?'

'Yes. It was the usual fare of Sally Lunn buns and bread.'

She wanted to storm off the dance floor and go over to The Fountain Head to demand to know why he had disregarded her request. As it stood, she was now dancing with her hands balled into two fists. Why was it so difficult for a man to realise that she knew what she was doing?

Clara stared off into the distance as she shouted things at Phillip in her head that no lady should ever say out loud. Then she caught the eye of a gentleman standing at the edge of the dance floor and her breath caught in her throat.

Mr Lane was here. And all she could think about were his parting words to her. *'The next time I see you I'm going to kiss you.'*

Chapter Seventeen

She was in green satin. Lane had wondered what colour Mrs Sommersby would be wearing on his walk over to the Upper Assembly Rooms. What someone was going to wear had never been any of his concern before, but tonight he kept trying to imagine what colour silk or satin would be against her skin.

When he entered the building, he was hoping he wouldn't find her in the ballroom. It would have been easier if she were in the card room. No one danced in there and he was fairly skilled at cards. But when he spied her on the dance floor with the impeccably groomed, middle-aged gentleman, he was not surprised. Mrs Sommersby would indeed be a woman who danced. And once he spotted her, he didn't want to look away.

The desire to kiss her deeply and passionately while holding her in his arms had not diminished.

If anything, in that gown and under the glow of the candlelight, he wanted her even more.

How she managed to spot him in the middle of the dance was a mystery. Lane thought he had blended in completely with every other man in the room dressed in fine black evening wear. Yet somehow during one particular sequence of the dance, she had turned her head and looked directly at him. And in her eyes, at that distance, he saw the spark of recognition and then a flash of excitement before she was forced to turn away with the movement of the dance.

Not wanting to distract her and risk her stumbling, he backed further into the crowd and was rewarded for the kind gesture by the fact that he saw her searching for him a few more times before the dance ended. When she gracefully lowered herself into the final curtsy of the minuet, Lane had the strongest urge to walk up to her, grab her hand and pull her out of the room to some secluded area in the building. He wasn't joking when he had told her he was going to kiss her the next time he saw her. He'd thought about it for most of the day.

As she walked off the dance floor with her partner, she flicked open her fan and surreptitiously scanned the room once more as they slipped into the crowd. Lane had no idea who the gentleman was. He had appeared to be very attentive to her, although he did notice that the gentleman had said something to her that had angered her. A protective instinct welled up inside him and he had to stop himself from going over there and demanding the man apologise.

He couldn't recall the last time he'd followed a woman around at a ball. There was a very real possibility that he never had. After leaving the Foundling Hospital his life had always been consumed with work. Entertainments such as this were infrequent and he usually spent them in the card room. But tonight, skulking through the crowd to watch her was his preferred way to spend the evening. Hell, she was the only reason he was here.

Somehow her eyes found him through the crowd when he got about twenty feet away from her. Something intense flared between them and he didn't miss when her tongue peeked out and briefly touched the dip in her top lip.

He wanted to taste that lip and the plump one below it. He wanted to savour the feel of her lips against his and slide his tongue over hers to see how she would respond. Two gentlemen came around from behind him and blocked Lane's view of her as they walked in her direction.

When she came back into view, she was standing in the very spot she had been in, looking stunning in her green-satin gown with her white-silk gloves that had fallen below her elbows. But now she was all alone. The gentleman she had been dancing with was no longer by her side. Whether it was intentional or not, he couldn't tell, but her gaze slid slowly down his body and it became impossible to swallow.

This was it. She was all alone now. This was what he had come here for.

He approached her slowly, holding her gaze and thinking that she might disappear back into the crowd if he rushed this. When he was less than three feet from her, Mrs Sommersby's gaze dropped to his mouth. Did she want him to drag her out of the assembly?

'Mr Lane.' Her voice was smooth like fine brandy and it had the ability to stir his soul with just the sound of his name. As she dipped into a shallow curtsy and lowered her head, he had the perfect view of the smooth, tempting skin of the upper swells of her shapely breasts and had to rub his gloved fingers across his palm to quell the itch to touch her.

'Good evening, Mrs Sommersby.' It came out surprisingly composed considering the inner turmoil he was in, knowing that somehow tonight he was finally going to kiss her. 'You look very fetching this evening.'

'Thank you. You look quite dashing, yourself.'

A deep sense of satisfaction came over him

when she called him dashing. He wasn't as impeccably turned out as her dancing partner. It had taken five tries to get the fall of his cravat just the way he wanted it. And it was obvious from his valet's expression that Winston had wanted to choke him with it by the time he left his room tonight.

Lane had never been a man who women fawned over. Whether that was from his appearance, his nature or his questionable birth he would never know.

'I saw you dancing,' he said.

'I saw you watching.'

'I couldn't help it. You are a vision in green.' He said it with a smile so that perhaps she wouldn't realise how true he found that statement. 'I was told by a gentlewoman with a rather rambunctious dog that this was a nice place to spend an evening.'

'You were?'

'Yes, she informed me of it behind a hedgerow near the Crescent.'

'You remembered.'

'I did.'

She turned her body and he walked beside her through the crowd, happy to allow her to set their course.

'Have you been here long, Mr Lane?'

'Not very.'

'I confess it surprises me that you are not spending your evening in the card room.'

'There is nothing that interests me in that room.'

'And in this room?'

'I find there is something in this room that interests me very much.'

She looked up at him from the corner of her eye. 'Something?'

'Someone.'

'Ah, I see. You seemed to have disappeared from the streets of Bath as of late. I thought you had left town. I was disappointed we hadn't had the chance to say goodbye.'

'I've been consumed with work.'

'Your investments.'

'Yes. Success only comes from long hours and dedication.'

There were four tiers of benches that lined the outer portion of the room and she headed towards them.

'And you're successful?'

'Very.'

'It hasn't escaped my notice how committed you are to your work.'

With her hand, she gestured towards the empty seats at the end of the second tier. 'Shall we?'

He might get a reprieve from dancing after all. Nodding his agreement, he waited for her to sit and then took the end seat beside her. She pushed the wrinkles out of her skirt and he couldn't help notice her thighs were outlined in green satin that shimmered in the candlelight.

The movement of her hand as she opened her fan broke his concentration.

'It feels nice to sit down. This is the first time I have taken a seat all night. One of the advantages of my age is that I do not need to stand about waiting to be seen.'

'You make it sound as if we have one foot in the grave.'

'*We* don't. But I am far closer to it than you are.' She continued to fan herself and looked about the room from where they were sitting. Her skin was smooth and she only had a few small lines by the corners of her eyes. There was no grey in her soft brown hair that was styled up, exposing the long curve of her neck. Her movements were spry yet graceful. She had so much energy that reverberated around her.

'That is the second time you've mentioned your status as an ancient crone to me.'

'I don't think I phrased it exactly that way.' The soft breeze she was making with her fan carried a hint of her fragrance on it.

'Why do you believe that we are so old?'

'I didn't say old. Perhaps just advanced in age. And I was referring to me, not you.'

'It's all the same.'

'No. It's not.' She turned at her waist to face him. 'How old are you, Mr Lane? If you don't mind me asking.'

'I turned seven and thirty recently.' There was no record of his birth. He knew the year and was told the approximate month. The date of his birth along with whether his mother had given him a name was something he had always wanted to know.

Her expression softened. 'I am five and forty. So perhaps I *am* an ancient crone to you.'

It couldn't be. She didn't look a year older than he was.

'Speechless, I see.'

'I just… I… I assumed we were the same age.'

'I will take that as a compliment.'

'You should.'

She leaned close to him and her shoulder pressed against his. Even through the satin of her gown and his tailcoat sleeve, Lane could feel the passionate heat spread from her body to him. She must have felt it, too, since she glanced at the area where their bodies were touching.

'Now that I have cured your desire,' she whispered to him behind her fan, 'please don't feel obliged to remain here with me. I understand.'

'That has changed nothing. If anything, sitting this close to you while you are in that gown has made me want to kiss you even more. And make no mistake, Mrs Sommersby—I will be kissing you some time tonight.'

Her eyes flew to his and then dropped to his lips. What he wouldn't give to kiss her right now.

'But how could you still want to? I am so much older than you.'

'You are not that much older and, in addition, you telling me your age has not changed anything about you. You are still the most captivating woman I know.'

'Then you must know very few women.'

'Do not do that. Do not try to diminish yourself to me. I will draw my own conclusions about you.'

'By the flattering glow of candlelight, you may think you have not changed your mind. But when the sun comes up, you will find you see a different portrait.'

'You truly have no idea how much I wish I could kiss you now and prove you wrong.'

Her breath caught. He heard it. And it gave him immense satisfaction.

As if to give herself time to regain her composure, she looked away from him and out into the crowd. Eventually her gaze settled on a small group of young dandies that were surrounding a tall, thin blonde woman whose hair was woven with a pale pink ribbon in it. He couldn't understand why this particular group had captured

Mrs Sommersby's interest, until he spotted Miss Collingswood, standing slightly off to one side. It was as if she were part of the group, yet somewhat removed at the same time. An outsider. He knew very well what that felt like, especially in grand places such as this with members of the *ton* practising their stinging judgements based on things that were out of your control.

'Who are those people with Miss Collingswood?'

'That's her sister Ann. The gentlemen are Mr Baxter, Mr Ross, Lord Harris, and Mr Warren.'

'*That* is her sister?'

'Yes, yes, I know she is a diamond of the first water.'

'I was going to say they look nothing alike.'

She looked over at his profile. 'Oh.'

Knowing that it was best if he kept his eyes on the group of young people and not on the woman beside him, Lane tipped his head closer to hers so their temples were almost touching. 'Do not interpret that to mean that I have designs on your Miss Collingswood. My desires, as you know, lie elsewhere.'

The fluttering movement of her fan stopped for a breath.

'If that is her sister,' he continued, 'why is she doing nothing to include Miss Collingswood in the conversation? I would think she sees that Miss Collingswood is being ignored.'

'That is my feeling on the matter.' Her attention was back on the party in question. 'Do you have any brothers or sisters, Mr Lane? Would you treat them that way?'

Any time anyone asked him about his family, it still brought a painful constriction to his heart, even after all these years. Some day he would find a wife, have some children and know what it was to have a family of his own. Until then, it was something he would not dwell on.

'I have no brothers or sisters,' he replied. 'And you?'

'I have an older sister.' Her eyes remained on Miss Collingswood's party. 'Mary was always the prettier one. She was always very comfortable conversing in crowds. I was not.' Their eyes met briefly and he sensed a sad nostalgic wave come over her. She adjusted her seat on the bench and looked back out at her young friend.

'I find it hard to believe that you are not accomplished in conversing in a crowd. And I also believe it isn't possible that your sister is prettier than you.'

'You flatter me again, sir.' She gifted him with a smile that shone in her eyes. 'Over the years it became easier to speak in groups of people. It happened after I married my husband, God rest his soul. But even now, I actually prefer smaller intimate groups of people I am well acquainted with than standing in a group with virtual strangers. I suppose I have become skilled at hiding that part of me from the world.'

Miss Collingswood looked sad. Everyone was laughing at something her sister had said, but Miss Collingswood looked lost in her own thoughts. No one seemed to notice. No one seemed to even see her standing there.

'I know what it is like to be ignored,' he said. 'To feel as though you don't quite have a place in the room. As though maybe your place isn't even in the room.'

He wasn't sure why he had admitted that to her. He never liked to think about what it felt like to be a bastard.

She reached out and squeezed his hand that was resting on his thigh. 'There are occasions when people can be so thoughtless.'

By the time he looked down, her hand was back on her lap.

The gesture was probably intended to be one of comfort. He hadn't had much experience with physical gestures of affection. But the brief contact of their gloved hands brought a warmth that spread through his entire body. It was too intimate.

He knew what he needed to do. Excusing

himself rather abruptly from her side, he strode through the crowd to a startled Miss Collingswood.

'Mr Lane!'

He gave her a very respectable bow. 'Miss Collingswood. Always a pleasure to see you.'

Her sister turned her head towards him and was eyeing him with her full attention. Apparently, she *was* aware her sister was beside her.

Miss Collingswood bobbed a curtsy. 'Have you seen Mrs Sommersby? She is here, you know. I spent a good portion of my time with her when I first arrived, but didn't wish to take up all her time tonight.'

'I'm sure she wouldn't have minded.'

It appeared Miss Collingswood's interest was with Mr Greeley after all. No woman with an interest in him would have tried to direct him to someone else. Greeley was sorely lacking if he had left her here alone tonight.

'I actually came to find out if you might honour me with the next dance. That is, if your dance card is free.'

With that, her entire face brightened and it warmed his heart to see genuine happiness in her eyes. 'I am free, Mr Lane, and accept your very kind invitation to dance.'

He held out his arm for her and in a few minutes found himself on the dance floor, trying to remember the steps to the damned minuet.

'That was really very kind of you to ask me to dance. I was hoping that Mr Greeley would be here tonight, but the Dowager said that she heard he'd had to go out of town to Plymouth to tend to a family matter. Not that I am not grateful that you have asked me to dance. I just thought I'd mention Mr Greeley…and my interest in him.'

'Uh-huh.'

'You never did say if you have seen Mrs Sommersby. She is here in a lovely green gown. It is very pretty and she looks so beautiful in it. I'm certain if you look around for her, you will find her. She is such wonderful company.'

'Uh-huh.'

'What are you doing, Mr Lane?'

'Remembering the sequence.'

'Of what?'

'The steps.'

They parted ways and he followed the gentleman on his right side as he walked around his particular group of four dancers.

'You don't know the minuet?'

'I haven't danced it in a long time.'

'Yet you decided to dance it with me?'

'My apologies for being a less-than-adequate partner.'

'Oh, Mr Lane, I think you are the finest partner I have ever had.' There was a brief shimmer of unshed tears in her eyes before she very quietly instructed him on the movements just low enough so only he could hear her.

Chapter Eighteen

'It does my heart good to see her dancing,' the Dowager said, taking Mr Lane's seat beside Clara. 'I spent some time with her—unfortunately, I was summoned into the card room to settle a debate between two old men with poor memories and couldn't have her remain by my side. That was kind of you to suggest that he ask her.'

'But I didn't. That was all his idea. I was going to suggest that we ask her to join us, but he left before I had the opportunity.'

The two women sat in silence as they watched Mr Lane and Harriet on the dance floor. His movements for the most part were smooth and measured. He had a presence about him, brought on by his perfect posture and the raised angle of his chin. It wasn't too high to indicate a sense of superiority, but it was high enough to say he wouldn't back down from a challenge. He was a fairly tall man. If she had to guess she would say he was about six foot, which, considering she was only five foot four, meant that there was a comfortable height difference between them and Clara didn't have to strain her neck too much when she was looking up at him. His athletic frame and broad shoulders were shown to his advantage in the cut of his well-made clothing. And through his white stockings she could see a pair of very nice, very defined calf muscles.

'He does seem to be concentrating quite a bit,' the Dowager observed in a low voice.

'I wonder what she is saying that he finds so interesting?'

'Perhaps she is talking about you.'

Clara eyed her friend. 'I don't know why he would find anything about me interesting? I am much too old for him.'

'I doubt Mr Lane feels you are. The two of you have a way when you are together. One gets the sense that in a room full of people, the two of you feel as though you are all alone.'

'What does that even mean?'

'It means that I have watched you at the theatre and tonight sitting here on the benches. You have some type of connection to one another. It's not something I see frequently. It's not something one can manufacture. It comes from somewhere in the soul.'

'Eleanor, have you been reading poetry again?'

The Dowager waved her gloved hand at Clara and the diamonds in her bracelet sparkled. 'That does not signify. I know what I see. I have been at this far too long to miss something as blatant as this.'

'And what is it that you have been at?'

'Why, matchmaking.'

'We are not a match. I am old enough to be his...young aunt.'

'Has it escaped your notice that I am the champion of unlikely matches? Just look at my grandson and his American wife. No other duke had ever married an American before. There was quite a to-do about his interest in her at the time. He knew there would be many things he would have to sacrifice if he married her. But they are happy. He is happy. Sometimes people just need a nudge. And when it comes to love, I know the early signs of it.'

'I am not in love, Eleanor.'

'Not yet. But you are on your way. Life is short, Clara. Take it from one as old as I am. Do not disregard what makes you happy. You don't always get a second chance when it comes to love.'

She opened her mouth to inform Eleanor that there was no place in her life for that kind of love, but Mrs Collingswood interrupted them when she approached the Dowager's side.

The woman was dressed in a fashionably cut

light-champagne-coloured gown with puce trim. The embroidery work alone projected how expensive the gown must have been. Three very large ostrich feathers, dyed puce, were attached to her champagne-coloured cap that rested on hair that was the same colour as Harriet's. Each one of the feathers had to be about a foot long, giving Mrs Collingswood, with her already tall frame, the appearance of great height. She was hard to miss in a room even this large. And Clara found the boldness of her appearance matched the boldness of her personality.

She curtsied to Eleanor, having been already introduced to her earlier in the evening, and appeared to be near bursting with suppressed excitement. 'Mrs Sommersby, I couldn't help but notice that the gentleman Harriet is dancing with was sitting with you a short while ago. Pray, can you tell me who he is?'

'His name is Mr William Lane and he is from London. I introduced them the night I took Harriet to the theatre.'

'London. Well, that is something.'

By the slightly crestfallen look in her eyes, Clara could tell she was disappointed that Mr Lane was not in possession of a title.

'I assume by the look of him and his manners that he is from a respectable part of town.'

Clara had no idea where in London he lived.

It had never come up in their discussions and the one time Harriet had brought up London when they were sitting having breakfast, he had left after barely acknowledging her comment. She also knew nothing of his family save for the fact that he had no brothers or sisters. For someone who had intended to arrange a match between the man and this woman's daughter, she truly had been remiss in finding out the necessary details to determine if he would have been a respectable match for the girl. But based on his character, she was certain he would check off all the other necessary points on her list.

'Will he be in Bath for long?'

'I am not sure how much longer he is to remain. He is here on a business matter.'

Mrs Collingswood turned to look at the dance floor once more. 'A businessman. What kind?'

'A respectable one.' At least she hoped he was. What had they been talking about each time they were together that she didn't know the answer to this?

The vague response seemed to perplex Mrs Collingswood, but she didn't press and once more she looked back at her daughter and Mr Lane. 'Well, at least she is on the dance floor. Thank you for arranging this.'

'Harriet is a dear girl. That dance was not done at my prompting.'

'But you introduced them?'

'I did.'

'Well then, we still owe you our gratitude. Harriet does not show as well as Ann does. The gentlemen never seem to have an interest in her. I suppose if she tried harder we wouldn't be faced with this situation. It's nice to see your Mr Lane's interest in her.'

The woman was looking at her much too keenly. She was waiting for some kind of reaction. There was nothing that Clara could say to that. Mr Lane had no romantic interest in Harriet. He had made that very plain to her when they'd had a few moments alone in Sydney Gardens. She doubted their turn about the dance floor would change that. He had asked Harriet to dance because he was helping a friend in need. At least she assumed that was the reason.

'I have advised Harriet to be more talkative like her sister is, but she simply refuses to listen. You know how children can be. They do try our patience at times.'

'I don't, actually. Mr Sommersby and I never had any children.'

'Oh, forgive me. I did not realise. I assumed your children were off at school or perhaps had married young. I myself was a very young bride. I married Mr Collingswood when I was just seventeen.'

After all these years, having to say that she was childless should have had no effect on her. However, when she did have to mention it the words still squeezed her heart for a life that at one time she assumed she would have had.

The Dowager opened her mouth to say something, but Mrs Collingswood ploughed on.

'Well, my dear, count yourself fortunate. They can be such a worry. For so long I have worried that Harriet would never find a man who would come to appreciate her unique charms. And now you have introduced her to Mr Lane. I would assume being a friend of yours that he is from a good family. One can tell he is in possession of a good fortune by the cut of his clothes.'

There was no sense in getting this woman's hopes up about Mr Lane and she might be able to save Harriet from being nagged by her mother about him if she could set the record straight. 'From what we can tell, they are only sharing one dance. You may find there are other gentlemen here in Bath who appreciate Harriet's charms and fine character. In fact, I am fairly certain of it.'

'I agree,' Eleanor said. 'There are other gentlemen closer to her own age who I have noticed have shown an interest in her.'

Mrs Collingswood looked sceptical. 'With all due respect, Your Grace, I shall believe that when I see it with my own eyes. Perhaps Mr King might know more about Mr Lane. As the Master of Ceremonies here, he does make it his business to know about everyone who comes to Bath.'

Just then the dance ended and Mr Lane returned Harriet to the vacant area of the ballroom where earlier her sister had been entertaining all those young men. Apparently Mr Ross had got up the courage to ask Ann to dance, because in a few short minutes they joined the couple and Harriet was extending introductions. Like a bee seeking some nectar, Mrs Collingswood excused herself rather quickly and made her way through the crowd to Harriet for her own introduction to Mr Lane.

The Dowager's gaze followed her as she approached the small group. 'That poor, dear girl.'

'Do you see why I have been avoiding them? That woman makes my head ache.'

'I believe Mr Lane is in for a surprise. Hopefully, she does not scare the man away. We may never see him again.'

Clara's stomach dipped with the thought that once again he would accuse her of playing matchmaker. She heard his voice inside her head.

'We want different things. I want to kiss you and you want to match me with Miss Collingswood.'

But she did want to kiss him. She wanted to

desperately. And now, thanks to Miss Collingswood, she might not be able to.

Ladies and gentlemen were continuing to move off the dance floor and find their places alongside it to talk in small groups which made Clara shift her seat on the bench in order to maintain a view of what Mrs Collingswood was doing. By the stiffening of his body, she could tell the moment Mr Lane realised he was meeting Harriet's mother. Did he believe that she had made some sort of arrangement with the woman to find a husband for her daughter?

'I do hope Mr Lane is not regretting asking Harriet to dance,' Eleanor said from beside her. 'The woman could have waited to be introduced to him. It was just one dance and they are in the middle of a public ball. Nothing untoward will be happening to Harriet with our eyes upon her even if Mr Lane was of questionable character. And if she is trying to entice him into courting her daughter, I fear she is off the mark. A gentleman like that needs to be approached with a bit of finesse.'

'I'm not sure the woman knows the word.'

'Well, I think I'll try to find a way for Greeley to spend time with Harriet away from the girl's mother for just a bit longer if I can. We don't need to have him running for the hills as well.'

Was Mr Lane going to run? Is this how their evening would end?

Eleanor nudged her arm with her pointy elbow. 'Ah, there is just something about a bachelor of a certain age,' she observed with amusement in her voice. 'They do become experts in extricating themselves from situations with matchmaking mothers.'

Mr Lane wasn't leaving. At least not yet. He was striding towards them in a purposeful manner.

Eleanor stood and adjusted her reticule on her wrist. 'That didn't take very long at all. Well, I see an old friend across the room. Do give Mr Lane my best and if, by some chance, I do not see you for the remainder of the ball, do have a lovely evening.'

'I'm sure you will see me. I always stay to the end.'

'I'm not so sure about that.' And with that, Eleanor left her to face Mr Lane alone.

The sight of him with his eyes locked on hers, stalking across the room, was stirring a heat inside her. From the look on his face he appeared to either want to grab her in his arms and kiss her, or ring a peel over her for pushing Mrs Collingswood in his direction. She was fervently hoping it was the former. Snapping open her fan, she attempted to cool any flush of passion that might be ready to colour her cheeks at the thought of it.

Eleanor was correct in her assessment of him. Mr Lane did not appear to have any qualms about expertly excusing himself from situations he did not want to be in. She had experienced that first hand on a number of occasions. The question was, would he be doing it again when he reached her? Was he just going to bid her a goodnight and leave out of exasperation?

The minute he reached her there was a palpable intensity radiating off of him as he looked down at her. Without even thinking about it she moved her fan faster.

'I had nothing to do with that.' It came out of her mouth so quickly that it was as if someone else had stated it. She tried to take deep, steadying breaths to fill her lungs so she wouldn't run the risk of rattling on and embarrassing herself.

His eyes narrowed before they dropped down and studied the movement of her fan. 'I think you and I need to find a place to talk.'

A knot formed in her stomach and it made its way up her throat. Unable to say anything, she motioned to the chair Eleanor had vacated. At least he could not yell at her in a room full of people.

He shook his head. 'Somewhere private.'

'There is nowhere private in this building. The

card room is always filled. The staff will be placing the finishing touches to the tea room and, if I know Bath Society, even the library upstairs will have small groups of people gathered in there.' Swallowing the lump in her throat, she prepared herself to defend her statement to him.

He held his hand out for her. 'The cloakroom.'

How in the world were they to have this discussion in the cloakroom? There were attendants there. People would still be arriving. It was no more private than anywhere else she'd mentioned. Still, as if by a force of its own, she placed her hand in his. Through the fine white cotton of his glove and the silk of her own, heat ran up her arm and across her breasts.

His fingers tightened around hers as he helped her to her feet and assisted her out of the row. But the minute she stood beside him, he dropped her hand, leaving it feeling cold.

They walked side by side through the crowd out of the ballroom, across the corridor and into the vestibule outside the cloakroom where two liveried attendants were there ready to take the coats, hats and walking sticks of the people attending the ball. No one else was about.

This did not constitute being alone in Clara's eyes. The two attendants were right there and people could enter the area at any moment. However, just as she was about to point that out to

Mr Lane, he walked up to one of the attendants and whispered something to him while he placed something in the man's hand.

While he strode back to Clara, the intensity of his gaze bore into her sending butterflies around her stomach. Before she was able to ask him what he had said to the man, he pulled her by her hand through the doorway that was a few feet away on her right and closed the white panelled door behind them. The small room he dragged her into was painted a celery green and was lit by four sconces on the wall. Tables lined the walls with stacks of coats and beaver hats and walking sticks on them. They were in the actual cloakroom. In all the years she had been coming to this building she had never seen this room before since only the attendants ever went in here.

She opened her mouth to once more explain her innocence to him, when he suddenly wrapped his arm around her waist and pulled her up against his hard chest. His hand rested in the small of her back and the tips of his fingers skimmed the top of her bottom. If she took a deep breath, which was currently impossible surrounded by all his masculinity, he would know because her breasts would press even further against him. Instinctively her hands went to his shoulders and then moved down to curve around his biceps. If he let go of her right now, there was a distinct possibility she would melt into the floor since her legs were turning to jelly.

The tips of their noses brushed against each other while his breath caressed her lips. Then his hand came up and cupped her cheek.

'I think it's about time we settled this once and for all.'

He could settle anything with her right now just as long as he closed that last inch and kissed her!

Chapter Nineteen

After all this time, Lane finally had her in his arms—and he wasn't going to let her go. Lowering his head for that final inch, he claimed her lips with a hungry kiss.

It was as if he had spent weeks in the desert and she was his last drop of water. He wanted to savour every moment of the feel of her soft lips against his and the way her body melted into his. She kissed him back with a passion that belied her normal refined demeanour. It surprised him for a second before he lifted her up, spun her around and pressed her back against the door—all the while never breaking their kiss.

She was clutching him with her fingers digging into his arms. He spread his legs and pushed his hand into the small of her lower back bringing her against his very hard length. There was no way to tell if the movement of her lower abdomen against him was intentional or instinctual. He wasn't about to stop kissing her to ask.

The need for her was becoming too strong and he let out a low guttural groan. The only place he could lay her down was on top of a pile of coats and he struggled with the notion of stopping their kiss to move them over there. He just wanted to get his hands and mouth on more of her bare skin.

A soft knock on the door behind her broke into his thoughts and both of them froze. The mixed sound of their breathing was the only thing to break the stillness of the room. She felt perfect in his arms and he wasn't ready to let go of holding her just yet.

'Someone wants to get in,' she whispered, sounding as if she thought they might barge in at any minute.

It took a deep breath to help him gather his voice. 'I asked the attendant to give us ten minutes. He won't come in.' Wanting to prolong holding her for as long as he could, Lane let his hands glide around the curve of her hips that were always hidden beneath her gowns. Now, he could envision what they might look like. It was a foolish move since now he was even harder than he had been a few minutes ago. He didn't want to, but knew that he had to release her and take a step back, otherwise there would be more knocking.

She was bound to be able to tell the effect she

was having on him. It was very evident with the current strain to his breeches—and his erection would never go down if he continued to watch her as she checked to see if any of her hair had come loose from the pins. Turning away, he stretched his neck from side to side and tried to take a mental inventory of the items in the stockroom at the coffee house in the hopes that would reduce his arousal.

'Are you ready to return to the ball?' Her voice sounded closer than it should which let him know she was standing right behind him.

'I just need another minute.'

Thank God she was a woman of a certain age and level of experience so that he didn't have to explain why. He heard her move away from him and he counted to ten. When he turned to face her, he cursed himself for not counting to twenty.

He just wanted to kiss her and lay her down on the coats all over again.

A loose curl hung by the side of her neck and he tucked it within the upsweep of her soft brown hair.

'Can you tell I've been kissing you?' she asked.

'Yes, you can. At least I can see it in your eyes.' He trailed his fingertip along her jaw. 'Go for a walk with me. I want to leave this ball…with you. I want us to find time to be without eyes upon us and without having to regulate our actions. You and me. Alone.'

It was what he had wanted for such a long time. She was what he wanted and if he didn't kiss her again soon, he felt as if he would go mad.

'I'll need my cloak,' was the only reply she gave him, aside from a smile that seemed to make his heart double in size.

They found her cloak and his hat, then slipped out of the room. The vestibule was still empty, aside from the two attendants, and he tipped his head at them, even though they were smart enough to keep their eyes averted from the couple who had managed to sneak away at a public ball. If he had to bet, he would say that he was not the first gentleman who had slipped them some money to take advantage of the very private cloakroom.

Mrs Sommersby remained silent as they proceeded down the short corridor and out into the evening air, although the rise and fall of her chest let him know their kiss had affected her as well. The soft breeze felt good against his skin and helped to cool some of the passionate heat that was still humming through him.

'Where shall we go?' she asked, closing the jewelled clasp on her cloak while he adjusted the brim of his hat.

'We could take my carriage to Sydney Gardens to watch the fireworks.'

She shook her head and a small smile lifted the corners to those lips that he was dying to taste again. 'I don't think it would be wise to be alone in a carriage with you right now.'

'And why would that be unwise?' He eyed her profile as she began to walk beside him down the darkened empty street.

'Because you, Mr Lane, are far too tempting.'

'I'm too tempting? You're the one who made it imperative that I find a secluded spot in that building so I could finally kiss you.'

They turned right on the pavement and began heading slowly down the deserted street.

'So where shall we go?' he asked after they walked in silence for a bit.

She gave a slight lift of her shoulder. 'Suppose we walk aimlessly all night long and simply arrive back at where we started?'

Lane stopped and stepped in front of her. She appeared to study him intently.

'I think we can both agree, we are far from where we started already. We are going somewhere. Why don't you tell me where?'

'We have just started out on this journey. I think it is too soon to tell.' Her voice faded in the hushed stillness.

There was something about talking with her

that made him smile. She had a quick mind and it was one of the many things he was finding that he liked about her. 'Fair enough. I shall let you take the lead.' He held his arm out to her and they strolled on the street known as the King's Circus.

This circular area in town had a round centre-gated garden surrounded by terraced town houses that gave the appearance of one long building. In the dark of the night with the warm lights coming from the buildings, it somehow felt as if they had stepped into a private haven. The roads were deserted at this hour with people already settled into their various evening entertainments. They were free to walk together without curious eyes upon them. However, Lane knew that could change at any moment. If only they could find somewhere completely private. As he looked over at her, he took note that she was very quiet, almost lost in thought, and he remembered seeing her on the dance floor with that well-dressed gentleman and how he sensed the man had angered her towards the end of the dance. Could she be thinking about that now?

'Do you mind if I ask you a question?'

The sound of his voice seemed to bring her out of her musings and she shook her head.

'Tonight, I spotted you on the dance floor with another gentleman. While you were dancing it appeared that he said something to upset you. What did he say?'

He was prepared for anything she was going to tell him, because no matter what it was he was going to find the man after their walk and make him apologise to her. He might even need to beat him to a pulp, depending on what he said.

She let out a sigh. 'It is nothing that you would understand.'

His mind raced with inappropriate scenarios. 'Why don't you tell me anyway?'

'There are times being a woman can be very trying. I had given instructions about an investment of mine and found out that those instructions were ignored.' Her brows drew together and the grip of her hand on his forearm tightened. 'I know that would never happen had I been a gentleman like yourself. No one would ever disregard your directions.'

She was right. No one would and if they did, they knew he'd ring a peel over them as soon as he found out.

'Do you normally manage your investments yourself?'

'Yes. I am not some woman whose head is filled with fashion and gossip without room for anything else.' The statement was made firmly and she was about to remove her hand from his sleeve except he held it there.

'I mean no disrespect. I am just trying to assess your involvement in the decisions that have been made in the past.'

'I have been involved in the decisions from the very beginning. Ten years ago, when my husband passed, our financial condition was less than ideal. After he died, I was free to determine how I wanted to invest my money and soon realised that my instincts were sharp. My decisions turned a profit.' As if she realised her agitation was being directed at him and that she had been discussing money, which was highly inappropriate in polite company, she looked away. 'Forgive me. As you can see, I am not one who likes to be ignored.'

'Then let him know that.'

'I will be writing him a sharply worded letter come morning.'

'That's not good enough. Make your feelings known face to face. Let him see that it is your money and that you will not be placated. State firmly that you will not have them go against your wishes or you will find someone else to handle your affairs. Let him see your anger.'

'Why are you not telling me that I should listen to him? That he must know more than I do about these things because he is a man?'

'Because I believe you are smart enough to know sound advice when you hear it and would not place any investment in danger due to vanity.'

'You can tell that about me?'

'I can.'

'If I show my anger, he will accuse me of being a hysterical female. That is why when I am angry with him I typically write him a letter.'

'Are you planning on sobbing and throwing yourself on the floor?'

She stopped walking, appearing highly insulted. 'Of course not.'

'Then let him experience your anger. Do not hesitate. Show him you are strong in your convictions and will not tolerate his interference.'

They turned on to the pavement that led to the Royal Crescent. This was where Hart was staying and where Lyonsdale was. He scanned the long row of thirty pale stone terraced houses that made up this curved row and tried to recall which one his friends were in.

'Well, I suppose there is no reason for me to return to the Assembly Rooms now,' she said, as she watched him search out the windows that were lit by the yellow glow of candlelight. 'I live over there.' She pointed to the fifth door.

Well, she must have been very good with her investments if she could afford to live here.

'What of your carriage?'

'As you can see, I am not far from the Assembly Rooms. I walked with some friends. It's how we do things here in Bath.'

The smile on her face made her eyes sparkle and he wasn't certain if her improved mood had to do with not returning to the ball or being close to her house with him. Her bedroom was just over there, possibly behind one of those windows that overlooked the large expanse of lawn and the wooded area beyond where he had encountered her stuck to a bush.

'So, it seems our journey has led us here. What do you think that means?' He shoved a hand into his pocket and waited—and prayed that she would invite him in so he could kiss and touch her some more. It couldn't be a coincidence that their walk had led them here.

'I think it means that you are a very lovely gentleman who was kind enough to walk me home. I enjoy talking with you, William.'

They strolled side by side slowly up to her door and then turned to face each other.

'It's actually Lane. My friends call me Lane. I never use William.'

'Really? I rather like your name—however, if you prefer Lane, I will call you that.'

'Does this mean you are giving me permission to call you Clara?'

'It seems fitting.'

'You mean since we kissed.'

It almost looked as if she was blushing, but in the dim light it was hard to tell.

* * *

Clara could feel the heat spread over her chest and up her neck. She was not a girl in her first Season. She was a grown woman who had been married—and yet just the mention of kissing him had left her all aflutter and was making her body hot with the need to kiss him again. Their brief time in the cloakroom was just long enough to make her crave the feel of his lips on hers once more—or all night long.

She had only been with one man in her life and that was Robert. Now, every piece of her wanted to be with Lane. That thought was both exciting and terrifying. It was exciting to imagine what it would be like to roll around the sheets with him and it was a delicious sensation to savour. And she would have, except part of her was terrified to trust her heart again. She knew it was easy to fall for someone who was all wrong for you. Perhaps Lane was all wrong for her? She wouldn't marry him, so where would this lead?

The sound of muted barking came through the window near them and a rapid soft pounding could be heard. It was Humphrey, who must have been standing up on the window seat, barking excitedly at Lane. Her wonderful puppy gave her something to focus on that did not have to do with her soft bed and Lane's amazing kisses. Her old butler, Darby, came to the window, wearing his dark coat and dark stock around his neck. He picked up Humphrey in his white-gloved hands and caught her eye through the wavy glass. She gave him a slight nod and a small smile. The man glanced at Lane before disappearing into the room.

'Thank you again for walking me home.' She took a step towards the door and removed a key from her reticule.

'It was my pleasure. I take it this is goodnight, then.' He was waiting to see if she was going to invite him in and she wished with every fibre of her being that she could. But her staff was still up and her neighbours might be watching…and her heart wasn't ready to commit herself to him that way. It was much too dangerous.

Placing the key in the lock, she turned to him with an almost bittersweet smile. 'It is. I wish I could invite you in, but as you saw my butler is about.'

'Yes, I saw.' He looked down at the ground and did not press the issue.

The door opened and a black-and-brown ball of fur came charging out, heading directly for Lane's leg. Humphrey jumped on to his calve and barked at him with his tail swishing back and forth. Lane picked the puppy up into his arms and scratched him behind his ears.

'Forgive me, madam,' Darby said now from the doorway.

'It's fine Darby. We know how Humphrey gets when he's excited.'

Lane placed him down on the ground and he continued to jump and bark. 'Stay, Humphrey.'

The small dog stood as still as he could, shifting slightly on his paws with his tail continuing to swish. He barked a few times and Lane bent down and held his muzzle closed gently between his fingers. 'Shhh,' he said while placing one of his fingers on his other hand up to his lips.

Humphrey's eyes widened, but he didn't try to bark.

'How did you do that?'

'He needs to understand who is in control. He needs to understand that he does not run the household. I could come back to help train him for you,' Lane continued. 'I believe I had mentioned it once before.' He looked up at her from where he was bent over Humphrey, still holding his muzzle.

'I don't know…'

When Lane released his hold on Humphrey and stood up, her dog barked up at him. But when Lane shushed him, the dog immediately quietened down. How was it that he had spent such little time with her dog and had made more progress with him than she or anyone of her staff had?

'Madam, if I may. This gentleman might be of some assistance.'

This would be a perfect way to see him during respectable hours and she really could use the help with Humphrey. 'Would you have some time tomorrow to work with him?'

'I could be here by two.'

Inside, she was bursting with excitement at the notion she would be able to spend time alone with him tomorrow. However, on the outside she tried to remain calm and composed. 'I will see you then.'

There was a flash of something in his eyes. Was he feeling the same way?

'And thank you for your advice earlier. I will forgo my letter-writing this time.'

'Excellent. You will feel much better afterwards. I assure you.'

Humphrey dropped his head down to rest on Lane's foot.

'My dog really does like you.'

'I'd say he has excellent taste,' he replied, appearing rather pleased with himself.

The moment standing there at her door with him and her dog had an indefinable feeling of rightness about it. With her back to the door she had no way to know where Darby had gone. If she was certain he was not standing within eyesight of her, she would have reached over and pulled Lane in for a kiss.

Perhaps he knew what she was thinking since he appeared to suppress a smile and glanced down at the ground…or maybe at Humphrey. She wasn't certain.

'Goodnight, Clara. Thank you for our walk.' He tipped his hat at her and held her gaze.

She liked the sound of her name on his lips. 'Goodnight, Lane.'

Their eyes held for a few more heartbeats before she coaxed Humphrey into the house and closed the door. Darby had been waiting at the end of the entrance hall, obviously not certain if he should have remained or disappeared to somewhere else in the house. He normally let her in at night. She always felt that it was his way of making certain that she arrived home safely whenever she went out. However, tonight was the first time she did not find a sense of comfort from his presence.

'Darby, do take Humphrey down to the kitchen to see if they can find a bone for him before bed.'

'Yes, madam.' He picked her dog up and headed out of the entrance hall.

Tonight, she would go to bed thinking of Lane's kiss. Shivers of desire raced through her and before she had a chance to think better of it, she opened her front door to go after him. Only he hadn't gotten very far. He was standing on the other side of the pavement, looking up at her house. Her appearance seemed to have startled him because there was a sudden stiffening to his posture.

'I forgot something,' she said, leading him back to her house by his elbow.

Thankfully, the entrance hall had remained empty when she pulled him inside. Once they both cleared the threshold, she closed the door quietly behind him. Lane remained silent and watchful the entire time, but she could tell he was curious about what she had forgotten. And what she had forgotten was for a way to kiss him goodnight inside her home away from the eyes of the neighbours and her staff.

Her entire body leaned into his as she wrapped her arms around his neck and pulled him in for a deep kiss. Within seconds his warm hands were cradling her waist and her hands were cupping his cheeks, needing to feel his bare skin. When they finally separated, he seemed pleasantly surprised by her boldness.

'I just wanted to kiss you goodnight,' she said, feeling the need to explain her actions as she placed her hand on the door handle.

'I'm glad you did. You gave me more to think about when I go to bed tonight. Sweet dreams,

Clara.' His pleasure at this unexpected end to the evening shone in his eyes before he walked out of the door when she opened it for him.

Chapter Twenty

The next morning Lane called upon Mr Edwards at precisely ten o'clock in the morning at the man's office on the first floor of The Fountain Head Hotel, which was the time the gentleman said he would be free to meet. After the night that he'd had with Clara, and knowing that he would be seeing her later in the day, he was in exceptionally good spirits. It was a sharp contrast to the mood he found Mr Edwards in when the man opened his door. Upon shaking his hand, Lane could see that the gentleman was distracted and on edge.

'What is it you wanted to discuss with me, Mr Lane?' he asked, showing Lane to the chair opposite his desk. 'I hope you have been finding your room to your satisfaction and you have not been having any problems with the staff?'

'No, my stay here has been exceptional. I've been very pleased. As I had mentioned to you the other day, Jack has been especially attentive. I wanted to meet with you because I have a business proposition for you.'

The moment Mr Edwards crossed his arms over his chest, Lane knew the discussion wasn't going to go as smoothly as he had hoped.

'What type of proposition?'

'Well, as you are aware I have purchased the coffee house next door and I've thought about the possibility of expanding the business. I cannot expand south since the church is there and I was wondering if you would consider selling your hotel?'

Mr Edwards blinked a few times as if he wasn't sure if he had heard Lane correctly. 'We... I... I am not interested in selling.'

'I realise that your hotel must do very well— however, I am prepared to offer you a substantial amount of money for it.'

'That is very generous of you, Mr Lane, however, as I said I will not sell this hotel.'

'But don't you want to even know the amount I am willing to offer you for it?'

There was a marked hesitation in his movement before he pressed his thumb along the surface of his large oak partners' desk and moved his gaze away from Lane. 'If you would like to present your offer I would be happy to oblige you by reviewing it. However, you should know that I will never sell this hotel.'

He said that now, but he didn't know how high Lane was willing to go with his offer. He took a piece of paper out of his waistcoat with the generous offer in writing and slid it across the table to Mr Edwards.

The man's eyes opened wider than Lane had ever seen them go as he glanced down at the paper. He swallowed hard and once more he refolded his arms. 'I am sorry, but as I stated before the hotel is not for sale.'

Lane took the paper back and crossed out the amount he was willing to offer and wrote a higher amount down. He was prepared to negotiate with the man. In fact, he expected it.

When he spun the paper around, the man shook his head.

How well could this hotel be doing if Mr Edwards would not even consider selling it? With the amount of money Lane was offering, the man could buy another hotel and still have money to spare. Once more he took the paper back and wrote a higher offer.

This time when he spun the paper back around he could tell that Mr Edwards was startled by the number, but he shook his head again.

'Mr Edwards, that is quite a lot of money that I have just offered you. Are you certain you would not like to think it over for a day or so? I am happy to wait for your answer.'

Mr Edwards opened his mouth to reply, but then looked once more to the offer. He appeared to be struggling over what to do. Lane knew it was not in his best interest to rush the man.

'Give me a day,' he finally said. 'I shall have an answer for you in a day.'

'Take all the time you need.'

If he was going to listen to his gut, then Lane already knew that Mr Edwards would not be accepting this offer, no matter what number he placed in front of him. Lane needed this hotel. Without it, he would never be able to build his spa. Without it, he and Hart would just own a coffee house in Bath and there was no need for him to stay. He would be returning to London in less than a week.

It was only two o'clock in the afternoon and already it felt as though an entire day had gone by for Clara. Sleep had eluded her and for most of the night she lay in bed, thinking about kissing Lane. She had stopped thinking she would ever be kissed again, ages ago. But ever since he'd helped her out of the shrubbery and their lips had been mere inches apart, she found she had thought about kissing him a few times each day. And now that she actually knew what it felt like to have his lips against hers, she knew she was going to have a hard time *not* thinking about it—and thinking about it made her practically giddy. That was completely out of character for her. While she did enjoy finding humour in a situation, no one of her acquaintance would ever accuse her of being giddy. She wasn't even giddy when she was Harriet's age.

When she finally did get out of bed she realised that if she didn't find a way to occupy herself until Lane arrived at two o'clock, she would go mad. She decided to take his advice and go to see Phillip and find out why he had disregarded her direction to change the menu at the hotel.

By half past eight she was waiting for him in his office at the hotel and when he walked in, she could see by the look in his eye he wasn't at all happy to see her at such an early hour.

'Why did you lie to me and tell me that you would adjust the breakfast menu?'

She was familiar with that placating look he started to give her and he opened his mouth to reply, but she held up her hand. 'Never you mind. I don't want your excuses.'

Because of her diminutive stature, she never liked to have important discussions with Phillip when she was standing up. It felt as if her height reinforced the opinion that she was a delicate woman who needed to be protected from the world. She was no delicate creature. She was a formidable woman who had kept herself and her husband out of debtors' prison by her cunning and determination. It was time that her cousin realised that about her. It was time that he saw her the way the rest of the world did. She was not a woman to be trifled with.

This time, she didn't ask him to sit beside her. She was taking Lane's advice and letting him see just how infuriated she was with him. She no longer cared if he accused her of being hysterical when she became impassioned and stood up for herself. They never accused men of being so when she witnessed them argue. Instead of asking him to sit, she stood up and marched up to him. 'This is my hotel. It is best that you remember that. The decisions that are made here are my decisions. If you would like to offer me your opinion as the manager of this establishment, I will take your opinions into consideration—however, I have the final say in what is done in this building. Do I make myself clear?'

His eyes widened with every increase in volume in her speech. 'I understand. I was only doing what I thought would be best.'

'Well don't. If I find that you take it upon yourself to act in direct contradiction to my wishes, I will be looking for someone else to take over managing this establishment.' Her hands were now balls of fists at her side.

'But you can't do that. People believe I own this hotel.'

'I can do anything I want.'

She didn't wait for him to reply. She didn't need to. The fear she wanted him to feel was in his eyes.

For the entire ride home, she had felt liberated and confident that Phillip would not go against her wishes again. He knew how much the hotel meant to her. She had made it clear to him numerous times that she would never consider selling it when they discussed his concerns that, if she did, he would be out of a job. Now she had let him know that just because she would not be selling the hotel it did not mean that his job would be secure no matter his actions. And thanks to Lane she had the satisfaction of seeing how her words had affected him. It was glorious! She had even received a note from Phillip later that morning, but she decided to wait until after Lane left to read what she assumed was a letter of apology from the man.

Now, as she watched for Lane on the window seat of her sun-drenched drawing room that overlooked the front of the Crescent, she was practically bubbling with her eagerness to tell him that she had taken his bit of brilliant advice and it had felt wonderful to do so. But when Darby had finally escorted Lane into the room at fifteen minutes past the hour it might have been in her best interest to offer him a glass of brandy or ale before she told him about her morning. While she had been having a wonderful day, it appeared that he had not.

His brow was all furrowed and his movements were stiff as he bowed his greeting to her as she stood. Clara had arranged for tea to be brought up when Lane had arrived, but now she wasn't certain if he planned to stay long enough to have a cup. Darby, on the other hand, looked as if he was trying his best to contain his pleasure that the man was here to help them deal with her small but energetic puppy.

'I do appreciate you coming here today to help me with Humphrey, but I know you are here in Bath for business. Please do not feel as if you are under any obligation to stay should you have other things that require your attention.' How she wished he would stay.

'No, I need to be here today more than you will know. It's nice to get away from my desk.'

'Is anything wrong? You do not quite appear like yourself.'

When she motioned towards her sofa that was along the wall opposite the three long windows, he joined her there and they took a seat beside each other.

He closed his eyes briefly and shook his head. 'Forgive me. I have recently received some disappointing news.'

'I hope the news isn't too distressing.' She reached out and gave his hand a reassuring squeeze.

He looked down at her hand as if he was surprised at the gesture. 'I fear it is about to get worse. I feel it deep in my gut. I will know soon enough.'

'You do not have to stay. We can do this another time.'

His features softened a bit with affection and there was almost a look of sadness in his eyes. 'No, I think it best if we don't delay this for another day.'

It almost sounded as if his time in Bath was coming to a close. It was something that on a day that had gone so well, she didn't wish to consider. They had never talked about when he was leaving. She had almost convinced herself that he would decide to leave London and take up residence here.

The tea tray was brought in and immediately she removed her hand from his before the footman lowered the tray to the table in front of them. The silver pot shone in the afternoon sun that streamed in from the windows.

'I thought I was here to train your dog.'

'You are, but you'll need to fortify yourself with tea before you start. Nothing is better than tea.'

'I beg to differ.'

He leaned forward and met her in a kiss. She had been hoping all day that he would kiss her again and she was contemplating kissing him first. The feel of his lips on hers sent a delicious sensation through her body and it didn't take long before she opened to him completely. Within seconds of deepening the kiss, she wrapped her arms around his neck and savoured the feel of his warm hands on her back and the silken waves of his thick blond hair against her fingers.

When he pulled his head back there was a devilish look in his eyes. 'Now that was better than tea.'

It warmed her heart to see him smile again.

'My mother always said that a good cup of tea can fix anything. There is magic in tea.'

With his warm fingers, he pushed away a tendril of hair by her neck, caressing her skin as he went. 'There was magic in that kiss.' As if to prove his point, he leaned forward and planted a provocative kiss on the hollow of her neck.

There was magic there because even though his lips were on a small spot on her neck, she felt his touch throughout her body. 'I thought you were here to train my dog,' she was just able to utter breathlessly.

He continued to trace a line of kisses along her neck. 'We can call this anything you like.'

His teasing comment made her laugh. What she *would* like would be for him to lay her down on the sofa and kiss the rest of her. Whatever he was doing to her neck had her imagining him doing it while he was lying on top of her with nothing between them. She could practically feel his bare skin against hers. She could just imagine what it would feel like to have him inside her. Just as Lane's hand settled on her breast, Humphrey came charging into the room as if he were a child who had heard his favourite relative had arrived. He ran right to Lane, spun in circles before him, then let out a series of barks accompanied by quite a bit of jumping up on to the man's boots.

'Stay, Humphrey,' Lane said rather firmly as they broke apart.

It didn't work. At least Clara didn't now feel too bad about her inability to get the dog to do what she wanted.

Lane stood up, giving her a lovely view of his muscular legs encased in black breeches that were tucked into his shiny black boots. Her attention travelled to the back of his burgundy tailcoat that covered his bottom.

'Down.' Lane's voice rumbled more firmly this time before pointing his finger at Humphrey and the dog melted into the floor with his head resting on his front paws. When the man had looked back at Clara and arched his brow, she realised her mouth had opened watching him.

'How did you manage to do that?'

'He needs to understand that you are not equals—that you are the mistress of this house. He is not the master.'

'But I've done that.'

Lane sat back down. 'You are too soft with him. You try to cajole him. I have seen it.'

'No, I don't,' she replied, filling his teacup and handing it to him with just a splash of milk as he specified. She was about to fix her own cup when Humphrey jumped up on to the sofa and snuggled in between them. Clara rubbed his little furry back while she poured milk into her tea.

'See, that is your problem. You are treating him like an equal.'

'I am simply rubbing his back.'

'On the sofa.'

'Well, that is where we are sitting.'

'He doesn't belong on the sofa. The sofa is for humans. The floor is for a dog.'

'But we cuddle up here.'

'Then cuddle with him down there.'

'On the floor?' *He was mad.*

'If you want him to understand that he needs to defer to you, you have to show him that you have certain privileges in this house that he does not. What else do you allow him to climb on? Do you allow him to sit at the dining-room table with you?'

'Of course not.'

'Do you let him crawl into bed with you?'

They were cosy that way. She liked how he would snuggle up beside her and rest his head under her chin while he fell asleep.

'You do, don't you?'

'What I do in my bed at night is of no concern of yours.' But deep down she wished it were.

'You do.' He let out a sigh. 'You must show him that you are the head of this household. You cannot do that if you are sleeping in the same bed.'

She picked Humphrey up and placed him on her lap to cuddle with him. 'Where is he supposed to sleep? And do not say the floor. It is much too hard down there for him to sleep there all night long.'

'You can arrange a cushion for him.'

'It's not the same.' Apparently, Humphrey agreed because he let out a series of barks.

'Do you want me to truly train him or did you

just want me here to kiss me?' The teasing sound was back in his voice.

'Can't I have both?'

'I am more than content to spend the day with you in my arms—however, at some point I can guarantee I will be wanting to do more than kiss you.' He tilted his head and looked at her, waiting for her reply.

She already wanted that, too, very much. It was what she had thought about last night. But could she trust herself not to give her heart to him if she gave him her body?

'Oh, very well. Show me how I can get this rascal to listen to me.' Using her best pouting face, she lowered Humphrey to the rug beside her feet.

Humphrey barked up at them and went to jump back on to the sofa, but Lane instructed her how to tell the dog no and how to get him to understand that she meant it. After twenty more minutes, they took a break for tea.

'You've impressed me with what you've been able to accomplish with him in such a short time,' she said as they sipped their tea and watched Humphrey sniff the legs on her pianoforte that was in the corner of the room. 'I think you've managed to wear him out. Look how slowly he is moving. How can I ever repay you for this?'

'I'm not leaving just yet.'

His gaze dropped down to her lips and her mouth suddenly went dry.

'I would hope not.'

'There is one more thing we need to do.'

Chapter Twenty-One

'How in the world did I allow you to talk me into this?' she asked, following him outside her front door. 'This is not a good idea.'

Lane could tell by the look on Clara's face that she was intrigued and terrified at the same time. They stood on the pavement in front of her home between the iron gates with Humphrey beside them without his leash. He was wagging his tail and looking up between them. Already he was able to understand that he could not run off and he needed to watch them for permission. Lane prayed there were no squirrels nearby. If there were, there was no telling how long he would find himself chasing Humphrey this afternoon.

'Whenever you are ready,' he said to Clara.

They turned out of her gate to the right and started to stroll along the Crescent to begin their short walk. There was no sense in keeping Humphrey out for a long time without his leash. It was too risky. They would just walk along for a bit to see if the dog would obey before taking him back home.

'Come, Humphrey,' she called out and the dog padded over to her side and then circled around to walk between them.

'My dog likes you.'

'I like him, too. You have a fine fellow in Humphrey.'

'You are generous with your praise. You know how he is.'

Lane glanced down at the puppy walking with his chin held high and knew that when he did leave Bath, he would miss his small, furry friend. It wasn't often he received the kind of greeting he received each time he ran into Humphrey.

'Yes, but it doesn't dim any of the brightness one feels from being the centre of his attention. I believe I shall miss him when I return to London.'

'Will you be returning to London soon?'

'Sooner than I would prefer, I believe. However, I am not sure of the date just yet.'

Over Humphrey's head, Lane placed his hand close enough to hers that he was able to secretly brush his fingers against hers hidden in the folds of the skirt of her blue gown. He couldn't help himself. This moment—this walk—felt oddly intimate since they were walking in broad daylight with the dog between them. It felt comfortable. It

felt natural. It felt as though this was how he was
supposed to be spending his afternoons.

He had been so certain that the owner of the
hotel would sell him the property that it never occurred to him that he might be leaving town in
less than a week's time and his dream of building a spa would die in the office of Mr Edwards.
He would find out soon enough. Glancing over
at Clara, strolling serenely along by his side, he
started to wonder if his profound sense of loss
had more to do with leaving her than it did with
not opening the spa.

They were approaching the corner of the pavement that would take them back on to the Crescent when she turned to him and broke the silence
that had surrounded them for the last ten minutes.

'I will miss you when you are gone.'

It was a short statement—just eight words. But
those words had hit him in the chest and meant so
much. He wanted to say it back to her. He wanted
to admit that he was not looking forward to the
days when he would wake in the morning without a sense of anticipation that he might see her
somewhere. His days would be darker without
Clara in them. She had every right to expect him
to say it back—and yet he couldn't.

Growing up in the Foundling Hospital had
taught him at a very early age that children could
be cruel and that admitting your feelings left you

vulnerable. Those two things had proved to be a devastating combination. Life was safer on your soul if you kept your feelings to yourself.

Their eyes met and held for several heartbeats. She was waiting for him to say it back to her. It was in her eyes.

Humphrey let out a series of barks, breaking into this moment that was crushing his chest. While it first appeared that Humphrey was barking up at them, he was in fact barking at the expensively outfitted landau with an official crest on its door that was parked in front of Clara's home and at the footmen wearing the burgundy livery of Clara's staff who were unloading trunks from it and bringing them inside her house. As if she could sense Humphrey's excitement at all the commotion, Clara picked him up and cradled him in her arms as they walked forward.

'Were you expecting guests?'

'No, but my nieces do have a habit of showing up unannounced. It might be one thing we Sommersby women pride ourselves on.' She picked up the pace of her steps and her obvious delight that she would be reunited with one of her nieces shone on her face.

It was a feeling that he could not relate to.

Just as they approached her house, three tall women between the ages of twenty-one and thirty-one emerged from inside, wrapped close together and talking over each other. There was no mistaking they were sisters with their similar features and forms. The older two had jet-black hair, but the younger one's hair was closer in colour to Clara's. It was interesting to see Clara pause to watch them before taking a step closer. He couldn't recall anyone looking at him with the expression Clara had on her face. It looked like a mixture of deep affection and pride.

The younger one spotted Clara and with a low squeal of delight she hurried towards her. With care, Clara placed Humphrey down on the pavement and met the girl halfway, enveloping her in her arms for a hug.

The young woman's eyes closed in delight as she held on to Clara with a smile that brightened her entire face. 'You always have given the best hugs. I'm so glad you have returned. We were wondering where you had gone off to. No one in the household seemed to know and Darby seemed quite perplexed you weren't in the drawing room.'

The other two sisters joined in the hugging and Lane was free to watch the dynamics between the women play out before him. The excitement proved to be too much for poor Humphrey and he began barking excitedly at the women who were back to talking over one another.

'Quiet, Humphrey,' he stated quite firmly, looking down at the dog.

The dog looked back at him, pleading his case with his big black eyes and yapping his explanation.

'You are too loud,' he said, picking the puppy up. He told himself he did it to ensure Humphrey didn't run over and paw at the women for attention. But he also took some comfort in holding the warm little dog that snuggled into the crook of his arm.

You knew your feelings ran deep when you would also miss her dog when you left.

When he looked back over at the women all four of them were staring at him.

'That dog looks like Ambrose,' the youngest one commented offhandedly, stepping back from Clara.

There was an apologetic look in Clara's eyes as she looked directly at him. 'It is Ambrose.'

'But this gentleman called him Humphrey.'

'It's a long story.'

'They always are,' the one with the finest clothes and the sapphire necklace said, eyeing him openly.

The younger one gave him a friendly smile and then turned to Clara. 'Is this gentleman a friend of yours?'

They were friends, he supposed...by definition. But he'd never had a friend whom he'd kissed before. He'd certainly never had a friend who he'd wanted desperately to bed—countless times.

The woman waited for a response and continued to glance expectantly between him and Clara. Humphrey took this opportunity to lick his chin as if to inform the woman that Lane was his friend as well.

Clara walked over and guided him by the arm closer to the woman as if she realised it would be better if they were introduced to each other without the entire Crescent having to hear the conversation. 'He is. Mr Lane, may I introduce my nieces to you. This is Elizabeth, the Duchess of Skeffington,' she said, gesturing to the one in the finest clothes and then turned to the other woman with black hair. 'And this is Lady Andrew Pearce.'

'You may call me Lady Charlotte, Mr Lane,' she replied with another warm smile.

The Duchess poked her with her elbow, showing her disapproval of her sister's request. He knew an Andrew Pearce. At one time the man had lived in the Albany, the building where Lane had his residence, and the man was a friend of Hart's. He had spent time with him at a number of races they had attended together over the years. He was a brother of the Duke of Winterbourne. Could this be his wife?

The youngest and most exuberant of the group,

continued to look at him with that friendly smile as she bobbed a curtsy, not waiting for Clara to introduce her. 'I'm Mrs Sommersby's youngest niece, Lady Montague Pearce. But you may call me Lady Juliet.'

'He can probably tell you are the youngest,' the Duchess called out. 'There is no need to announce it.'

Lady Juliet turned to her sister with a teasing grin. 'You are just jealous you cannot use that title as well.'

'I'd rather the one I have.'

'We know,' Lady Charlotte and Lady Juliet said in unison.

'Girls, this is my friend, Mr William Lane' There was an affectionate glow about her when she said it that spread warmth throughout his chest.

Lady Juliet was keeping her eyes on him as Humphrey continued to shower him with wet kisses all over his chin.

'We should go inside and have tea,' Clara said. 'Are your husbands with you?'

'No,' Lady Charlotte said, taking Clara's hand and giving it a pat. 'We have left them at home as we decided we wanted to spend time with you like we used to.'

The Duchess began walking through the opening of the black wrought-iron gates that led to

Clara's front door and lifted the skirt of her purple gown to take the step. 'You always have the best tea. It's just what I need after that ride.'

He put Humphrey down and was just about to shoo him into the house and take his leave to return back to the coffee house when Lady Juliet called out, 'Isn't Mr Lane going to join us?'

'Oh, please do, Mr Lane,' Lady Charlotte added. 'We did not mean to impose on your visit with our aunt.'

To hear Lady Charlotte refer to Clara as her aunt was strange to his ears. He didn't think of Clara as anyone's aunt. He didn't think of Clara as being related to anyone. 'I'm sure you ladies have much to discuss. You don't need a gentleman about.'

'Nonsense. We will be here for a week. That is plenty of time for us to visit with our aunt.'

'You are staying for the week?' Clara said, her eyes widening as she looked between Lady Juliet and Lady Charlotte.

'It has all been arranged.'

Lady Juliet looked pointedly at Clara and cleared her throat. 'Don't you think Mr Lane should come inside?'

'Of course I do,' Clara said, dropping her niece's hands. 'Won't you join us for some tea?'

'I should be off. I've been here long enough.'

'Then perhaps Mr Lane can join us for dinner tonight?' Her youngest niece was very eager for him to stay. There was no telling if that was good or bad.

'Tonight I am having a musical recital here. Had I known the three of you were coming I would not have arranged it.'

'Is Mr Lane attending?'

Lady Charlotte stared at her sister with wide eyes. 'Juliet!'

'Why don't you girls go inside?' Clara said, walking towards him as she scooped up Humphrey in her arms. 'I will meet you in the drawing room.'

Behind Clara's shoulder he could see Lady Charlotte pull Lady Juliet into the house.

'Do not feel obligated to extend an invitation to me. My skin is thicker than that.'

'No. I would like you to come. It's just…' She averted her gaze. 'I've invited the Collingswoods and Mr Greeley as well, you see. And the Dowager.'

'I see. And does Greeley know that he is to be ambushed when he arrives?'

'I have left it up to Eleanor to break the news to him.'

'I see.'

She tilted her head and offered him a rueful smile. 'Mr Greeley might appreciate having you there.'

'Mr Greeley would?'

She stepped closer to him. 'And I would. I am sorry that our afternoon has had to end so quickly. I had hoped we would have been able to return to the drawing room.'

'And what did you hope we would do in there?'

A flicker of passion flashed in her eyes. 'I'm sure we could have thought of something.'

'I'm sure we could have.'

'Then you will come back later? It begins at seven.'

'Very well…for Greeley I will return.'

The look of joy on her face just from finding out that she would see him later gave him an odd full feeling in his chest. It was an unexpected re-action and one he contemplated on his long walk back to the coffee house.

Chapter Twenty-Two

Never before had Clara been disappointed to see her nieces. However, once the excitement of knowing that they were back in her home after all this time had subsided, she found she was sad that her day with Lane had been interrupted. She was beginning to realise that he would be leaving Bath soon and that she did not have an infinite amount of time with him.

A deep sense of melancholy washed over her. Her nieces were here—however, part of her wished they had not come. A twinge of guilt hit her as she entered her home and placed Humphrey down on the floor. He scampered off, probably to take a nap, and she notified Darby that she would be serving tea to her nieces.

Walking up the stairs, she recalled the times she had spent in this house with Charlotte, Lizzy, and Juliet. She had no children of her own, but she couldn't have loved these girls any more than if they were her own daughters. She recalled Charlotte running to her here when she received word that her husband had been killed at Waterloo. She could see herself sitting on these stairs, comforting Juliet when she brought her here after the girl's heart had been broken in London. And she remembered the times she'd spent shopping and sharing much-needed laughter with Lizzy when the Duchess would find refuge here from her loveless marriage. There were countless other moments as well. Getting ready for balls. Taking turns reading novels to each other. Chatting endlessly over pots of tea and needlework. Having them here knowing Lane might be leaving soon should be a blessing. Her heart should feel comforted. So why was it aching? She pinched her cheeks and pasted on a smile before taking a deep breath and walking into the room.

'Tell us about Mr Lane,' Juliet said without any preamble the moment Clara crossed the threshold.

The urge to turn and walk out of the room was overwhelming.

'Juliet, allow her to sit first before you pepper her with your questions.' Charlotte always had been the most level-headed one of the three.

'I am simply asking the question we all want an answer to. Your dog seems very taken with him. Where did you meet?'

Clara took a seat between Charlotte and Juliet

on the sofa where an hour before Lane had kissed her. She hadn't realised how much she liked this pink sofa with gold-painted accents until now. 'We met in the Pump Room.' She busied herself pushing out the wrinkles from her gown. She didn't want to talk about Lane. Their relationship was too complicated.

'Did you bring the baby?' she asked Charlotte.

'Yes, he is asleep in my room. My maid is watching over him should he wake. I think the ride tired him out.'

'And did you all ride here together in Lizzy's carriage?'

Lizzy sat back in her chair across from them. 'No, Charlotte and Juliet arrived in Charlotte's. I followed them in mine.'

'What Lizzy is not saying is that there wasn't enough room for all of us to travel together in her carriage, so I took mine as well. She has too many trunks with her. I honestly don't know how she travelled to Sicily without the ship sinking from the weight of her luggage.'

'I managed to travel lighter than you would believe.'

'And yet here you are at Aunt Clara's for a week with enough luggage to stay for three months.'

'I like to be prepared.'

Juliet was uncharacteristically quiet. Of all her nieces, Clara had spent the most time with Juliet.

The girl had lived with her for years here before her recent marriage. Juliet knew her very well. If she needed to fool anyone that she was happy at this moment, it would be Juliet.

Turning to her, she made sure she was smiling. 'And how is married life?'

There was a soft blush that filled Juliet's cheek. 'It is everything I could have wanted.'

Clara reached out and squeezed her hand. 'I knew it would be.' But when she went to remove her hand, the girl held on to it.

'Now tell us about Mr Lane. Does he live in Bath?'

'No. He is visiting.' Once again she was reminded that he was leaving and it became hard to speak.

When the tea tray arrived, she was relieved that arranging the cups on the table and preparing the tea gave her something to do. Unfortunately, it also reminded her of making tea for Lane and how she thought she would be having another cup with him right now.

'You are too quiet.' This time it was Lizzy who spoke.

'I am not one to always fill the room with the sound of my voice.'

She felt Charlotte's hand at her back. 'The three of us have shown up on her doorstep unannounced, claiming we are staying for a week. I think that would leave most people speechless.' Charlotte gestured to the large bouquet of flowers that Clara had placed on the harpsichord after she had cut them from the garden when she returned home from the hotel. 'Those roses are lovely.'

Clara handed her a cup of tea. 'The roses in the garden are beginning to bloom. You must spend time out there while you are here.'

'I'm looking forward to it.'

She kept her eyes on the cup of tea she was fixing for Juliet. 'How did you all manage to get away like this?'

'When I saw Juliet and Charlotte in London we all agreed that we have missed you terribly and thought to surprise you. Thankfully our husbands understood.'

'I would love to hear more about your travels. I enjoyed receiving all your letters.' She handed a teacup to Lizzy.

'I would love hearing more about Mr Lane and why that puppy I gave you is now called Humphrey when we agreed he bears an odd resemblance to Uncle Ambrose.' Juliet was proving to be just as stubborn as the puppy she had given her.

Clara didn't want to talk about Lane. She didn't want to think about him. Because now, each time she did, she was picturing him walking away for the last time and it made her want to cry. When had she fallen for him this deeply?

She thought she had her emotions under control, but then a small tear drop slipped out and landed on her lap. With her head bent down to fix Juliet a cup of tea, she hoped none of them had noticed.

They had.

At once, Juliet's arm was around her and Lizzy gently reached across the table and took the teacup out of her hand. She refused to look up at them for fear that once she did her tears would begin to flow and she would have a hard time stopping them.

Charlotte took her hand and stroked it in a comforting gesture. 'Talk to us. What has made you so sad?'

The words were stuck in her throat and would not come out.

'Have you been so lonely without me here?' Juliet asked gently. 'I thought the dog might have helped. I've written to you several times a week, but I could write every day.'

'It's not that.'

'Then what is it?'

'Mr Lane will be leaving Bath soon. I know I am all wrong for him. I am too old. But once he leaves I will probably never see him again and I find it hurts my heart.'

'Come now,' Juliet said, 'you are not that much older than he is.'

'But I am old enough. A gentleman his age is thinking about starting a family. A gentleman his age wants to have children. I cannot give him that.'

'Has he talked about wanting children?'

'Well, no. We haven't talked about any of that.'

'Then how do you know that that is what he wants?'

'What man doesn't?'

'I'm sure there are some.'

'Has he given you any indication about what he feels for you?' Lizzy asked with a sympathetic voice.

'I think there is true affection on his part as well as attraction,' Charlotte chimed in. 'One can sense it. Don't you think?'

'I do,' Juliet replied. 'And by the way he was looking at you, it was very apparent to me that he is taken with you.'

'But just now before you arrived I told him that when he was gone I would miss him.'

Juliet squeezed her hand. 'That's a lovely thing to tell someone.'

'But he didn't say it back. Why would he not say it back?'

Charlotte lowered her head to catch Clara's eye and gave a small shrug. 'We have never seen you like this. You have been strong for all of us in our times of need. Do not concern yourself with us. We will give you all the time you need with him while we are here. We can occupy ourselves very well when we are together. This is far from the last time that we will all be together again.'

'And you will get to see him later this evening,' Juliet said in an encouraging tone. 'You never know what he will confess to you then.'

Chapter Twenty-Three

Lane had planned to take his carriage to Clara's house that night, but after he received a letter from Mr Edwards shortly before he left, he knew a walk would help him work through his anger.

What man turned down an offer to purchase his hotel for that amount of money? It made no sense—and it destroyed Lane's dream of opening a spa here in Bath.

Now he would have to inform Hart, Lyonsdale and Lord Musgrove of it in the morning. It was not something he was eager to do. He took great pride in his business accomplishments. His reputation was built on his ability to consistently find sound and profitable investment opportunities. And while the coffee house would turn a decent profit, it wasn't nearly as large a profit as the spa would have brought. And Lord Musgrove was going to take back news to London that Lane hadn't been able to fulfil his part of the contract.

That cut deep. But as he walked closer and closer to Clara's house, he began to wonder if the pain and anger he was feeling had more to do with knowing that, within the week, he would leave Bath. His time with Clara was coming to an end.

He could have sent word to her that he was not going to be able to join her tonight. Hell, he probably should have after he read Mr Edwards's letter. However, the thought of spending this evening without her, knowing that they had such little time left together, was not an option. By the time he reached her door, the walk had helped to get his anger under control—even if it would only last for a few hours. He had no doubt that by morning it would be back again in full force.

Standing outside Clara's home, he tried to shake off his melancholy and brace himself for being around this many people when all he wanted to do was be alone with her. It seemed that this was the very definition of his relationship with her.

It was Darby who opened the door and welcomed him into her home. Lane scanned the parquet floor for signs of Humphrey and was disheartened the small dog did not charge him with his normal unconditional exuberance.

'I believe if you are looking for Humphrey, sir, he is probably still asleep in Mrs Sommersby's bedchamber. Lady Juliet had been playing with him out in the garden earlier and, between your training and her playing, he appeared to be quite worn out.'

A very large vase of roses was on a round table in the middle of the entrance hall that scented the air so it smelled like Clara. He knew he had walked past it earlier in the day, but only now did he feel the impact of the scent on his soul. He knew he would think of her whenever he smelled roses from now on.

After Darby took his hat and walking stick, he showed him into a small parlour, where people were talking in small groups. This room, with its pale yellow walls and patterned rug, wasn't as ornate and formal as her drawing room. There was a small table with four chairs near the fireplace, where the three Sommersby sisters were deep in conversation, and at the other end of the room were two small sofas that faced one another. Standing around them were the Collingswoods, along with Clara, Mr Greeley and the Dowager. When he took a step further into the room, Harriet took note of him and whispered something into Clara's ear. When their eyes met, it felt as if a soothing balm was placed on his emotional wounds of the day.

Her face brightened and she left her party to approach him. Lane wished with all his heart that he could take her in his arms. He had missed her already and they had only been apart for a few hours.

Clara took him around and reintroduced him to her nieces, each one more welcoming than the next. Greeley appeared relieved to see another gentleman aside from Mr Collingswood in attendance and the Collingswoods were all cordial, but he could sense the mother and father were trying to determine what to make of him and sizing him up against poor Greeley. In all, it wasn't horrible company to be in, but he still would have preferred to be alone with Clara.

It appeared he was the last to arrive and, within a few minutes, the party made its way through a doorway into her dining room. This room was painted the same colour with royal-blue curtains on the tall windows and portraits of men and women from centuries past on the walls. He assumed that some were Clara's ancestors. He searched each face for any resemblance he could see to her. There was a woman in a blue gown with elaborate lace sleeves holding a basket of flowers who looked somewhat like Clara. He could see it in the shape of her brown eyes and that pert upturned nose. There had been times when he was younger when he had wondered if he had looked like either of his parents. He had seen familial resemblances in the children of his friends and he could see it tonight in the Sommersby sisters. Did he look like his mother or his father? Which one had dark blond hair? And which had blue eyes?

He must have been staring at the portrait of the woman for an inordinate length of time because Lady Charlotte, who was seated beside him, commented about it to him.

'That's Baroness Cecily Reynolds. She is my aunt's grandmother.'

'I can see the resemblance.'

They sat shoulder to shoulder, studying it.

Lady Charlotte removed her napkin from the table and placed it on her lap. 'It's the eyes.'

'And the nose.'

She looked up at the portrait again and tilted her head. 'You're right. I never noticed that before.' Moving her attention away from the portrait, she looked over at Clara, who was speaking to the Dowager, seated across from him on Clara's right. 'I always liked that portrait when I was a young girl. It hung in the dining room of the town house my aunt and uncle lived in in London. I always thought she looked like a woman who I would enjoy having tea with…one who had a good sense of fun and liked to laugh.'

Whether she realised it or not, she had described her aunt.

He had never given much consideration to the fact that Clara was a widow and that meant she'd had a husband. He scanned the portraits again, looking for a gentleman dressed in more current fashion who might be the man she had married. His gaze settled on the portrait over the fireplace behind Clara. The gentleman in question appeared to be a bit younger than Greeley and was dressed in a scarlet coat with black lapels and a long pale-coloured waistcoat, white breeches and black boots. His cravat had more lace to it than was fashionable now, as was the cut of his coat. He was leaning against a tree, standing beside a horse and looking directly at the viewer with a bemused expression. The position in the room showed the significance of the sitter to Clara.

'That was Uncle Robert,' Lady Charlotte replied in a low voice.

He looked back at her and found her staring at the portrait with a nostalgic smile on her face. 'My grandparents had it painted not long before he married my aunt.'

'He appears to be a genial man.'

It didn't matter how genial the man was, Lane didn't like him.

'Oh, he was. Uncle Robert was our father's youngest brother and very affable. He was one of those lucky people who had the true gift for storytelling. When we were little he would love to tell us these absolutely outrageous tales and as children he would have us all believing them, until he would say this one funny twist at the end of it that let us know it was a Banbury tale.'

'When did he die?'

'I think it's about ten years now.' She picked up her glass of wine and took a sip while appearing to count the years in her head. 'Yes, that's right. Ten years. Time does seem to move at a different pace once you get older, does it not?'

She appeared to be about five years younger than he was, if he had to estimate, and she was right. It was moving much quicker now. He always thought that he would have a wife and children some day in the distant future. It was only since he had spent time with Clara that he had truly pictured what that life might be like. He tried to think what he was doing ten years ago. He recalled living up in Liverpool for the year and being completely absorbed in the shipping industry. His eyes drifted down from the portrait of Robert Sommersby over to Clara. How had her life changed after her husband died? How had she taken his death?

'You mentioned that your aunt and uncle lived in London. When did she move here?'

'Aunt Clara grew up here in Bath so she has always had a connection here. They lived here when they were first married and moved to London when I was about ten. She moved back here shortly after my uncle passed. My aunt has told us that you reside in London. Do you mind if I ask what part?'

He leaned back, allowing the footman to ladle white soup into his bowl. 'On the edge of Mayfair.'

Her surprised expression brought a smile with it. 'I am very familiar with Mayfair,' she replied, bouncing up a fraction in her chair, appearing eager to find out if they shared any acquaintances.

This was what he didn't want. He didn't want his past infringing on his present. Not with Clara. She didn't need to know he was a by-blow. Once more his eyes landed on the portrait of Robert Sommersby and then travelled to the Baroness, who was Clara's grandmother. They would have thought they were so far above him that it would have been funny to see how they would have reacted to having a bastard at the dinner table. It would have been funny—except right now it was making him sick just thinking about it.

He didn't want anything to diminish what Clara was feeling for him. Even though he would be leaving her, he wanted to believe that she would miss him for a time and that if his name ever drifted through her mind years from now, it would be accompanied by fond memories.

He was saved from continuing the discussion with Lady Charlotte when the Dowager enquired about the health of her sister-in-law, the Duchess of Winterbourne, and of the work the woman was doing with the Royal Academy. Their discussion gave him the opportunity to turn to his right and steal a glance at Clara, who was sitting next to him at the head of the table.

His heart felt larger when he found her watching him. For how long her eyes had been on him he didn't know, but knowing he had captured her attention somehow made his shoulders go back.

She leaned towards him and lowered her voice. 'I could have placed you beside Mrs Collingswood, but seeing how you and Greeley are of the same rank, I took the liberty of placing you beside me instead of that seat going to her husband, both saving you and me from tedious conversation.'

But he wasn't the same as Greeley and Mr Collingswood, and his prominent place beside the hostess was a sham. Suddenly he was feeling their difference in rank acutely.

'You aren't quietly thinking of dull things to discuss with me, are you?' She gave him a teasing smile. 'If you are, then I assure you that I can think of topics that are duller than yours.'

He leaned closer so their heads were almost touching. 'I doubt that. I have been accused of being as dull as a doornail.'

'You have not.'

'I have.'

'Who would accuse you of such a thing?'

'My business partner. He does so each time I begin to discuss problems with things like inventory.'

His disclosing he was in trade did not seem to scandalise her in any way. There was still a glint of amusement in her eyes. 'And what types of problems do you have with your inventory? Do you believe the horses are stealing the hay in your stables?'

'They might be. I will need to do a thorough check of the books when I am there next.'

'Horses stealing hay in the dead of night does not sound dull to me.'

'I never said they were doing it in the dead of night. They might be brazen beasts and slipping it away in the middle of the day.'

'That's more daring. Sorry but your attempt at being dull has failed. I am far duller than you.'

'But you have yet to try to bore me. I doubt you can.'

'Oh, I can.'

'I don't think so.'

'I will be taking my nieces shopping tomorrow.'

'That's not dull.'

'We will be shopping for ribbons and gloves. And perhaps new slippers. And one can always use a new bonnet. Something fresh and different.

And have I mentioned that I have a passion for reticules? I do. I don't know why.'

'I think you might have won.'

'Ah, I told you. I am far duller than you are. Quite forgettable.'

'One could never accuse you of that.'

There was a ripple in the air between them as they sat looking at each other while he tried to memorise her with his eyes.

The sound of the Dowager's spoon lightly hitting the inside of her bowl broke the spell between them and they finished their soup course without speaking further.

The remainder of the meal went by pleasantly enough with delicious food and interesting and congenial conversation. As an array of jellies, syllabubs, and fruits were brought to the table, the discussion turned to music.

'Do you remember the last time Lizzy played the harpsichord for us?' Lady Juliet asked, directing her question to Clara.

The Duchess, or Lizzy as her family referred to her, raised her chin. 'Well, I might not have had the patience to practise the harpsichord to play it proficiently, but at least I have a pleasant singing voice.'

Lady Charlotte looked at her sister Juliet. Their

exchanged expressions were enough to have the
Duchess raise her chin.

'I do. Simon has remarked upon how lovely
it is.'

'Simon is in love with you. His opinion does
not signify,' Lady Juliet said with a wave of her
hand.

'My daughters are accomplished in both singing and playing piano,' Mrs Collingswood said to
no one in particular, which made Harriet redden
and her sister look down at her lap.

'I, for one, would love to hear them,' Greeley
chimed in from his seat beside Harriet. 'My parents had arranged for me to have lessons on our
pianoforte so I would be more than happy to accompany them should they choose to sing.' His
eyes were on Harriet. 'Or any of you ladies,' he
said, breaking his gaze and looking around the
table.

'And what of you, Mr Lane?' Mrs Collingswood said across the table. 'Do you possess any
musical talents we should be aware of?'

'I can sing,' he admitted, although he wasn't
sure why he had even bothered to say it.

'Really? How lovely,' she responded. 'Is your
skill learned or did you discover it on your own?'

He could lie. It would be so easy to do, but that
was not the kind of man he was.

'I had a music teacher.' All the children in the

Foundling Hospital had music lessons. It was part of the curriculum.

'What a wonderful thing for your parents to do for you and how lucky for them that they could enjoy your talents.' She scooped her spoon slowly into her syllabub. 'Tell us about your parents, Mr Lane. I don't believe I have heard anything about your family. Harriet has informed me you are from London. Is that where you were raised, or do they have a place in the country?' She took the spoonful of the sweet dessert in her mouth.

All side conversations stopped at the very forward probing of Mrs Collingswood. Harriet sent him an apologetic look while turning red with a deep flush. Once more he was faced with lying about his past or telling the truth. He had never lied about who he was before. He might have avoided talking about it, but he would never lie about who he was when asked directly.

This would change everything. He felt it in his bones.

'I was raised in London, not in the country. As for my parents and my family, there isn't anything I could really say. You see, I was raised in the Foundling Hospital there. I have no knowledge of my parents.'

Mrs Collingswood's mouth and hand went slack and she almost dropped the spoon that she was holding. Her eyes darted to Clara, who he had yet to look at. He didn't even want to see her out of the corner of his eye. Everyone who was in his line of vision was staring at him. It was obvious that his response was not what any of them expected.

'Why don't we go up to the drawing room now?' Clara said, ending dinner rather abruptly. Her voice was even, but he knew her well enough now that he could hear the suppressed strain in it. 'The harpsichord is in there and you can all decide what it is you would like to perform tonight.'

Juliet was the first one to her feet, followed by the rest of the guests around the table. As if someone else had possessed him, he took a drink of his claret and stood as well. Clara walked behind his chair on her way to the door as was customary for the hostess to lead them out of the room. He was the last one to leave and he looked back at the portrait of her husband and scanned the room that he was certain he would never see again. As he stepped into the parlour, Lady Charlotte, who was walking in front of him, turned and gave him a slight sympathetic smile.

This was how things would end between them. This was how she would remember him. He was the bastard who had sat at her table and pretended to be a gentleman to her and her guests.

The day that he had believed couldn't get any worse suddenly did and he didn't think he was in the mind frame to deal with the consequences. The crushing disappointment that he had felt at not being able to buy the hotel was nothing compared to the pain inside his chest right now. There was no sense in staying and being ignored. It had happened to him before. He had spent nights at small gatherings like this off to the side, feeling like an outsider in a room full of people.

Lady Charlotte was almost at the top of the stairs when, while standing at the bottom, he decided to leave. He turned away from the wooden banister and began to walk to the front door. He didn't even care if he left his hat and walking stick behind. He could afford new ones.

As he stepped outside, a cool breeze hit his face. The moon, high in the night sky, was casting blue light on to the grassy lawn before him. It would be a long walk home and he knew he needed the physical exertion if he had any chance of falling asleep tonight. Tomorrow he would make final notes to leave for Mr Sanderson. Then he would pack his things for his return to London. He didn't need to spend more time in Bath than was necessary.

He turned to his left to walk down the pavement along the Crescent, when the door to Clara's house suddenly opened and she hurried outside.

'Where are you going?' she asked, running up to him.

'I thought I would save us both the awkwardness of my saying goodbye, especially in a house full of your guests.'

'But you told us you could sing.'

'It's best if I go.'

'But I don't want you to. I want you to stay.'

How he wished she meant that. A thought flashed through his mind that he wished she wanted that for ever.

'There is no need to do this out of politeness, Clara. You know what I am now. I don't belong in there.'

'I determine who belongs in my home. Now come back inside with me.'

Was she going to make him explain it all to her? Did he have to tell her and see the look in her eyes when he did? When he didn't move, she placed her hands on her hips and raised her chin, looking like a warrior preparing for battle.

'You will leave then, before you and I have had a chance to talk about any of this or say our goodbyes…since it appears you are determined to go. I never took you for a man who walked away when life becomes difficult, but it appears I was wrong. If that truly is the type of man you are, then I do believe it is best that you leave. However, I have proper manners and will wish you Godspeed and not simply disappear.'

Her words made his blood run cold. He was

not a man who walked away from his problems. He never was and never would be. As she spun around and stormed back to the house, his opportunity to let her know that was slipping away.

'I am not running away,' he insisted, catching up to her before she reached her door.

She stopped in her tracks and turned to him, vexation shone in her eyes. 'Then prove that to be true and talk to me.'

'You have guests. This is not a conversation fit for anyone else's ears but your own. I owe the Collingswoods no explanation of my origins.'

'Then talk to *me*,' she said, poking herself in the chest so hard it had to have hurt. 'Go in that house and talk to me. There are many places we can have a private discussion.'

If it didn't bother her that she was being negligent to her guests and hosting a bastard, then it damned well wasn't going to bother him. 'Fine. After you.' He tossed his hand towards her door and followed her inside.

The sound of voices travelled down the staircase, but she took him by the hand and practically dragged him into the parlour where they had started the evening. He watched her first close the door that led to the dining room, ensuring that any servants that were in there cleaning up did not have the opportunity to see or hear them. And then she marched past him and closed the door they had just walked through. The fact she was leaning against it and had not offered him a seat was telling him what she thought of having him in her house. He would make this brief.

'There is nothing for us to discuss,' he said, planting his feet firmly on the ground, not about to allow her to make him feel small for what he was.

'I beg to differ and I will stand in front of this door until we are finished so there is no possibility of you leaving.'

That was why she was standing there?

'I will not leave, but when I finish telling you all of it, you may wish you had let me go the first time.'

'Whatever it is that you need to tell me, I will listen. It is better that we have a clear understanding of each other than be cowards and slip away into the night without a word.'

Her words pierced his pride, but he could not deny she was right in what she said.

'I was trying to avoid creating a spectacle in front of your guests, a number of whom I am sure are grateful I left.'

'Do not concern yourself with my guests. That is my responsibility and I couldn't give a fig what any of them think right now. I thought we had come to mean something to each other. I thought we were friends. And then you leave like that without a word?'

'Clara, you're the granddaughter of a baron. Your husband was the brother of an earl. I grew up in a Foundling Hospital. Do you know what that makes me? Do you know what that means? I am not just an orphan whose parents have died. I am a bastard—a by-blow of some man who couldn't be bothered to marry my mother. Or was married already when he took her. The only children who are taken in by the Foundling Hospital are bastards. Don't you see? I don't even know on what day I was born or what my real name is—if I was even given one. I am not William Lane. It's the name the Hospital gave me when they took me in. For all I know, my mother didn't even give me a name. For all I know, she never bothered because she couldn't wait to give me away. So, you see, every day my name is a constant reminder that I was discarded and unwanted in the event I ever forget.'

She walked up to him and took his hand into her two delicate ones. The gesture held him in place when in truth he wished he was the type of man to run.

'Is that why you didn't want me to call you William?'

'There is no reason I should have two false names. One is a sufficient enough reminder.'

In her eyes, instead of pity, he saw compassion. Which one was worse he couldn't say, because right now instead of running he wanted to stay with her for ever. And that very thought scared the hell out of him.

When she reached up and slowly ran her fingers through his hair in a comforting gesture, he had to look away. But she guided his jaw gently so he was facing her once more.

'The circumstances of your birth do not change anything. They do not change what kind of man I think you are or the feelings I have for you. I am truly sorry that that horrid woman put you in a position at my dining table where you felt obligated to confess it like that in a room full of strangers. I am sorry that you had to endure a pain all these years that was none of your making.'

The tips of her warm fingers caressed his brow and without thinking he wrapped his arms around her, holding her close and wishing that this moment of complete acceptance wouldn't end. He was not a man who saw a point to physical affection. It probably was because he hadn't had any since he was a small boy, living in the countryside. But right now, with her touch, he felt some of the wounds to his soul begin to heal.

Raising herself up on her toes, Clara touched her lips to his and he opened to her kiss. The kiss was slow and thoughtful, filled with something he couldn't name, but didn't feel like passion. And with each nibble to his lips and slide of her tongue against his, his world started to be pieced back together. Nothing mattered any more except for this moment and the woman in his arms. He broke the kiss to trail his lips along her jaw, down her neck, to the base of her throat, where he swirled his tongue against her soft, fragrant skin while his hand moved over her ribcage and settled on her left breast.

For the first time in his life, he felt as if he was exactly where he belonged.

He kissed his way back to her lips, knowing that they needed to end this—knowing that she needed to return to her guests. When their lips met once more, she deepened the kiss for several more moments before moving her head back and touching her forehead to his.

'I'd like you to stay.'

'I don't want to leave.'

She ran her hands over his shoulders and settled them on his chest. Without a doubt, she would be able to feel the rapid beating of his heart.

'I will not allow anyone to treat you unkindly in my home. I would just as soon ask them to leave—no matter who it is.'

'I do not need you to champion me, Clara. I am a grown man and have years of experience dealing with people and their prejudices.'

'But I want you to know I will not place you in a position where you have to do that here.'

He cupped her jaw and kissed her one last time before they left the parlour and made their way to her drawing room. She was telling him that she accepted him enough to have him in her home, yet their stations in life were so very different. If he thought he could forget that fact, he was reminded of it in vivid detail when he entered the drawing room with her a few minutes later and the entire room stared at him. Mr Collingswood's dark bushy brows drew together and his wife raised her nose.

'We did not realise how late it was, Mrs Sommersby,' the man said. 'I believe that it is time that we headed home.'

'Thank you for this evening,' his wife added, gathering up her daughters.

Lane walked to the window overlooking the moonlit lawn and could see them bid their farewells to everyone else in the room except for him in the reflection in the glass. Harriet had looked his way a number of times, but was ushered out of the room by her parents. The Collingswoods could go to hell for all he cared—however, the cut still stung and he hated himself for that.

He waited to see who was next to leave the room.

'I had to get married.'

A woman's voice broke the silence and he turned to find Lady Charlotte looking directly at him. 'It's true. While I love my husband with all of my soul now, we had to wed.'

He didn't understand why she had decided to reveal that to the room, half of which was her family and probably knew that already—until Lady Juliet spoke up.

'When I was seventeen I tried to convince a gentleman to run away to Gretna Green with me to elope. I hadn't cared that it would have created a scandal.'

They were sharing their scandals with him. Showing him that they were not perfect either. He didn't know what to say. He had never experienced anything like this before.

The Dowager tilted her head with assessing eyes. 'My grandson, the Duke, married an American...an *American*. And it is one of my favourite matches. Birth does not truly define who a person is, Mr Lane. Do not let anyone make you believe any differently.'

The Duchess of Skeffington pinched the bridge of her nose. 'Oh, fine, I had to pretend to be married to my husband for three days before he asked me to marry him.' She looked up and met him in the eye. 'It's a long story.'

'I don't have anything scandalous to share, but

if I did I would gladly share it now,' Greeley said to him.

'I think you'll have scandals soon enough,' the Dowager replied to him.

Clara hadn't said a word, but stood there watching her family with a hand on her heart, appearing as touched as he was. When her gaze left Mr Greeley and settled on Lane, there was such affection for him in her eyes. 'I have a secret, too. After Robert died I needed an investment that would make me financially stable. I didn't want to be dependent on my relatives or become a lady's companion. So, I took all the money I was left with and purchased a hotel. It is what has allowed me to live this comfortable life here in Bath.'

'What?' the Duchess cried in disbelief. 'You're an innkeeper?'

Lady Juliet turned to her sister. 'Why are you so surprised? Surely you knew.'

'No. I did not know. You knew?' Her agitation had not subsided.

'Well, yes, I thought you both knew.'

They both turned to Lady Charlotte, who shook her head. 'I was not aware of this.'

'This is why I never told you. This and the fact that your uncle while he was alive refused to buy one saying it was far beneath our station in life to do so. That if it was known it would affect Juliet's ability to launch well in Society even with a sister who was a duchess. He feared we would lose the friendships of prominent families we knew and the men he went to university with. And he knew your father would have forbidden it. I have kept it quiet to protect you all from any shame it might have caused.'

'I can't believe you're an innkeeper,' the Duchess said again.

The women were talking so quickly it was almost hard to keep track of what they were saying. But the fact that she owned a hotel was stuck front and centre in his mind.

'I'm not an innkeeper, Lizzy. I own The Fountain Head Hotel here in Bath and have someone manage it for me.'

If his brain exploded right now he would not have been surprised. Certainly he hadn't heard her correctly? 'You own The Fountain Head?'

She turned away from her niece, who had gone from standing up to sitting down on the sofa, to face him. 'Yes. Are you all right? You look as if you could use a brandy.'

'It's as if I don't even know you,' the Duchess said in a faint whisper, reclining back. 'You've been leading this other life.'

'Lizzy, she owns a hotel, not a brothel.' Lady Charlotte went and stood over her sister.

The Duchess looked up at her. 'I realise that,

but this is a completely new side of her that I wasn't even aware of. I've spent a significant amount of time in this house. How could I not be aware of this?'

Lane was still trying to wrap his brain around the fact that the woman in front of him—the one whom he thought of day and night—was the person who had turned down his offer to buy that hotel. She had to have known that he had placed the offer for it. She had to have known he wanted it. His legs felt weak and he took a seat on the bench by the harpsichord that was beside him.

I could use that brandy.

The Dowager approached his side with a bottle of port and two stemmed glasses. 'I found these on the table.' She handed him the glasses and poured a good amount of port in each. After tucking the bottle under her arm, she took one of the glasses, and toasted him with it before taking a drink. 'It's not brandy, but it will do.'

Apparently, he had said it out loud.

Greeley walked over to them with his shoulders hunched and trying hard not to look at the animated discussion going on over by the sofa between the Sommersby women.

'Elizabeth,' the Dowager called out. 'Do you love your aunt any less over this?'

The Duchess sat up and looked between the Dowager and Clara. 'No, of course not.'

'Then pull yourself together. It's not as if she's murdered anyone. She is a woman who, without a husband, has managed to find a way to financial security and she has not had to become a man's mistress to do it. That should be celebrated.'

'It's just so unexpected. That is all.'

'So are many things in life, my dear, but that doesn't mean that they are bad.' She arched her brow at Lane and finished her glass of port. 'Something tells me that you and Mrs Sommersby will have things to talk about tonight. Greeley, I find I am feeling a bit tired all of a sudden. Would you care to walk me home?'

'Of course, Your Grace.'

'It was a pleasure seeing you once more, Mr Lane. I do hope I will see you again soon.' She smiled up at him and patted his arm as she walked past him on her way to say goodnight to Clara and her nieces.

'Goodnight, Mr Lane,' Greeley said, shaking his hand. 'Will you be in Bath for long?'

Now with the knowledge that Clara owned The Fountain Head Hotel, his life had been turned upside down and he didn't know what he would be doing. 'I couldn't say. I was planning on leaving by week's end.'

The man appeared genuinely disappointed. 'Well, I have enjoyed making your acquaintance. If you are ever in town again, please do send your card around. It would be my pleasure to see you again.' He tipped his head one last time and walked across the room.

Staring at the ruby liquid in his glass, Lane tried to remember if she had ever said anything that would have given him any indication that she was aware about the offer he had made on the hotel. Was she partners with Mr Edwards? Perhaps he had never told her about the offer. Perhaps he had turned down the offer without her knowledge. If she knew that he had made an offer on her hotel, wouldn't she have said something? He was beginning to feel like an emotional wreck inside after admitting he was a bastard and then finding out she owned the hotel.

When he looked up his eyes met Clara's across the room where her niece Elizabeth was hugging her. He needed to find out what Clara knew about the offer he'd made. When her eyebrows furrowed and she gave him a questioning look, he signalled to the doorway with his head. With a nod, she disengaged herself from Elizabeth, excused herself from her nieces and met him out in the corridor.

'We should talk.'

Chapter Twenty-Four

With the support of her family, it felt as if a giant weight had been lifted off Clara's chest—a weight that she hadn't realised she had been carrying around. She was proud of the business she had built up and she was relieved that she no longer felt as if she had to hide it.

Yet the relief ended the moment she looked across her drawing room to see the unreadable expression on Lane's face. It reminded her how isolated he must have felt growing up without a family. Her heart broke for him because she knew that he had lived in that Hospital without anyone to love and comfort him when he needed it the most. She had been inside that Hospital and seen what it was like. It was where she had met the Dowager while working on a committee to raise funds for it.

When she showed him into her small library

that was next to the drawing room, she gestured to him to join her on the sofa and she took a seat.

'I am sorry about the Collingswoods. I am sorry that they made you feel anything less than welcome in my home. You know I do not share their feelings on the matter.'

He sat down next to her and searched her eyes. 'You own The Fountain Head Hotel?'

This was what he wanted to talk about?

'I do.' She waited for him to say more except she was getting the impression that he was waiting for her to continue.

He tilted his head and his thick blond hair slid across his forehead. 'Is this the investment you were referring to when you said that the gentleman handling your affairs does not listen to you?'

'Yes, that's right, and your advice to me was very helpful.'

'Mr Edwards is the gentleman you were referring to?'

'Yes. He's my cousin. We grew up together here in Bath as children. I think that is why we have the problems at times that we do. I think part of him still sees me as the little girl he would tease, even after all these years.'

'Has he told you about anyone wanting to buy your hotel from you?'

The hairs on her arm stood up. 'How do you know about that?'

'Then you don't know?'

'Don't know what?'

'I was the one who made the offer to purchase it.'

'*You?* Why would you want my hotel?'

'I didn't know it was your hotel.'

'Phillip sent me a letter regarding the conditions of the offer, knowing I would need to be aware of it even though he knows full well I have no desire to sell it. His letter said the offer was made by the gentleman who had purchased the coffee house next door.'

'That's me. I own the White Bear.'

'But you said you owned a racing stable?'

'I do, but that's only one of my investments. I purchased the coffee house a month ago along with a business partner of mine.'

'None of this is making sense. If you own the coffee house, why would you want my hotel as well?'

'Why didn't you accept my offer? It was a very substantial one.'

'Because I do not wish to sell it. And you didn't answer my question.'

'But you could buy another hotel with the money we are offering.' The words came out clipped, taking her aback.

'I don't want the money to purchase another one. That one is doing very well for me.'

He was not being forthcoming with her and it was leaving a prickly sensation running up and down her spine, making her very uneasy.

Suddenly, Lane got up and walked away from the sofa. 'You are being unreasonable,' he declared, pacing the rug in front of her.

That one word enflamed her temper and she stood up as tall as her petite stature would allow. As she planted her hands on her hips, her fingers dug into her skin through her gown. He was not about to accuse her of being unreasonable… or hysterical! 'On the contrary, I am being very reasonable.'

The breath he let out was audible and she could tell he was struggling with what to say.

After all they had shared together, she couldn't understand why he could not explain himself adequately. Marching over to him, she blocked his pacing. 'Talk to me. Tell me why you want my hotel with such fervour. There is something you are not telling me.'

Finally, he met her in the eye and she could see the moment he decided to confide in her. Lane raked his hand through his hair and gestured for them to sit back down. 'Shortly after we purchased the White Bear, we discovered an underground hot spring that had been capped off ages ago in the cellar. I want to take the coffee house and your hotel and convert them into a spa. The coffee house would serve as a pump room, much like the one that we met in, and the hotel would be used for bathing.'

'That seems to be a large amount of effort and expense to create yet another spa in this town.'

Before he answered he pinched the bridge of his nose for a few breaths. 'I have studied the comings and goings of the people who go to the King's and Queen's Baths. The potential profits make it worthwhile.'

'It is an interesting proposition for your coffee house. You would not have to pay for the supplies you are currently using. The water is in the ground with no cost to you aside from the cost of designing and constructing a way to pump it out of the ground.'

'Exactly, although without the bathing facilities I have strong reservations that people would travel outside the centre of town just to drink the water when it appears most people prefer to both drink and bathe in it.'

It was an ingenious idea. 'If you offered rooms like a hotel above the bathhouse and pump room, you would attract a significant number of people who didn't wish to travel far to their lodgings all wrapped in blankets in their sedan chairs after they leave the baths for the day. Those rooms could be let at a premium price.'

'That never occurred to me. I just thought of

turning your hotel into the baths. Now do you see why I need your hotel? I cannot expand towards the church. Your hotel is my only option. I've offered you a substantial amount of money to buy it. Clara, you can take that money and invest it in another hotel.'

She didn't want another hotel. There was no guarantee that another hotel would be as successful as this one. She could not take that chance. The fear of losing all her money was still very real for her and the thought of losing her hotel was making her physically sick.

She took his hand in hers. 'I know that this is going to be hard for you to understand, but I cannot sell my hotel. I will not. Too many people are employed there. Those people need their jobs. I will not be responsible for placing them in positions where they will be unable to support themselves or their families.'

'I have no wish to place your staff on the street. I intend to find other jobs for them in the spa.'

'I still cannot sell it to you.'

He removed his hand from hers and rubbed the back of his neck. 'Why? I am giving you a chance to try something new.'

'I don't want to try something new. Don't you see? I am good at making the decisions for *this* hotel. I am good at finding ways to improve the profits that this hotel steadily brings me. It is safe.'

'Safe will not make you rich. Safe will not expand your wealth to a greater degree. You are living very comfortably here, but I am giving you an opportunity to live grander than this.'

'I do not need to live any grander than I am. I have no wish for a country house, or more carriages, or jewels. I am content.'

There was a desperation in his eyes that she couldn't quite understand. He would eventually find another venture to go after. She could not find another Fountain Head Hotel. There was only one.

'I wish you knew how much opening this spa means to me,' he said.

'And I wish you could understand that owning that hotel means everything to me.' She didn't like to discuss her past with Robert. It felt as if she was ruining his memory. Her nieces didn't even know how horrible their life had been the last few years he had been alive. There was no reason that they should think any less of a man who was a loving uncle and a good man. But maybe if she let Lane know, then he would understand why she could not sell the hotel and he would stop asking her to.

'Let me try to help you understand. Before I begin, I need you to know that my husband Robert was a good man.' She let out a deep breath, preparing herself to remain steady while she told Lane things that she hadn't told anyone else before. 'While he was a good man, he did not have the skills for making wise investments with our money. As was expected of him as the younger son of an earl, he had served time as an officer in the King's army. After a number of years, he found the service did not suit his temperament and he returned home and convinced his father to give him some money which he would invest and earn his living that way. He was fairly successful for a time, but during the last three years of his life in particular, his choices proved to be disastrous. I tried to offer suggestions about ventures I'd heard about during drawing-room conversations, or things I had read in the papers, but Robert was a proud man and did not believe that a woman could know more about such things than he did. I continually saw the opportunities that I had suggested to him succeed, while those that he put our money into fail.

One night he took to playing cards at his club and by chance won a substantial amount of money. I had wanted us to purchase a hotel back here in Bath with it, knowing there was a demand for a quality establishment to cater to the *ton* that gathered here regularly. He saw owning a hotel as beneath our station and refused to consider it each time I brought it up. He decided to invest the money with an old friend from Oxford and lost it all.'

She took a deep breath, recalling the day he arrived at their London town house with the news. She could see how broken he was and how these failures were taking their toll on him.

'The last year of his life, our financial situation became so bad that I lived in fear that we would find ourselves in debtors' prison.' The memories began flooding back and she had to rub her chest to help alleviate some of the squeezing she felt around her heart. 'It's by the grace of God that we did not. After Robert was killed in a riding accident, his older brother discovered the financial state we were in. He was kind enough to settle our debts and provide me with money to secure a new husband—those were his words, not mine. I decided to take that money and instead buy the hotel. And I haven't looked back since.' She leaned closer, needing him to understand. 'That hotel provides me with enough income to live comfortably. That hotel allows me to go to sleep at night and not fear that I will be carted off to prison when I wake up in the morning. You see it as a way to increase your income, but I see it as my protection from the cruel fate that can befall many women in my circumstances. I cannot sell it to you. I'm sorry.'

There was a long pause while he sat forward and rested his forearms on his thighs. He rubbed the thumb of his right hand into the palm of his left and looked down at the rug. She prayed he would let the matter rest and not bother bringing it up again. It only made her relive the reasons she would never sell it in the first place.

Finally, he looked back at her and arched his brow. 'Suppose I do not need you to sell it to me. Suppose you were responsible for running the lodging portion and I took care of the pump room. We could work together on the baths, since they would be available in the building of your hotel. You could join in our corporation and we could all split the profits equally.'

'That's less money in your pocket.'

'Yes, but it gets me the spa so there is more money than I am currently making with the coffee house.'

'I don't want to be beholden to any man again. It is why I will never marry again and place my future in the hands of a husband. I want control of what is done with my money. I want to make my own decisions.'

'Success is made through compromise. I cannot guarantee that everything you want to do with the property you will be able to. But everything will always be up for discussion.'

'I don't even know how wise you are with

money. You appear successful, but I understand more than many that looks do not always tell the true story. And I do not know anything about the other gentlemen who are in this venture with you.'

They sat together and he patiently answered all of her questions and offered to bring her his calculations about turning the properties into a spa. The more they discussed it, the more excited they both became at the prospect of creating something new together.

She already suspected she was falling in love with him. And if they were going to turn both their properties into a spa, he wouldn't be leaving Bath for months. She would have more time with him. And if what he told her was true, he was financially sound with his investments. The idea of giving up some of her control was terrifying, but so was the thought of not seeing Lane again.

Chapter Twenty-Five

The next morning a note from Clara was slipped under Lane's door just as he was getting out of bed. He had lain awake most of the night, thinking about what she would do. When he left her house, she said she would be interested in having him bring his papers with his financial projections to her home so she could review them. He feared she had changed her mind, but instead she requested to meet the other investors as well before she decided if she would enter into this partnership.

He had to admire her for her willingness to consider this after all she had told him. How his chest had ached while he listened to her tell him about the struggles she had gone through. Her request proved she would be an intelligent, level-headed business partner. It was all he could ask for.

She was everything he could ever want in a

woman and that thought frightened him down to his soul. He'd always imagined having a family of his own some day. On those nights when he'd had a particularly horrible day, he would lie awake in bed in his dormitory room that he shared with forty-nine other boys and picture the family he would have once he grew up. He would imagine a kind and loving wife and four sons who he would take fishing and they would give him hugs. He had seen that family perfectly in his mind for many years and he could still picture them today. However, now the kind and loving wife had a face—and it was Clara's. And while that should have felt like such a relief, the reality of it was terrifying.

He had been an unwanted child. What was there to say Clara would want him as a man?

By ten o'clock it was arranged. They'd meet in his office in the coffee house at two. Luckily Lord Musgrove had not yet returned to London and agreed to come to Lane's office for the brief meeting. Since Lyonsdale had just offered to loan them some money to help with the construction, there was no need to include him in this discussion. He would not be involved in the day-to-day responsibilities of running the spa and hopefully soon they would be giving him back the money he'd loaned them with interest.

* * *

At ten before the hour, Lane met Clara outside the back door to the coffee house and smuggled her inside, probably in a similar fashion to the way Hart's wife had entered the establishment not long ago. They agreed that he would meet with Hart and Lord Musgrove first and then, when the plan was explained to them, Lane would bring her in. For the time being, she would wait for him in the stockroom opposite his office. It all felt rather clandestine and not at all like the way he was normally accustomed to doing business.

By ten minutes after two, he was sitting behind his desk, trying to convince Lord Musgrove that having Clara as an additional partner would be a good idea. The man wanted none of it. Thank God Clara was still in the stockroom so she was not subject to his hostile dismissal of going into business with her.

'In all my sixty-two years, I have never once listened to the advice of a woman…about anything,' he stated and slammed his fist on the table. 'When I agreed to this idea of yours, I agreed that you would be the one to handle the details of this spa and I would be regularly receiving my share of the profits. Hart told me of the successes you have had in the past. Our agreement did not include a woman. Our agreement did not include splitting the profits from this spa four ways.'

Hart held up his palm to Lord Musgrove in a placating gesture. 'If this is the only way that we can make this enterprise possible, then I think it is worth exploring. Lane is presenting us with an alternative arrangement based on unforeseen circumstances. I think it is in our best interest to consider it.'

'The hell I will!' Lord Musgrove's face was starting to turn red. 'I will not be in partnership with a woman. I gave you plenty of money. Buy her off.'

'I can't,' Lane said. 'She does not want to sell.'

'Offer her more money.'

'I have. Money is not the issue.'

'Then what is? If this woman is foolish enough not to accept your offer to buy the hotel, then she is too foolish to do business with.'

The urge to plant the man a facer was getting stronger with each word he spoke and now Lane was standing over his desk with his face close to Lord Musgrove's. 'She is not a foolish woman.'

'All women are foolish. The sooner you realise that the sooner you'll become good at what you do.'

Hart jumped up just in time to move between Lord Musgrove and Lane. 'Perhaps we should take a moment to sit back down and behave like civilised gentlemen.'

'I am a civilised gentleman,' Lord Musgrove spat. 'I don't know what you would call him. This is what I get for trying to do business with a man of no consequence.'

The vein that ran along Lane's temple began to throb and a warm rush of anger heated his face. He went to move around his desk to throttle the man, but once more Hart stepped in the way.

With his back to Lane, he pointed his finger at Lord Musgrove. 'Sir, I will not stand here and allow you to disparage my friend.'

'Well, you won't have to,' Lord Musgrove shouted. 'I am leaving. Our contract stipulates there are three parties involved, not four. It does not include a woman. I will have my secretary contact your solicitor. I am backing out of our contract!'

'You don't need to contact anyone. I'll take care of it for you!' Lane grabbed their contract off his desk and ripped it up.

Lord Musgrove's body stiffened and there was rage in his eyes. He jerked his hat on to his head. 'Barbarian,' he said through his teeth before he stormed to the door and flung it open.

Through the doorway, Lane could see Clara out in the hallway, standing against the wall opposite his door, with a startled expression on her face. Lord Musgrove took one look at her, rolled his eyes at Lane and stormed off to the front door in a huff. Lane would have done anything to go back in time and somehow save Clara from hearing Lord Musgrove's comments.

'Well, that went well,' Hart said, dropping himself into his leather chair and throwing his head back. 'If it wasn't clear before, it is painfully clear now why I am much better at getting investors than you are.'

Lane's eyes were still on Clara. 'You couldn't have done any better with him and you know it.'

'You're right. The man is an ass.' He rubbed his hand across his brow. 'What do we do now?'

From where he stood, Lane saw Clara raise her chin. She marched across the hall and into his office, closing the door behind her. The sound made Hart turn around and he got his first look at who their potential partner would have been. It took a lot to surprise Hart. In fact, Lane had only seen him truly surprised less than five times in all the years he had known the man. There was no doubt that Clara had taken him completely by surprise. In true Hart fashion, he recovered quickly.

He stood and offered her a bow. 'Mrs Sommersby, this truly is a surprise. Either you have a sense of uncanny timing or there is a facet to the diamond you are that I somehow missed years ago.'

Taking a step further into the room, she bobbed a quick, efficient curtsy to him. 'Lord Hartwick, you have always appeared to be the soul of discretion—however, some facets are best not brought into the light.'

Her comment made him laugh and Lane wondered how his friend could feel any humour after enduring the storm that had just destroyed their plans. They both waited for her to take a seat beside Hart before sitting down. Lane sat forward and rested his forearms on his desk, clasping his hands together to stop himself from reaching out to her in Hart's presence.

'I take it you own The Fountain Head?' Hart asked, tipping his head to the side and watching her.

She cleared her throat and nodded. 'I do.'

'I see. Well, for the longest time I pictured you as a balding man approaching fifty, so this is a pleasant improvement. I understand why you would not want your association known. I will not tell your tale.'

'I am through with hiding this. My nieces are all married now and no longer have a need for me to chaperone them in Society. They have assured me that it is of no consequence to them what people think of their eccentric aunt.'

'The Sommersby sisters are wise women. They take after their aunt—'

'I am sorry,' Lane broke in. 'I had no idea Lord Musgrove would react as he did. Had I known, I wouldn't have suggested any of this to you.'

'Do not blame yourself for other people's actions. This is not your fault.'

From the corner of his eye, Lane could see that Hart was studying them and he recalled how his friend had once fancied Clara.

'Lane informed us you're a shrewd businesswoman, responsible for the success of that hotel. Seeing the reputation it has, I would heartily agree.'

'It was kind of him to say so.'

Hart rubbed his hands together. 'So, we are back in search of a partner. One who has deep pockets and an open mind to investments. Let me talk with Sarah tonight. She might have some ideas.'

'There is no need,' Clara replied, shaking her head. 'I will not be able to go forward with this. I will not sell my hotel or go into any agreement with you gentlemen.'

Instinctively, Lane clasped his hands tighter. 'But we do not have a problem with partnering with you. We will let you make decisions and have a say in what is done.'

'I know you believe that and that might be what happens, but some day something might happen and all that could change. I am not willing to take that risk.'

'Clara, please. Do not let Lord Musgrove have you believing that every gentleman agrees with his ideas.'

'He just reminded me that enough do—and sometimes, it's not horrid men like him that do.'

There was a shimmer in her eyes. It was brief, but it was there. She knew what this meant. She knew that, without her hotel, there was no reason for Lane to stay in Bath. She knew that in making this decision, she would be ending whatever this was between them. Although she was the one who would be staying, she was leaving him.

When Hart stood up, it served as a distraction from the pain Lane was feeling in his heart.

'Well, I am sorry we will not be working together on this, Mrs Sommersby, but you have to follow your gut. It's what Lane likes to remind me from time to time. We need to trust our instincts. If we do that, things will work out for the best.' He tipped his head at her and a lock of his black hair slipped close to his eye. Then he turned to Lane, pulling Lane's attention away from Clara. 'Send word when you return to London. I will be there with brandy and a good meal waiting for you.' As they shook hands, Hart held Lane's a moment longer than necessary and patted him on the shoulder before he walked out of the office and closed the door quietly behind him.

They were alone—and deep down Lane knew that this would be for the last time.

'Is there anything that I can say that will change your mind about this?' He would say anything, if she would just let him know that she wanted him.

She shook her head and it felt as if his heart was ripped in two. She didn't want him. Once again, he wasn't wanted.

Having to look at the top of her head as she stared at her lap was painful. He wanted to work on trying to forget her as quickly as possible, because he knew it was bound to take him years. However, he was grateful that he was not forced to stand just yet while she walked out on him, because his legs felt too weak to support him.

When she did look up, she swallowed before she spoke. 'Thank you for believing that this could have worked. For giving me the chance to see if this would have been something that I could have wanted. Knowing that you believed in me means more to me than you will ever know.'

He knew why she was walking away from this. He understood what owning that hotel meant to her. He cared for her with every fibre of his being and never wanted her to fear for her future. She deserved peace and security.

'If I had the money and this place was mine,

I would create the finest spa Bath has ever seen with you. But I am not the sole owner and I don't have the money on my own to make all of that happen. I wish I did. You don't know how much I wish I did.'

She didn't say anything back. She just nodded.

'I'll be returning to London in a few days. I'm not needed here at the White Bear. Mr Sanderson is competent and trustworthy. He will send me regular reports at the Albany. He doesn't need me looking over his shoulder. I would need another reason to stay.' Their eyes met and he waited. He waited for her to tell him that she wanted him. That she was his reason for staying and that she wanted to have a life with him.

He waited.

And then she looked down.

'I understand,' she said softly as she ran her thumb over the rose embroidered on her reticule.

Who knew that two words could hurt so much?

'Will you come by the house to say goodbye to Humphrey before you leave? I'm sure he will miss you when you are gone.'

'I won't have time, but I'm sure he has already forgotten all about me.'

She looked up at him then and in her eyes he saw a sadness. 'He will never forget you.'

Abruptly, she stood and shook out her skirts and Lane managed somehow to stand. This was it. His time with her was over. Somehow, he would need to find a way to forget her which wouldn't be easy since he was certain a ghost of her would always remain with his soul.

'I will leave you to your work. I know you are a busy man.'

He couldn't let her go without kissing her one last time. He wished he could tell her how much she meant to him, but even if he worked out how to express his feelings, it wouldn't change the fact that she didn't want him enough to ask him to stay.

When he stepped around his desk, she stood, frozen. He watched her as her gaze travelled slowly over his face before settling on his lips. She lifted her face up and he brushed a gentle kiss on her forehead, before lowering his mouth for one last kiss. He drew her closer to him, savouring the warmth of her body one last time, and a lump formed in his throat when her hand caressed his cheek as she deepened the kiss. He couldn't imagine ever wanting to kiss another woman again. She pulled her head slowly away and it was impossible for him to speak.

'Godspeed, Lane. I will never forget you.' She spun around and rushed out the door, not stopping to close it.

For the first time since he was a child, Lane felt a soul-crushing loss that he knew would take him years to get over.

Chapter Twenty-Six

For three days Clara had stayed in her room. For three days, her nieces had tried to get her to talk to them, but it was much too painful. For Lane to have the life he deserved, she had to let the man she loved go. She had to give him the chance to find a woman to bear him the family he'd never had—a family that, at her age, she could never give him.

More than anything Clara wanted him to be happy, but knowing that meant that he would fall in love with someone else was breaking her heart. As if sensing the magnitude of her grief, Humphrey remained by her side, snuggled against her in bed, giving her much-needed kisses. She knew that Lane would not have approved and would have told her that Humphrey belonged on the floor. The only time Humphrey left her side was when Juliet would take him for his walk. Clara would watch from her window as her niece took him on his leash to the wooded area at the end of the large expanse of grass where Lane had freed her from where she had been stuck, weeks ago. How was it possible to lose your heart so quickly?

On the fourth morning after she kissed Lane for the last time, she knew she needed to leave her room. Her nieces would be gone in a few days and she knew she would regret it if she didn't spend time with them before they left. It was time to face the world again and doing so surrounded by Charlotte, Lizzy, and Juliet would help ease her pain.

Maria, her maid, was in the best of spirits seeing that her mistress actually wanted to get dressed and might consume more than tea. She had styled Clara's hair with perfect ringlets near her face and suggested her new pink gown which would add colour to her pale complexion. In all, she did a miraculous job hiding Clara's heartache behind a fashionable artifice. At least Clara thought so until she walked into the parlour which was set for breakfast.

All activity at the table stopped and her three nieces stared at her. Humphrey let out a series of excited barks as if to inform them that, yes, their aunt had finally emerged from her solitary confinement and was rejoining Society and they should thank him because it was all his doing.

Life was about to go back to the way it was before Mr William Lane appeared in her life.

'You look terrible,' Lizzy said, then shrugged at Charlotte when her sister eyed her sharply.

'I thought Maria had managed very well with my hair today.'

'Your hair is lovely—however, you have dark circles under your eyes.' There was true concern in Lizzy's expression. 'I am worried about you.'

'I haven't been sleeping.'

Juliet held out a chair for her and kissed her cheek when Clara sat down. 'Don't listen to Lizzy, you look beautiful.'

She knew she didn't look anywhere near beautiful and that Lizzy with her honest statements was expressing her concern for her. Sitting at the table, she settled in and studied the breads that were offered. Each one made her throat close up.

'I think I'll just have tea.'

Humphrey laid down beside her and rested his chin on her slipper.

'You have to eat something. I don't think you've eaten anything in three days.'

'Four,' she replied, correcting Lizzy.

'At least have some bread.' Lizzy cut a Sally Lunn bun in half and reached for the butter.

Clara's stomach rolled over and instead she accepted the tea that Juliet had poured for her. It was her favourite oolong blend and she smiled her thanks to her niece, knowing that Juliet would know that.

'Are you cold?' Charlotte asked her. 'It feels like rain today and there is a chill in the air. I was going to go and write to Andrew, but I would be happy to go upstairs and get your blue cashmere shawl for you instead. It will look so pretty with that dress.'

Before she was able to reply, Charlotte was already out of her chair and heading to the doorway.

'Girls, please stop fussing over me. I have a broken heart, but I am fully capable of managing myself. In time, this melancholy will lift and I will find I miss him a little less. I will be fine.' Her gaze landed on Lizzy and she saw tears in her niece's eyes. 'Do not feel sorry for me. I am stronger than I look today.'

'We just thought he loved you.'

'Maybe he does.' She toyed with her cup in its saucer. 'Maybe he came to realise what I already knew…that a woman my age cannot give him the family he wants.'

'Did he tell you that?' Juliet asked.

'No, but you all know about his life. You know that he has never had a family to love and cherish him the way we have. Everyone deserves to experience that. Everyone needs that kind of unconditional love. He needs children. I can never give him that.'

Charlotte placed her hand over Clara's. 'You truly do love him, don't you?'

'I do. I just want him to find some peace with his past and be happy.'

'He seemed happy when he was with you.'

The warm tea was comforting, but for the first time in her life she didn't think she could take another sip. She pushed the cup and saucer away.

'You've been inside the Foundling Hospital when you worked on the fundraising committee,' Juliet stated, eyeing Clara's discarded cup. 'What would it have been like for him growing up in there?'

'He would have been left there by his mother because she was unable to keep him. If she intended to return for him in the future, she would have left a small token with him that could be used to identify him as her child since the Hospital changes the children's names.'

'So, his real name is not William Lane?'

She shook her head at Charlotte's question. 'No. He has no idea what it is or the day of his birth.'

'How very sad. How did they manage to take care of all the infants in the Hospital? That is a lot of hungry mouths to feed.'

'He would have been given to a wet nurse while he was an infant and lived with her family in the country until he was five. Then they would have taken him back to the Hospital where he would live with hundreds of other children until he reached the age of fifteen.'

'Then would they just release them into London with no contacts and no prospects?' Juliet asked with wide eyes.

'No, for the boys they would either begin military service or they would become an apprentice of some sort. Lane had received an apprenticeship with a London bank.'

'He had such a different childhood from us. I can see why you feel that he deserves a family of his own.'

He did deserve to experience what it would be like to be part of a family. Her heart ached for not being able to give him that.

Chapter Twenty-Seven

Lane had been riding in Hyde Park when he passed a flower border alongside the bridle path of Rotten Row and the scent of roses drifted up on the warm breeze. This was normally his favourite time of year in London. The Season had ended and the streets and parks were less crowded with the carriages of the *ton*, whose members had left town to spend their summer in the country. It was mornings such as this when the sky was clear and the air pleasant that Lane preferred to go for a ride or walk before he would settle in at the desk in his study for a day's work. Today's ride should have put him in good spirits with the ideal weather conditions. But the minute he smelled the scent of roses, his heart constricted in his chest and he cursed himself for deciding on this ride.

Two weeks had passed since he left Bath—two very long weeks. And although he tried daily not to think about Clara, this morning all it took was one whiff of her familiar scent to darken his mood and make him chastise himself for not being able to put the past behind him.

Now he was wondering if the weather in Bath was as pleasant as it was in London and, if it was, would she spend most of the day with Humphrey outside. Not only did he miss her, but he missed her dog as well. He really was a fool to be in love with a woman who had let him leave town without trying to stop him. He had been right to devote all of his time to work. It was much safer for his heart that way.

Out of frustration at his inability to forget her, he took off at a gallop down the sparsely populated dirt path and out of the park. Even though he had to slow down on Piccadilly, it didn't take him long to turn into the courtyard of his residence and jump down from his horse. He had racing reports to go over and log into his ledger. He would have coffee brought up to his suite of rooms from the Albany's kitchen. That rich smell would surely dispel the scent of roses that he could swear he still smelled.

Just as he handed the reins of his horse over to one of the stable hands who were stationed outside the three-storey building that housed apartments for some of London's most eligible and well-to-do bachelors, he heard someone call his name. Turning, he spied Lord Andrew Pearce walking towards him on the pavement. The man was tall and built like a mountain. Although he had been nothing but genial to Lane when they had spent time together with Hart, who was a mutual friend, from the sheer size of him he was not someone you would want to cross.

'You saved me a trip inside,' Lord Andrew said as he approached Lane and gestured to the brick building in front of them. 'I was asked to deliver this here to you.' He handed him a small brown-wrapped parcel no bigger than the size of Lane's palm. Lane didn't recognise the handwriting, but assumed it must be from Hart.

Lord Andrew looked up at the building with a nostalgic expression. 'This place was good to me before I settled into married life.' The expression on his face cleared and he looked back down at Lane and adjusted the brim of his hat over his light brown hair. 'Not that I regret a day that I've spent with my wife. Best decision I've made. Tell me, does Brewster still play his violin at five in the morning? I can think of many a day that I wanted to shove the instrument down his throat and I am an early riser.'

'He does and Lord Allum tried to do just that last week. I take it you never told the man about your old neighbour's violin habits.'

Lord Andrew gave a careless shrug. 'It might

have slipped my mind.' A flash of humour crossed his face and reached his hazel eyes.

'Convenient for you, not so much for Lord Allum.'

'I suppose you're right.' He shoved both his hands into the pockets of his brown frock coat. 'Give my best to Roberts and Jeremy,' he said, regarding two of the porters. 'It was good to see you again, Lane.' With that he tipped his head, turned and strolled back towards Piccadilly.

As he entered the building, Lane's curiosity got the better of him and he shook the parcel as he made his way down the corridor to his set of rooms. Nothing shifted. Nothing rattled. He turned it over in his hand and once again puzzled over the unknown handwriting.

After unlocking his door, he was greeted by Burrows, his butler, who took his hat and gloves and went to see about arranging coffee for Lane. Since the day was warm, he slipped out of his green-linen frock coat and tossed it over the chair beside the sofa in his parlour. On warm days like this he would work in just his shirtsleeves and white waistcoat. A gentle breeze was blowing in through the window, making it a comfortable place to spend the day. He had intended to get right to work in his study, but instead he dropped down on the sofa as his poor mood was proving hard to shake. Resting his head back on the sofa, he stretched his legs out and crossed his booted feet at the ankle and tried to crowd his mind with thoughts so he would no longer be imagining Clara walking Humphrey, which is what she was probably doing at this hour.

Picking up his head, he looked over at the parcel that was beside him on the green-damask seat of his canapé sofa. Hart had made distracting people an art form. Perhaps the arrival of this package was fate's way of reminding him that he needed to get back to his old life—a life where Clara did not exist.

He picked it up and turned it over. His name was neatly scrawled on the front. It wasn't Hart's hand, but perhaps he had had someone else forward the contents to Lane. His curiosity was most certainly sparked as he untied the string and unwrapped it. To his surprise, he uncovered a rectangular red-leather jewellery box. No one had ever given him jewellery before. What in the world was Hart up to?

Sitting up, he opened the box and found a folded piece of paper covered the contents. Under it was a small silver circle the size of a shilling, resting on the white-satin lining. A small hole had been drilled near the top of it. The currency and image had been rubbed away and were replaced by one line of swirly script. He had seen tokens like this before. Some people gave them as love tokens. Taking it out of the box, the metal felt smooth in his hand and he rubbed his thumb over the etching. His finger stilled when he read the line of script.

William

His heart started racing and he flipped it over, but there was nothing on the other side. The denomination had been rubbed off and it was just a smooth, plain surface with a few scratch marks on it. He turned it over in his palm so his name appeared face up once again.

Hope started to blossom that it might be from Clara—that maybe, just maybe, she still thought about him. She had told him once that she would miss him. Maybe after all this time she still did and this was her way of letting him know.

With his one hand, he flicked open the folded paper he had placed on his lap and scanned the handwritten contents to find the name scratched at the bottom. It was Clara.

His heart skipped a beat and for the first time in his life he had to clear his vision to read his correspondence.

Dear Lane,
I hope with all my heart that this letter finds you well. I realise I am taking the risk that this might never reach you, but it is a risk I

*must take since I am not able to deliver this
to you in person.*

*Lord Andrew Pearce is Charlotte's hus-
band and he has informed her that he is an
acquaintance of yours. Knowing him to be
a man of honour, I am certain that he will
deliver this to you unopened.*

*You once told me that the one thing you
wished for most in the world was to know
if your mother had given you a name when
you were born. I hope this token clarifies
that for you. It was pinned to your blanket
when she gave you to the Foundling Hospital all those years ago.*

*I hope you see that this means your
mother had every intention of returning
for you some day. If she hadn't, she would
never have left it as a way to identify you.
She wanted you back, William. She must
have had no choice but to leave you.*

*I hope this token gives you some sense
of peace.*

Yours,

Clara

His vision had blurred with unshed tears. His
mother had named him. His name really was William. All these years, he had never wanted to use
it and it was truly the one thing that was his. And

this token was the only connection he had to the woman who bore him—a woman who, he finally knew, had wanted him back. He had been wanted.

As he clutched the token in his palm, knowing that his mother had once held it in her hand, a tear scorched a trail down his cheek. It was the first time since he was a child that he had allowed that to happen.

There were so many new questions running through his mind about this woman who had given birth to him. But the most pressing question was how in the world had Clara ever managed to get this?

Chapter Twenty-Eight

June was Clara's favourite month. The weather was warmer, her favourite roses were in bloom and the days were longer. Except this year, she would have preferred shorter days so she could have spent more time in bed, asleep. It was only while she was sleeping that she didn't feel the daily pain of missing Lane. Aside from being with Humphrey, tending to her roses was the only bit of joy she could find lately.

On this particular morning, she had spent time in her garden cutting roses with Juliet, who was in town with her husband looking for a house to buy. Now that her niece had left, she was arranging a bunch of pink and yellow roses in a green Sèvres vase that rested on the harpsichord in her drawing room when Humphrey attempted to gnaw on the leg of the instrument.

'Humphrey, no.' She used her firmest voice and he stopped what he was doing and looked up at her with his big dark eyes. 'You have already destroyed my favourite slippers. You will not be attacking my furniture as well. Go play with your bone.'

Humphrey tilted his head, his black ears flopping with the movement, and looked back to where she was pointing with her clippers to the bone that Darby had brought up for him from the kitchen. He let out what could only be described as a sniff and then went back to chewing on the wooden leg.

'No!' She nudged him gently with her foot.

Finally, the little scamp walked away, but not before letting out a few yaps in protest first. He wasn't even gone for five minutes before he starting barking again and ran to her side to tug at the bottom of her white-muslin dress with his teeth.

'Humphrey, stop! You will rip my dress.'

He let out a series of more barks and, if the commotion brought Mrs Collingswood to her door, complaining that he was disturbing the woman's nap again, she would not allow her dog out in the garden for the rest of the week.

'Humphrey!'

He finally stopped barking and ran away. A peaceful stillness descended on the room and she took in the soft sounds coming through the open windows of the birds chirping in the distant trees and faint voices carrying on the wind. This was what her life had sounded like before that dog came into it.

After a few minutes, the bucolic sounds became too peaceful. She snipped another stem and stuck the yellow rose into the vase, listening for any sound behind her. If Humphrey was this quiet, it might mean that he had found something else to chew. As she turned around to see if he had perhaps left the room, she spotted him standing near the door with his tail wagging. Her entire body froze. Crouched down in the doorway, Lane was rubbing Humphrey behind his ears and watching her intently with his lovely blue eyes. At the very sight of him, it became difficult to breathe.

His eyes remained on her as Humphrey continued to lick his hand before he gave the dog a final pat on the head and stood up and adjusted the cuffs of his navy-linen coat. Humphrey let out a series of happy barks as he took a few steps back. All the while his tail continued to swish from side to side and, like Clara, his attention did not waver from the man in front of him.

They stood twenty feet apart and it was as if neither of them wanted to take a step forward for fear of breaking this perfect moment. Slowly he walked towards her and the highly polished leather of his black boots shone in the sunlight. Clara had to blink a few times to make certain she wasn't imagining things.

He stopped about a foot away from her and seemed to study her as if he was savouring this moment of seeing her once more. She didn't think they would ever be in the same room together again. She didn't think if he ever came back to Bath that he would seek her out. The shock of being this close to him ran through her body and she placed her hand over her ribs in the hopes of steadying her heart that was thundering in her chest.

'I don't even know how to begin thanking you for what you did for me.'

The token. Of course, that was why he was here. It had nothing to do with his feelings about her. He knew she was all wrong for him. For all she knew he had already found some woman to replace her—someone younger.

'How did you get in here?'

'Lady Juliet let me in. She was leaving your home just as I was about to knock. She told me that there was a chance you would not agree to see me and that she thought it was important that I did.'

It was impossible to take a deep breath even though she was trying.

'Why would you not have wanted to see me?'

Because my heart cannot take the additional pain of having you leave me twice. And you need to leave again...for your own happiness.

She was saved by Humphrey, who sprang up from where he had been lying next to Lane and raced out the door. The smell of the evening roast from down in the kitchen was drifting into the room and she knew where he was headed. Needing a reprieve from Lane's masculine presence, she walked over and closed the door to the room.

'I take it you received the package I sent,' Clara stated on her way back to standing near him, knowing that was the only thing that could have brought him back to her door.

'I did. Lord Andrew delivered it as you requested. How did you know where I lived?'

'You had mentioned it the last time I saw you.'

He took a step closer so they were less than two feet apart. 'Clara, there are no adequate words to express how grateful I am to you for what you have done for me...how important that token is to me.'

Taking her hand in his, he brought it to his lips and kissed it. The brief touch spread a rush of warmth throughout her entire body. Needing to protect her heart, she pulled her hand out of his and clasped both her hands together in front of her.

'I hope that token helped you find some peace in answering some of the questions you had.'

His attention was on her hands. 'It did.'

'Would you care to have a seat?' She gestured to the gilded sofa and held her breath, afraid he would say he was too busy to stay.

Thank heavens he nodded and followed her to the sofa. Even though he was raised as an orphan, he possessed exceptional manners and waited until she was seated before he sat down beside her.

'I have to ask, how were you able to find it? How did you even know it existed?'

She fiddled with the white muslin of her dress that covered her knee because it was becoming too painful to look at him. 'I didn't know for certain, but I knew there was a chance your mother had left something with you.'

There was an intensity in his expression when she looked up at him, as if he were paying close attention to every syllable she uttered. 'Years ago, I had been on a fundraising committee at the Hospital. I'd been through the building a number of times and know the procedure for how the children are taken in. I was shown tokens that were left with some of the children who had been admitted that week. Not all look like yours. I've seen scraps of cloth and single playing cards. All sorts of things, really. And not every mother leaves something. I only hoped that your mother had.'

'But I don't understand. How did you even find it? How do you know it's mine?'

'I knew the year of your birth. The information that was taken when you were admitted was sealed in a billet with that token and your new name. It took some time going through all the billets for 1782 and 1783.'

'I was told that information about me would never be released.'

'It's not supposed to be.' She looked away, embarrassed to admit the next bit. 'We might have circumvented the rules.'

For the first time since he arrived a hint of a smile was on his face. 'We?'

'I met the Dowager Duchess of Lyonsdale while we both were raising funds for the Hospital. She is still currently on the committee and knows where the records are kept and I asked her to help me. She was the one to find your billet and slipped the token into her reticule.'

He blinked and she didn't know if it was from shock or from the sunlight in his eyes. 'She stole it?'

'Let's just say it's on permanent loan to you.'

Her heart was beating so fast she was certain it was visible through her fichu. Part of her had hoped he would come back here after receiving the token. But another part of her had feared it. She had no future with him. It would have been better if she could have just let him go, but she had wanted to give him this gift. And now she knew for certain that watching him leave her this time was going to hurt more than the last.

He searched her face. 'Why did you go to all that trouble for me?'

'You deserved to know the truth.'

It was the only reason she was willing to confess to him. There was no sense in letting him know how much she loved him. His future was with someone else.

'What made you want to help the Hospital? It's a far enough place from Bath.'

'When I had lived in London I had another friend who would donate money to it on a regular basis. It was her favourite charity. She suggested that I become involved with it because she thought it might bring me some comfort.'

His forehead wrinkled and he shifted in his seat so he was facing more of her. 'Comfort? How so?'

She could lie. She could invent an excuse that would have seemed plausible. But that was not who she was. She was done hiding things from the people she cared about. And it was better that he knew this about her in the event her gift to him had him considering that they had a future together.

'I came to help the Foundling Hospital because I could not have any children of my own. You see, I never was able to carry a child to its birth. My womb has some kind of defect. That is why I never had any children.'

He stilled and, even though he was looking at her, Clara didn't think he saw her.

'Is that why you took the waters in Bath?'

She swallowed before nodding slowly. 'I was advised the waters might strengthen my body. It never did work, but it became a bit of a habit, I suppose. I don't do it now for that reason, of course. Now it just helps with the occasional ache or two.'

'I'm sorry. That must not have been easy for you.'

A sympathetic expression showed in his eyes that touched her heart and she had to look away.

'It wasn't easy, but in time both Robert and I came to accept it. I wasn't able to give the Hospital any funds. We frequently didn't have any to spare. However, being able to help those children in any way I could somehow helped my soul heal from the loss of not having a child.'

'So, you truly do understand where I come from. That night when I admitted it at the table and we talked afterwards, you knew I was a by-blow before I even informed you of it.'

'I did and told you that it did not change how I felt about you. I doubt anything could.'

'Felt…you no longer feel the same way about me?'

'That night feels like a lifetime ago.'

'And now?'

He was asking her to explain her feelings to him. How could she when every day she prayed that what she felt for him would soon become a distant memory? She didn't want to love him. She didn't want to go through life feeling as if she had lost a part of her heart. 'Now, I hope that we remain good friends.'

His features hardened and he shook his head. 'You are telling me that all there is between us is friendship.'

'That's all it can be. I am not what you want in life. I am too old for you.'

'Why don't you let me decide what it is I want in life?' His voice was sharp which took her aback.

If she left it up to him, it would mean that her heart would suffer even greater pain when he re-alised he wanted a family and not her. She didn't know if she would be able to endure that.

Lane had kept the token on his person ever since he had opened the parcel three days ago. It was a relief to find out his name, but the reason he had kept it with him was that it was a constant reminder that Clara had not forgotten him…that maybe, just maybe, she loved him the way he loved her.

But carrying a token around would not mend his broken heart. Only Clara could do that. She was all he wanted in his life. Everything else dimmed in comparison. He didn't have much experience expressing his emotions. He had done everything he could in his life to hide any sign of vulnerability. But for Clara, he couldn't allow this thing between them to fade away. He wanted her and he was going to do everything he could to make her understand that.

He let out an uneven breath and held her gaze. 'I think what is between us is more than friendship.'

She closed her eyes. 'Please don't.'

'Don't what?'

'Letting you go is hard enough. Don't make it worse.'

'Then don't let me go.'

When she opened her eyes, he saw pain there. 'We have no future together. It is better if we don't prolong this.'

'You don't want a future with me?'

'I didn't say that.'

'Then what are you saying?'

'I'm saying you deserve more in life than I can give you.' There was a catch in her voice.

'You are what I want in my life. You are the only thing.'

'You say that now and maybe you mean it, but you will not feel that way ten years from now. You deserve to have that family that you were denied years ago. I cannot give that to you.' There was a pleading sound in her voice as she turned away from him. She was asking him to end this conversation and she might even be wanting him to leave.

He wasn't going anywhere.

'All I want is you.' He placed his hand gently on her clasped hands when what he really wanted to do was hold her tightly and not let her go. 'Clara, look at me... Clara.'

She turned with tears streaming down her beautiful face. His heart twisted a bit more as he placed soft kisses on her eyelids in an attempt to stop her tears.

'You are all the family I need. I have never had a father and have no idea how to be one. While I have thought of having children, I cannot miss anything that I have not had. I cannot miss children that do not exist. We don't need children to be a family, Clara. You and I are all the family I could ever want.'

'You may change your mind.'

'Clara, if having children in my life were that important to me, don't you think I would have made an effort to have them by now? I have been out on my own for over twenty years now. In all that time, not once has there ever been anyone who I have wanted to carry my child. I have never found anyone who I care about as much as I do you. I love you.'

He had thought when he finally said those words to her they would feel awkward on his tongue. Yet saying them now, saying them to her, just felt so natural. He needed her to understand how much he loved and cherished her. He needed her to know that she meant the world to him and that he knew she always would.

Leaning down, he softly brushed the tears from her cheeks and placed his lips on hers for a gentle kiss. It was a kiss that was meant to convey all the things that he felt about her that he could not put into words. In his heart, he hoped she loved him, too.

She moved her head back and their eyes met. He had never seen anyone look at him the way Clara was looking at him now. 'I do love you,' she said. 'I love you so much and I am terrified that I will lose you.'

The words hit his chest. In all his life, no one had ever told him that they loved him. He wasn't prepared for how much those words would affect him.

'You will never lose me, Clara. I want to be with you always.'

What started out as a gentle caress of his lips against hers became much more urgent as she opened herself up to him and pulled him in closer. Their tongues glided over each other's with a passion that had him wanting her so much more—needing her so much more. Her hands slid up into his hair and with each stroke of his tongue against hers, she tangled her fingers through his hair and gave a gentle tug.

He wanted to possess her completely. His hands moved to her breasts, confined in her stays and in her soft cotton gown. The passionate need inside him was growing. He needed to touch her bare skin and broke the kiss to trail his lips down the column of her neck. She smelled faintly of roses and it had become his favourite scent.

She was working at the knot of his cravat and her breathing was becoming laboured.

'I want you,' he said into her collarbone, licking her skin and gently squeezing her full round breasts. 'I want to be with you more than anything.'

His cravat was tossed to the floor and she worked his coat over his shoulders. 'I want that, too,' she replied, breathlessly tilting her head to give him better access to the base of her neck.

She clung to him as he laid her down and trailed his hand up her leg. His desire for her was overriding everything else as he skimmed his fingers up the soft skin of her thigh until he couldn't go any further and he sank his fingers into her warmth. He could feel her work the buttons of the fall of his breeches as she periodically arched her back as he moved his hand faster.

When she climaxed with a soft cry, he was aching for her. He was aching to fill her and claim her as his own. Her delicate hand encircled his length with a firm grip and slid up and down.

'I want this. I want you,' she said in between kisses.

And as he slid himself inside her for the first time, she grasped his forearms while they watched each other intently with their foreheads touching. It didn't take long before they found a rhythm all their own through their laboured breathing. Being inside her was something he had been imagining for weeks. The reality of it was so much better. A hot tide of passion claimed them both and when they came together, his primal groan filled the room.

He rested his forehead on her shoulder as they both tried to catch their breath. She played with the waves of his hair near his collar, content to lay in his arms.

Eventually he picked his head up and looked at her. 'The next time we do that, we will do it in a proper bed and neither one of us will have a stitch of clothing on.'

'You sound rather confident that it will happen again.'

'I am. When I sleep beside you every night, it's bound to happen again a time or two.'

'Only a time or two?'

He wanted this. He wanted her. For ever. And the fact that she wasn't dispelling the notion made his heart feel as though it had grown in size.

'A time or two each night.' He needed her to know he was serious about this. He needed her to know that he wanted her for ever with every fibre of his being. 'I love you. I did not say that to get under your skirts. I meant it.'

'I know you did.'

He moved off her and help her up so that they were sitting side by side. They took their time fixing their clothing in silence for which he was grateful since he had to compose his thoughts. When he was ready, he turned to her.

'I know you said you would never marry again for fear of losing control of your financial independence. That in order to feel secure, you need to own your hotel. We can draw up contracts and whatever is needed to indicate that you would remain its sole owner should you marry me. I will do anything for you not to fear for your future again. And I meant that you are everything in this world that I need. I don't need your hotel. I need you and want to spend the rest of my life with you in my arms. I want to marry you, Clara, if you'll have me.'

There was a catch to her breath and she brought her hand up to her lips. 'You mean that, don't you? You truly do.' In her eyes, he saw it. He saw that she knew for certain there was no hesitation on his part. She knew he was earnest in his proposal.

'I will marry you, William. I will.'

He hadn't had anyone call him by that name in years. The sound of it on her lips touched a part of him that he didn't even know existed. His heart was ready to burst. And more than anything he was grateful that he had found her and that she would be calling him that every day for the rest of their lives.

Epilogue

Two months later...

Clara stood on a chair in the storeroom of the White Bear, counting out the coffee pots that were kept on the top shelf on the wall opposite the closed door. Below her, her husband stood with his ledger book and pencil, waiting for her to tell him how many pots were in this room.

'That's twenty-seven. Although this one might have a crack in it,' she said, turning with the white-porcelain pot in her hand and tilting it towards the window. 'It's either not been washed well or that is a crack.' Rubbing her finger over the line, she was able to confirm that there was indeed a crack in the porcelain.

William wrote the number down in his ledger, took the pot from her hand and placed it on the lowest shelf. 'I suppose one out of this entire storeroom isn't too bad.'

'The crack is very small. I could see how someone else might have missed it. Especially if they were putting them away late at night.'

Just as she lowered her hands and wiped them on her apron, he stepped closer and trailed his fingers under her skirt and up the back of her leg. The sensation sent a delicious shiver to her most intimate places.

'I thought you said you needed my help with inventory since Mr Sanderson is visiting his sick mother.'

'I did. We are finished and I thought I'd show you my appreciation.'

'We are in the storeroom.'

'That never stopped us before,' he offered with a lift of his brow.

His hand travelled up over her knee and Clara had to hold on to his shoulders to steady herself. A small satisfied smile lifted the corner of his mouth. Just as his hand begin to skim up her thigh, there was a knock on the door behind him. His hand froze.

'Yes,' he called out, not breaking their gaze.

'There is someone here to see you, sir,' Hatchard replied through the door. The young man who they had hired from the Foundling Hospital was settling in nicely, assisting Mr Sanderson here in the coffee house.

The disappointment on William's face was obvious as he removed his hand from Clara's thigh and helped her down from the chair.

'Did you have an appointment?' she asked, shaking out her skirt.

'No.'

He opened the door and startled the slight, dark-haired young man who immediately averted his eyes. Did all of their employees assume when they were spending time in the storeroom that they weren't exactly working? She had only been in that room four times with him.

'Do you know who it is, Hatchard?'

'Yes, sir, it's the Dowager Duchess of Lyonsdale.' From the expression on his face when he said Eleanor's name it was apparent that this might have been the first time he had spoken with anyone of her elevated station in Society.

'Where did you put her?' he asked.

'She told me she would wait for you and Mrs Lane in your office.'

'Very good. Thank you for coming to get me.'

His smile of encouragement seemed to bolster the young man's spirits since Hatchard stood a bit taller when he tipped his head respectfully at William and then at Clara before heading down the corridor to the shop.

William looked across at his closed office door and then over at Clara. 'For a woman who wanted to be a silent investor in our spa, she seems to want to talk about it a lot.'

'She is excited about the prospect. You should be happy. This spa was your idea.'

'I am and you know how much I like her, but if the two of you are going to discuss colour choices for the walls again, I think I'll find something else to count in the storeroom.' He turned as if to go back inside and Clara tugged him around by his arm.

'We were enjoying ourselves.'

Talking with Eleanor about the decorating scheme for the hotel after the ground floor was converted to a bathing spa was fun. She enjoyed picking out colours with her friend. But after a half an hour of their discussion two days ago, she could see her husband's eyes glaze over. This was not the aspect of the business he enjoyed the most. Fortunately for him, it was one of her favourites.

'You have my word. If she is here to bring me samples of paint, you can find any excuse you like to leave. I will not think you rude.' She kissed his cheek for good measure.

'Very well. I will take my paperwork from the stables and head home. I can work at my desk in our parlour just as easily as I can here.'

When he opened the door, they found Eleanor standing by the window, looking outside. She turned with a smile when she saw them.

'You have been spending quite a bit of time here this week and I wasn't far so I thought I would see if you were here first before I went to your home.'

'Please, have a seat,' Clara said, gesturing to the pair of chairs in front of William's desk. She knew that look in Eleanor's eyes. Some exciting bit of gossip was about to make the rounds of Bath.

'Do you recall the other night you said the Collingswoods had been particularly quiet and you thought they might have returned to London without saying goodbye?'

Clara and William exchanged glances. Now they would find out why the house next door had been dark for the past week. Eleanor always seemed to find out things other people could not.

'Well,' she continued, sitting on the edge of her chair, 'I received a letter from Greeley today. He was writing to thank me for introducing him to Miss Collingswood. It seems that your Harriet had been introduced to another man while you were on your honeymoon and Greeley was away working on Lyonsdale House. This gentleman had just become a baron and showed interest in Harriet. Her parents had favoured the match and were actively attempting to keep Harriet and Greeley apart.'

'That's terrible! Why did Harriet not write to me in Paris and tell me this?'

'My dear, you were on your honeymoon. As young as Harriet is, I think she is wise enough to know not to bother you with her problems during such a time.'

'But she is my friend. I would have tried to help her.'

Eleanor waved her comment away. 'Nonsense. Besides, if you would have helped her we would not have this exciting news.'

William leaned forward on his desk and rested his forearms on the polished oak surface. 'What news?'

Excitement was evident in Eleanor's eyes as she looked between them. 'Greeley and Harriet have run away to Gretna Green and got married over the anvil. They have eloped.'

Clara felt her eyes widen as William let out a burst of laughter.

'Why are you laughing?' she asked.

'I didn't think he had it in him.'

'It was *her* idea,' Eleanor interjected. 'Greeley told me so in his letter. The family had gone after them to try to avoid a scandal, but they didn't reach them in time. Now Greeley and Harriet are married and plan to settle here in Bath. I told them that they can stay with me on the Crescent in the home I am leasing for the next few months.' She tugged up her gloves near her elbow. 'I knew that boy was destined to have a scandal of his own. I told him as much that night, months ago, when we were dining at your home. It seems I am the better matchmaker after all. I was able to match Harriet and Greeley, and the two of you.'

'You didn't match us together,' Clara said, glancing at her husband.

'Of course I did. I could tell the moment that you both were standing around that fountain in the Pump Room that you needed to be together. I could tell then and there by the way you looked at one another. Why do you think I left you alone during that ball in the Assembly Room? Why do you think I barely spoke to you during the performance of Mr Sheridan's play? I know a love match when I see one.'

Clara wasn't certain she would give Eleanor credit for bringing her and William together. She liked to think that fate had something to do with it that day at the Pump Room. If he had arrived an hour earlier or if she had chosen to stay home that day, they would never have spoken. And when her dress had got caught in the shrubbery in the park, fate had chosen that path for him to take that day.

She had a lot to thank the heavens for. But the one thing she was grateful for more than anything else was that she had been given a second chance to find love in her life. And she could not have asked for a better man to share this part of her life with.

Their voices must have woken Humphrey, who had been sleeping under Clara's chair. He lifted himself with a yawn and slowly padded over to the other side of the desk. She could tell by his languid movements that he wasn't finished with his nap yet and Clara knew that right now he was resting his head on William's booted foot. There was a special bond between that dog and her husband and she would bet good money that William would not be reviewing his reports from the stable at home. He never would disturb their dog while he fell asleep on him. She wondered if he ever marvelled at how much his life had changed in such a short amount of time all because of the water here in Bath.

* * * * *

Historical Note

The Foundling Hospital, where Lane grew up, was the first children's charity in the UK. It was established in 1739 by philanthropist Thomas Coram to help care for and educate children who had been abandoned by their parents due to severe poverty or illegitimacy. Joining him in this venture were the artist William Hogarth and the composer George Frideric Handel.

Later, admission to the Foundling Hospital became restricted to the first children of women of good character whom the father of the child had deserted. In placing her child with the Hospital, the unmarried mother would be able to earn an honest livelihood.

By the time the Foundling Hospital closed, in 1954, it had taken care of approximately twenty-five thousand children.

To find out more information about this important part of London's history and the tokens that were left with some of the children, visit my website at *www.lauriebenson.net* and search my blog. You can also visit the Foundling Hospital museum, as well as browse their website.

COMING SOON!

We really hope you enjoyed reading this book. If you're looking for more romance, be sure to head to the shops when new books are available on

Thursday 22nd August

To see which titles are coming soon, please visit

millsandboon.co.uk/nextmonth

MILLS & BOON

Coming next month

THE LORD'S HIGHLAND TEMPTATION
DIANE GASTON

Mairi stopped and gazed across the river. 'The mountains look so beautiful. It is hard to say what time of year is the most beautiful in Scotland, but right now I'd say October.'

Lucas agreed. It had its own unique beauty. Like her.

The faint sounds of gunfire wafted in the wind.

'The hunt is still on,' she said sadly.

Lucas had heard the gunfire on and off throughout their walk. He pushed away memories the gunfire provoked. 'Maybe that is why we see so many deer on this side of the mountain. They are hiding.'

'Hide well, deer,' she murmured.

They continued walking, crossing a patch of grass. The ground was uneven and again Lucas held her arm to steady her. When he released her, she threaded her arm through his and held on to him as they continued walking.

After a while she asked, 'Will you talk to me about last night, Lucas?'

He knew instantly what she meant. He searched for the right words to say.

'To beg your forgiveness? I should not have touched you.' *Or almost kissed you*, he added silently.

'Why?' she said softly. 'It is not as though you are really a servant, are you, Lucas? You were a soldier.'

This was his chance to tell her who he really was, but the gunfire sounded again.

'I was a soldier, but I grew up in a great house.' Let her believe he was John Lucas. 'In any event, I should not have behaved as I did towards you. It was wrong of me.'

She let go of him and walked a little faster, putting herself a step or two ahead of him. He caught up to her.

'I know you are right,' she said, but her tone was sharp.

Had she wanted the kiss? He'd thought so. He'd been too familiar with her. In his father's house he would not dream of becoming so involved with—say—one of the maids. But she was not a maid and he was not really a butler. How had this become so complicated?

Continue reading
THE LORD'S HIGHLAND TEMPTATION
DIANE GASTON

Available next month
www.millsandboon.co.uk

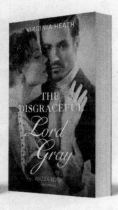